Cover Design: Deranged Doctors

Editing: Tamara Mataya

Print ISBN: 978-1-7350961-5-5

❀ Created with Vellum

Finally Falling

book three

FIX it

JESSIE HARPER

1

Kat

"There's no way you're ever going to convince me this was how you wanted to spend your birthday." I scowl at my brother over the rim of my glass and wait for him to contradict me. He doesn't even bother as he gives me a giant grin from the bar stool next to mine.

"What?" Zach shouts, pretending he can't hear me. He cups his hand around his ear and shrugs his shoulders, laughing. "Karaoke!" he tells me and then goes back to watching the poor woman up on stage belt out Madonna's *Like a Virgin*. I'm pretty sure it's been a few decades since this lady knew much about virginity. She's rocking some late '80s hair and some serious pelvic thrusting to go along with her musical stylings.

Mercifully, the song ends and Dime Store Madonna starts taking her bows. My brother puts his fingers up to his lips and whistles. I curse his overzealous encouragement, bracing for the next performer. After an hour of neighborhood karaoke I've truly reached my limit, but I'm saved by the band's announcement that they're going to take a break.

Yes, this bar has a band to accompany anyone who wants to get on stage and sing. Welcome to Nashville, folks.

"Whoa, that was kind of intense," my brother's wife tells us as she makes her way back from the edge of the stage. Julia's never been subjected to karaoke night at this fine establishment either, but she seems less shell-shocked than I would have imagined. "We're really going to need to up our game if we want to get on the list. Zach, are we still doing a duet? I've got the song list right here."

"You guys are going to sing?" I ask, slightly mortified.

"Sure, Kit Kat. It's fun. You and Amy could sing something together." My brother gestures toward the other end of the bar where my twin sister sits deep in conversation with some tatted-up dude. I'm pretty sure she's not in the mood to make a fool of herself tonight by joining me on *Eye of the Tiger*. She's the sensible one, anyway, and neither of us can carry a tune in a bucket.

"Do you have the song list?" Julia's best friend demands as she reaches over me to grab it. "Graham and I call dibs on anything from *Grease*."

Cassie's in on this too? I watch as her giant ex-football-star husband comes up behind her and agrees.

"You guys cannot be serious," I say more to myself than to any of my assembled family and friends.

"Do you want something from *Grease*? We could try to choose something else, I guess." Cassie turns to her husband and she and Graham pore over the piece of paper in front of them. "Oh, we could do something from *Frozen*! We know all those songs by heart."

"What other Disney have they got?" Julia demands. Of course they're all going to go down the Disney rabbit hole. They've all got kids eight and under.

"You want to spend your one night with a babysitter

singing all the songs from the movies your kids torture you with on a daily basis?" I ask, incredulous, and four confused faces stare back at me.

"Well, if we want to really kill it, we need to pick songs we know," Graham explains, shrugging. "You should really think about getting up there. You know, introducing yourself to your new neighbors."

I frown as Zach and Graham high five.

"I guess that would be one way to make sure everyone remembers me."

"Who needs drinks?" Julia asks and scans the crowded bar for someone to take her order. There's not a bartender in sight.

"I could use another beer." Graham drains the last of the amber liquid in his glass. "Do you need anything, babe?"

Cassie shakes her head. "I'm still good, thanks." Cassie's been nursing that glass of water since we got here while the rest of us are hitting the sauce. No one mentions the fact that our resident party girl has decided to get serious about her eight glasses a day.

"This end is too crowded," Julia groans. "I'm going to try farther down." She pushes her way through the crowd to find an opening closer to a bartender.

It *is* surprisingly crowded in here for a Thursday. I wouldn't have thought karaoke night would be such a big draw. A mix of old and young patrons mingle in front of us. More than a few of them give my brother a fist bump or clap him on the back.

"Is it always this busy?" I ask him once he's back to sipping on his beer. Zach would know better than anyone. It's crawling distance from his old house—the one he lived in after his divorce and before he married Julia. *My* house after officially moving in this afternoon. So I guess this is now my local, for better or worse.

"Not always," Zach shouts over the hum of drink orders and laughter. "But everyone comes out for karaoke at Smitty's."

"Great," I say and don't really mean it. I'm not sure if I can acclimate to a neighborhood that loves karaoke night the way this one does. But part of moving into my brother's house is to give this whole neighborhood thing a try. Instead of living downtown in my old loft I'll be learning the ins and outs of yard maintenance and water heater repair. And karaoke, apparently.

I'd initially pitched the idea to Zach as a way of getting out of my rent increase. He hadn't wanted to sell his place once he'd moved out to the suburbs with Julia, and my land-lord had decided he could bump my monthly rent up to astronomical levels. But in truth, I'd wanted the chance to see how life might be if I slowed down a little. Zach's old house has everything in walking distance, a great yard, and plenty of space. Just not enough for his family. He went from a single guy running to work every day to a father of four in the blink of an eye. Between Julia's two boys and now their set of twins, it made sense for him to move into her larger house and rent his out.

Suddenly everyone's coupling up and starting their families. Cassie and Graham already have a toddler and if her beverage selection tonight is any indication, he's managed to convince her to have another. I can't help but be envious of the way he keeps putting a protective hand on her belly every now and again. Which sucks because for me these feelings are coming out of the blue. Zach is my younger brother but somehow he's the one with a house full of kids. Amy and I are both still single and, up until about five minutes ago, I was loving it. Until my biological clock decided to flip itself over to something closer to the doomsday clock.

That ticking is getting damn near impossible to ignore and I'm screeching up to forty in a few months. Without a partner in sight, I thought maybe dipping my toe into the shallow end of parenthood might start with moving into a more kid-friendly neighborhood. Although, if I'm serious about it, I might need to start swimming in the deep end sooner rather than later. But I haven't told anyone else about this little experiment yet. Not even Amy knows that I'm seeing emoji hearts whenever I think of squishy little babies. I'm keeping that to myself. I've spent so much time focusing on other things that everyone's probably written off children in my future.

"Is that guy cute?" Zach asks me, pointing down to the other end of the bar.

"What guy?" I squint in the direction of his finger. I can see Julia down there talking to the owner of a surprisingly broad back. When he turns his head a bit, I get a handsome profile.

"Yes." I wait for my brother's reaction.

"Is he hot?"

I laugh. Zach is not the jealous type. He literally works at the gym and has the kind of face most girls appreciate. I'm sure he doesn't have anything to worry about. If some guy is talking to his wife, he can probably just count the seconds until she makes her way back down here to kiss him on the mouth.

"Is he?" he demands and I take another look as the man turns further.

"Yep." From what I can see Julia's having a nice chat with an exceptionally attractive man. Dark hair, strong jaw. When he tilts his head back to laugh at something she's said I get a glimpse of dark eyes and white teeth.

"Go down there and talk to him," my brother orders and I give him a look.

"I'm not going down there. If you need to collect your wife you're going to have to do that yourself. I'm not getting in the middle of some sort of caveman death match."

"I don't want to get aggressive with him, Kat." Zach looks at me like I'm an idiot. "I just need you to go order me another beer." He takes his nearly full glass and tips it back, draining the whole thing. "I'm empty."

"That's a pretty drastic measure just to make sure your wife doesn't get thrown over someone else's shoulder. Remind me not to let you drive home." I slide off my bar stool. "You owe me, Neanderthal."

Zach gives me a thumbs up as I weave through the crowd. Julia isn't that far away, but it takes time to meander through all these bodies, avoiding errant elbows. I try to smile at people when I pass—no use upsetting my new neighbors. When I finally get to Julia she's loading up the drinks to haul them back.

"Hi," I announce way more brightly than the situation calls for. Julia turns to look at me at the same time her new friend does. Did I say he was hot? Because up close he is so much more than that. He's got just a little bit of dark stubble and chocolate eyes that have me losing my train of thought. Other parts of me perk up and my brain just sits there humming along. Julia looks at me like I have two heads and cocks one eyebrow. Right. I was on a mission.

"I'm here to tell you that Zach would like a beer and that he's apparently unable to sit over there by himself without pining for you." I roll my eyes and Julia laughs. She motions for the bartender and orders another beer for my stupid brother.

"Who's your friend here?" I ask, moving my arm forward to touch the mystery man's back. Unfortunately, that's the exact moment one of the patrons scrambling to get their name on the karaoke list bumps me from behind. As Mr. Handsome leans back, my hand makes solid contact with the muscles on his upper arm.

And I jam my thumb into his armpit.

2
———

Michael

Well, fuck me.

One minute I'm hanging out, chatting with a woman at the bar and the next thing I know I've got someone's thumb lodged between my arm and my ribcage.

I jump once her thumb makes contact. I'm not ticklish exactly, but the surprise of it sends my ass right off the bar stool I'm sitting on. The sound I make can only be described as a yelp, and not a particularly masculine one either. If anyone tries to tell you that the armpit is some kind of erogenous zone you should tell them they're wrong. There's nothing sexy about getting poked in the armpit. And having a stranger's digit do the poking? That's just unsettling.

Luckily, my beer gets delivered immediately after the poking. I could really use something to take the edge off after that.

And, luckily, when my eyes pop back into my head, the woman on the other end of that thumb happens to be extremely pretty. The look of shock on her face matches mine, and her full lips pull themselves into a horrified gasp. She's kind of leaning forward on me a bit so our faces end up closer than expected for casual conversation but not as close as you might expect for having your thumb in someone's armpit. Her eyes are the most amazing shade of green, and the long dark hair that comes spilling over her shoulder and onto mine has me wondering if I've ever really seen that combination before.

"Oh my God!" she yells almost directly into my ear. "I'm so sorry!"

She's mortified but she doesn't remove her hand from my back or, by default, her thumb from my armpit. I'd gone home to shower and change after work so I'm relatively dry, provided my antiperspirant has done its job. I hadn't been paying much attention to my armpits before I found her hand in one of them. I'd been complaining to her friend about the slow service. Smitty's has karaoke every week. It's not like they couldn't have anticipated a crowd. But my beer was slow in coming so I was making small talk with the woman standing next to me. Now I'm trapped in a game of twister with this beautiful woman who's stumbled into our conversation.

"Let me just..." She works to get her balance, using her other hand to push off the middle of my back. Again I'm thankful for the clean T-shirt I'm wearing. If I'd come straight from the job site I'd be a sweaty mess. Sometimes when we finish late the guys and I come straight to the bar for a round or two. But tonight, I'm smelling less like I spent all day on top of someone's roof and more like I spent the day enjoying an air-conditioned office.

Her friend looks on while we struggle, biting back a laugh.

My new friend scowls at her as she extricates herself. Once we're separated she sticks out her hand and mine comes out automatically to meet hers. "I'm Kat. We should at least exchange names now that I've assaulted you."

I laugh because what else can you do when someone introduces themselves like that? "I'm Michael." I close my hand around hers. Her skin is silky where it touches mine, definitely a contrast to the calluses I've got going on.

"I'm Julia," her friend interjects. Reluctantly I let go of Kat's hand to shake the one Julia offers. "If you'll excuse me, I need to deliver these beers." She turns on her heel and disappears into the crowd, leaving me with an annoyed and still a little flustered Kat.

"Do you want to sit?" I ask because like magic there's now an empty stool next to mine. Sometimes the universe has a way of looking out for me. Kat hesitates for a second but then slides onto the stool. "Drink?" I'm not sure if I should be offering to buy her a drink this early in the conversation but after our little wrestling match from earlier, I'm feeling like we've skipped a few steps.

"I should probably be buying you a drink, actually," she says. "It isn't every day that someone comes up and just—"

And I'll be damned if she doesn't shove her thumb back in my armpit.

"Jesus!" I fly off my seat again.

"Sorry, I'm kind of committed to it now. Whatever you're using seems to be working nicely, by the way. No sweaty pits for you." Kat stares right at me and I swear I stop breathing. Who is this person?

"Should I be worried you're going to keep doing that?" I can already feel myself hugging my arms tighter to my sides.

"Probably not. I mean, I might do it once more, but after that it'll just seem weird." She smiles at me and cocks her head to the side. I almost expect a wink but she straightens up and motions for the bartender.

"Put that on my tab," I say and Kat whirls around to look at me again.

"I was putting *your* drink on *my* tab." She narrows her eyes at me, daring me to argue.

"That's just because you think I'm going to let you touch my armpit again," I tell her, trying to keep my face straight. "But two times was my limit. I'm old fashioned like that." And I'm a little old fashioned about letting a pretty girl pay for my drinks.

Kat considers this, lips pursing. "No more armpit?"

"Nope."

"Fine, but just so you know that's probably going to be one of my go-to fantasies for a long time." She gives me a wicked grin.

I swallow. Hard.

When the bartender slides her drink along the smooth surface in front of us Kat picks it up and clinks her glass with mine. "Cheers."

I want to follow this up with something memorable— something profound, but Kat's already moved on. Her emerald gaze roves around the bar, taking in the crazy karaoke night scene. "Do you make a habit of showing up at Smitty's for karaoke night?" she asks me, turning completely around until her back leans against the wood of the bar.

"Not usually. But this is a good place for after work and it's pretty entertaining," I confess. It's probably not the nicest move to tease my neighbors, but they are pretty hilarious once they hit the stage. "It's my neighborhood bar."

"Mine too!" Kat's eyes go wide with excitement and I can't help but hope this means we'll be running into each other frequently. "I just moved into my brother's house. It's right down the street. So, who are you here with, Mike-of-the-perfectly-dry-armpit?" she asks, taking a drink of whatever I've just bought her. Vodka tonic, maybe? Something with gin? I could lean over to get a sniff of it but I'd really only be trying to get my face closer to hers again.

"Those guys over there." I point toward the corner of the bar where my work buddies are engaged in a serious game of darts. I had been too until I realized how much more interesting it was over here.

"Those guys?" Kat squints. "Are they even old enough to get into this bar?"

"They're all over twenty-one," I counter, not sure where this is going.

"Not by much. Look at that one! I bet he doesn't even need to shave."

Right on cue the guy in question turns and gives me a thumbs up. Kevin is pretty baby-faced, I guess. "He's like twenty-three or something," I protest.

"Twenty-three?" Kat basically crows, taking another sip of her drink. "And that one's what, like, twenty-five?"

I look over at my unsuspecting friends. "They're all in their twenties, sure." I take a gulp of my beer and Kat regards me warily.

"You're here with a bunch of twenty-something guys?"

I nod. Nothing wrong with that, right? But the way Kat keeps eyeing me has me thinking she disagrees. "Who are you here with, Kat-of-the-roving-thumbs?" I deflect the attention back to her.

"That bunch over there," Kat points down to the other end of the room. "And my sister. She's over there." I look to my left and see another version of Kat a few seats away.

"Twins?" I give her a look I'm sure she gets all the time, one that makes her scowl just a little.

"Seriously? Not a chance. There's no twin fantasy happening here no matter how cute you are."

"Ah, but you think I'm cute." I pounce on the sliver of interest.

"If you like muscles, I guess." She looks down at my arms and I involuntarily flex. Her eyes widen. Oh, she likes muscles.

We sit for a minute, sipping our drinks as the band makes their way back to the stage. Kat groans.

"Not excited for the rest of karaoke night?" I tease.

"My brother and his wife are probably going to make our ears bleed in a second. I hope you've enjoyed your last few minutes of excellent hearing."

"I've enjoyed these last few minutes immensely." I mean it. I'm already plotting all the ways I can try to convince Kat to hang out with me again. Soon the bar will be too loud for conversation so I go ahead and take a chance. "Can I get your number? I could give you a tour of the neighborhood hot spots."

Kat hesitates and I feel the first ripple of disappointment. I don't always get the girl, but I'm successful more than I strike out. Maybe I've misread the banter we've had going here, mistaken politeness for interest. One side of her mouth quirks up and I have the urge to nip at it, to graze my teeth over her lip. I don't, of course, because Kat doesn't want me to kiss her; she doesn't even want to give me her phone number.

"Can I ask you a question?"

"Sure." I turn my body to face her. "Ask me whatever."

"How old are you?"

"Twenty-eight."

Kat startles. "Wow. Okay."

"What's wrong with twenty-eight?"

"Nothing." *Obviously something.* "How old do you think *I* am?"

I recognize this for the trap it most certainly is. Guessing a woman's age? She might as well ask me if she looks fat in that outfit. There's no sane man alive who would answer those questions. I stall, hoping the band will save me. I search Kat's face for the right answer. What even *is* the right answer here?

"Twenty-eight?" I know that's not going to be right, but I figure it's safer to hedge my bets than to start making wild guesses.

Kat scoffs. "There's no way you believe that." She rolls her eyes and looks at me like I'm the dumbest man she's ever met.

"Okay then, are you sixteen and you're telling me you snuck into this bar? Is your dad going to come bursting through those doors any minute and threaten me with a shotgun?"

She shakes her head. "I'm definitely older than sixteen."

"Seventeen?" At least that gets a hint of a smile. "Are you trying to tell me you're two hundred years old? Three hundred? Am I sitting next to the world's oldest woman?" I hedge and hedge but she won't just put me out of my misery.

"I'm forty years old, Michael."

I blink. That was not what I was expecting. "You're forty?" I try to keep the surprise out of my voice but I obviously fail miserably.

Kat sighs and takes a gulp of her drink, the condensation running along the side of her glass.

"You don't look forty."

"Technically I'm still thirty-nine, but I'll be forty in a few months." Kat tells me this like it's a cancer diagnosis. "So, you should head back over to darts now and find someone more age appropriate." With that, she slides off her stool and starts moving toward her friends. "Thanks for the drink, though. Maybe I'll see you around."

She's *forty*? Wait, she's walking away? Fuck that.

3

Kat

As I walk away, I can feel his eyes boring a hole in my back.

Turn around! Go back! part of me yells.

You're leaving a gorgeous and willing man!

I get it, internal voice of good times. Really, I do. But for some reason the new little whisper that's started to dominate my life has completely taken over.

That's not a man; that's a boy! she shouts, along with a new one I've never really heard before:

He's not daddy material!

That, plus the way his face had frozen when he found out I wasn't the twenty-something girl he thought I was—yeah, I'm not sticking around to see where this goes.

"What are you doing back over here?" Cassie asks me like I'm a kid in the principal's office.

I stop and four sets of eyes stare me down. "I can't come over here and sit with you guys?"

"Not if you're leaving that"—Cassie gestures with her

hand—"over there, you can't. Did you at least get his number? Are you meeting up later?"

"He asked for mine, but I didn't give it to him," I tell them, suddenly very interested in the bottom of my glass.

"What?" Cassie and Julia say simultaneously.

"Why?" Julia asks. "He's so cute."

"He's more than cute. Look at his butt in those jeans." Both Cassie and Julia lean away from the bar to get a better look at Michael's backside. He's throwing darts with his buddies now, the fabric of his T-shirt stretching tight across his back as he lines up his shot and then releases it. Once the dart goes flying, he looks back over toward me. I look away too late; he knows we're talking about him.

"Can you ladies keep the objectification to a minimum over there?" Graham jokes. "Some of you are supposed to be married."

"We're married, not dead," Cassie counters. "Let us live vicariously through Kat for a minute."

"He seems like your type, K. Did he turn out to be a jerk or something?" Julia asks like she can't quite make the puzzle pieces fit. I'll admit it isn't normally my style to walk away from an opportunity so early in the evening, particularly one who looks that good in jeans and a T-shirt.

"He turned out to be a kid, that's the problem."

"A kid?" My brother's all ears now. "He's underage?" He's already prepping for a hilarious story. I can just picture him telling our parents about the time I picked up a high schooler at the neighborhood bar.

"Not like a real kid, dumb ass. He's under thirty." Everyone looks at me and waits for there to be more. The general consensus concerning my bombshell announcement seems to be a resounding *so what?*

"And you were hoping for someone more geriatric?"

Graham's eyes twinkle. "You could go chat up those guys over there. I think I overheard one of them talking about his grandkids. But you better hurry up. Those guys probably have to get home for their Metamucil soon."

Graham and Zach roar with laughter. For two guys who were once basically competitors for Julia's heart they sure are getting along great tonight. Already they're scanning the crowd for other possible love connections for me. All of them sixty and over.

"I don't see what the problem is. He's young, but it isn't like you want to marry him and have his babies, right?" Julia's question hits me harder than it should. *Right. No babies.*

"He didn't seem so cool with the age difference once he found out," I lie. I never really gave him much of a chance to get over his initial reaction.

"Screw him, then," Cassie says. "Should we get another round to loosen us up for our big singing debut?"

"I could go for another drink," Julia says and then gives my arm a shove. "Uh oh, incoming."

I turn just in time to come face-to-face with a pair of brown eyes and the perfect amount of facial hair. Michael takes two breaths while we stand staring at each other; I hold my breath, unsure of what's about to come out of his mouth.

"Can I talk to you for a second?" His hand shoots out to touch my upper arm. The skin there comes alive, making my brain send all the wrong signals to the rest of my body.

"Sure," I manage but don't move when he slides his hand down my arm and gives my hand a tug.

"You want to do this here?" Michael takes in the extremely interested audience of my friends and family. I stay put so he really doesn't have a choice. "Fine," he sighs but keeps holding my hand.

"I'm guessing you think I'm too young for you. I'm going to go ahead and say I think you're wrong. The last thing I'm thinking about when I look at you is your age. So, if you change your mind and want to get together some time, here's my number." He hands me a round cardboard bar coaster, his number scrawled above the Smitty's logo. I take it in my free hand, eyes still glued to his.

"That's all I needed to say," he finishes and then slides a hand around the nape of my neck and presses his lips to mine.

The contact is so unexpected I almost jump. Almost, because once his mouth is on mine the surprise wears off and there's nothing but bliss. The stubble from his chin scrapes my cheek as he pulls away and I find myself wanting more, missing it once it's gone. Good lord, I did not need a sample of that.

He moves out of my space and taps his finger on the coaster. "See you around, neighbor." And then he stalks out of the bar, the glass door swinging shut behind him.

"What the hell was that?" my brother asks.

"I don't know, but I think it just got about ten degrees hotter in here." Cassie fans herself with her hand. "We should come to this bar more often."

I'm pretty sure I'm never going to be able to come to this bar again. Either that or I'm never going to leave it. Hello, new neighborhood.

4

Michael

"And then he just walked out of the bar!" Danny shouts it loud enough for the entire world to hear. "Just like 'thank you very much, I'm outta here'! Most interesting thing that happened all night."

I scowl from down at the bottom of the ladder. I can't deny my actions, but I'd love it if the guys who witnessed it would keep some of the details to themselves. Or make me sound more badass and a little less like a petulant kid. Sure, I planted one on Kat and then left her standing there, but I'm reliving it in my own mind enough as it is. I don't need everyone else's version of events to torture myself with too.

"I don't know, that lady who got up to sing that Missy Elliot song was pretty entertaining," one of the other guys ventures, trying to change the subject. I peer up at the roof trying to decide whose lunch I should buy.

"Sure that was _interesting_, but not in the same way, dude," Danny argues. "I'll bet the girl sings that song every time she gets up there. It isn't every day that Mike kisses some woman against her will."

"It wasn't..." I shout up, basically outing myself as an eavesdropper. I wince as I hear the other guys hoot.

"You down there, Mikey? Wanna tell us your side of the story? Because I know what I saw and that girl was more than a little surprised when you puckered up." Danny slides over to the edge and leans over just enough for me to see his gap-toothed grin. Fucker.

"What did she do after he left?" another one of the knuckleheads asks in between the hammering.

"Well," Danny starts like he's telling the world's most anticipated bedtime story. "She stood there for a second or two, kind of gettin' her bearings you know? And there was a bit where it looked like one of the guys she was with might go tearing out after our boy Mikey but then things settled down. Nobody called the police so there's that, I guess."

None of that gives me the information I want to know. I've been thinking about Kat since I left Smitty's. The kiss was impulsive and she may not have enjoyed it nearly as much as I did. I gave her my number and my phone's been silent ever since, so I guess that gives me all the answer I really need. She told me she wasn't interested; I pushed it a bit and the answer's still no. I'm probably lucky she didn't slap me.

"Was one of those guys her husband or something?" Danny asks, not quite ready to leave this conversation alone.

"No, she's not married." I think. *Did I even ever ask her?* Not wearing a ring doesn't mean anything. Kat could be married. I roll that idea around in my head for a minute. "One of those guys is her brother, I think."

"Then you're doubly lucky no one chased you out of the bar. A husband probably cares less than a brother. If some dude just came up and kissed my little sister?" Danny whistles low. "That'd be that for him."

"Sure it would," I yell up at him. We all know Dan's all talk and no walk. You could probably get away with way more than kissing his sister before he took offense. "And he's her little brother." Because somehow she's forty years old which still makes no sense and no difference to me. But to her it means things are over before they've even started.

"Little brother? Well then, I guess you're off the hook."

There's more hooting and hollering from up on the roof. I know the guys can work and talk, but I let their badgering get the better of me. "How about less gossiping like a bunch of church ladies and more hammering?" I shout. The laughter only gets worse.

"Not used to being rejected, boss?" one of the guys shouts down, and I decide to make myself scarce. I consider taking the ladder with me and stranding them on top of the house but that wouldn't look too professional. And I am the boss, after all.

Boss. That still sounds weird to me. After being one of the guys on the crew I'm still not used to being the one in charge. They aren't used to it either if their ribbing is any indication. Half those guys are older than me, some old enough to be my father. It isn't easy moving from being one of the grunts to being the one who makes the decisions. But those guys all knew what they were getting into when they came to work with me. I can put in the hours like the rest of them, but when I had the chance to move from worker bee to the one cutting the checks, I took it and I'm not apologizing.

I head back to my truck and slide behind the wheel. We've got two jobs today and I'm moving between them. Stacks of papers and old coffee cups fill the passenger seat. I'm having to learn the ins and outs of managing things quickly and I'm the first to admit I'm not doing a great job of it. The roofing business had been my grandfather's and no one was more surprised than I when he left it to me. But he was old school, so while his work ethic brought in customers, he was never that savvy with promotion or marketing. I need a crash course in taking it to the next level, but I can barely keep up with my receipts.

I try to put all of that out of my mind and let myself think about the future. This opportunity fell into my lap, but I'm determined to prove that my grandfather made the right choice. My father would have just sold it off. Cruz and Sons never actually had anything to do with sons. My grandfather knew I would keep it and try to build it up, to make it even more successful. He had faith in me so I try to have a little faith in myself.

My mind finds its way back to Kat like it has every day since she slid up next to me in the bar. I give myself two minutes to dwell on the heat of that kiss, the way she melted into me, the little sigh she made that made me want to drag her out to my truck instead of leaving her there. Of course, if I'd tried to take her home she would've seen the mess I'm currently sitting in. It would only have been proof she was right about me being a kid. That thought takes me right out of my fantasy and back to reality. I cannot be sitting here daydreaming about an unavailable woman while minutes tick away in an already busy day.

I grab one of the old receipts from my last coffee run and flip it over. At the top I write: *TO DO* and then I get to work making a list. First order of business—something to organize all this paper. I keep writing until all the tasks I have jumbled in my brain are there in black and white. At the bottom I write *MARKETING* in all caps and then shove the receipt in my back pocket before moving back into the midday heat.

5

Kat

Drip, drip, drip.

That is not the sound you want to hear inside your house the morning after a heavy rainstorm. I cover my head with my pillow, but that isn't going to make the situation magically go away. Zach's house has charm in spades, from its cute little fireplace to the wraparound front porch, but all that charm comes at a cost. This house is old and that means things break. My brother had warned me about all the little tricks he occasionally had to use to get things to work. The toilet in the half bath always needs a little jiggle of the handle. The back door sometimes requires more force than it should to get the bolt to turn. But I haven't been given any special instructions about dripping water and I'm sure what I'll find when I crawl out of bed isn't going to be good.

Sure enough, when I make it into the living room the plaster above the fireplace bulges in a way a wall never should. Even in my first week of pretend homeownership I can tell that a huge bubble of plaster is out of my skill set. I think about poking it, but the slow trickle of water that I see running down keeps me from touching anything. Instead I call Zach and get ready for a day of dealing with this emergency.

"I have a problem," I spit out the second he answers the phone.

"Well, good morning to you, too," Zach answers and I can hear the chaos that is four young children in the background. They're probably in the middle of breakfast.

"Sorry," I say and then try again. "Good morning! I have a problem."

"Some random guy come up and maul your mouth again?" I can hear him already laughing at his own hilarity. Zach cannot let go of his now week-old joke.

"First of all, that guy wasn't random and second, that wasn't exactly what I would classify as a problem." My lips tingle just thinking about Michael's mouth on mine.

Zach grunts. The kissing did not sit well with my brother. "Alright. What's your problem, then, if it isn't unwanted advances from strangers?"

"I think there's a leak in the living room." I move closer to the giant plaster bubble.

"It did rain pretty hard last night," Zach says. "Is there water in the house?" I hear him shuffling between rooms, the sounds of kids shrieking getting fainter.

"There's water on the floor and more of it coming down the wall, but the main thing is this giant place in the plaster. I'm not sure what to do about it." I nibble on my lip. "I'll take a picture and text it to you." I snap a few photos from different angles and press send.

"Shit," Zach says once they go through, hopefully out of earshot of the kids. His daughters will be talking any minute and he and Julia have been working to make sure their first words aren't all vulgar. "Whatever you do, don't touch that. See if you can mop the water up from the floor and then put some towels down. Try to keep the floor dry so the hardwood doesn't get ruined. I don't want to replace that on top of whatever we have to fix already."

"Do you need me to call around and find someone to come and look at it?" I don't want Zach to get caught up in soccer games or whatever they're doing today and forget. "What do we need? A roof guy?"

"A roof guy and then someone to repair the plaster and repaint. Two different people, probably. But I can make the calls. You can just live in ignorant bliss for a little bit longer. I'll let you get through your first month before I hand over the house responsibilities completely to you." He chuckles like it isn't going to be a huge pain in the butt for him.

"I can do it," I tell him but he doesn't back down.

"No worries. Just let me know when you're available to have people come by the house. I know you're busy." Not any busier than Zach. He's got a family to take care of and a business to run.

"Just schedule the appointments and I'll be here. See if you can get one for today and I'll pay the emergency fee. I'll work from home if I have to next week. I can swing that no problem." That's a bit of a white lie. Working from home is sometimes tricky, but that's what I'd have to do if this was my house. And if I had a kid in daycare? Part of finally being the boss means I can breathe a little bit easier about dictating my own schedule. It's time they get used to me being flexible. No time like the present to test the waters because no one's ever died from a public relations disaster. Their careers have, maybe, but no real fatalities. I'm not exactly out there saving the world. Although, coming from someone who can count the number of days she's missed work on one hand, I haven't exactly been acting like it.

The crash I hear in the background has me wincing. Poor Julia. I love her kids, but I can't imagine what she and Zach are dealing with on a daily basis. They've got diapers and elementary school homework, dinners to cook and lunches to pack, and all of that while they both try to have careers. Julia's photography business isn't a nine-to-five thing and Zach's gym has some flexibility, but they're still two of the busiest people I know.

"I should go before this house falls down, too," Zach tells me. "I'll let you know once I get some magicians lined up for you. I can see if we can get someone to come over today. And I'll try to stop by and take a look."

I hope it doesn't take magicians. I'm keeping my fingers crossed that this is the easiest fix in the history of roof repair. "Thanks, Zach," I say. "I promise I'll be ready to run the show over here before you know it."

"Enjoy your kid-free day!" he yells at me before hanging up. I'm surprised at how much that actually stings. Zach doesn't know he's hurting my feelings, doesn't know I've been dreaming of those hospital blankets with the pink and blue stripes.

I take a deep breath and go to refill my coffee cup. Caffeine is something I'm going to have to give up if I go through with this pregnancy idea, right? I'm pretty sure coffee is a no-no when you're growing a tiny human, but there's no one I can ask other than the Internet unless I want to let everyone else in on my secret. I'm an almost forty-year-old woman who's always put her career first. I'm not quite ready to try to explain this sudden change to my friends and family. It's been brewing for a while, but to them it will be a shock. There are boxes to unpack and all sorts of client work I should try to catch up on, but when

I crack open my laptop, I fire up Google and let my fingers fly. Where to start? I type in *single woman wants* and before I can even finish my thought I'm greeted with a slew of options.

Single woman wants a baby

My finger hovers over the trackpad. That's what I want. A baby. I put my hand on my stomach and try to imagine something—someone—moving around in there. I can't. My stomach unleashes a growl because I haven't had breakfast yet. Yes, I'm fabulous mother material—I can't even feed myself on time. I click return and I'm provided with even more suggestions.

Having a baby alone

Desperate for a baby but single

Having a baby alone at 40

The last one punches me just the tiniest bit in the gut. It looks like I'm not the only one asking Google for advice. I click on the first link—a private fertility clinic with a long glossary of terms in the left-hand margin. *Is your biological clock ticking?* some unseen narrator asks me. *There's more than one way to have a family!* it counsels.

I have a family. A brother and a sister. A mother and a father both still spry enough to give me hell about not showing up to Sunday dinner, a tradition that sounds very family-oriented if you ask me. And I've got my two nieces and two nephews thanks to Zach and Julia's ability to procreate. The nephews technically have to do more with Julia's ability to make cute babies, but those boys are family no matter how they ended up calling me Aunt Kat. Still, there's something to be said for having a baby of my own and the gnawing that I keep trying to ignore has gotten to be impossible to tamp down. I don't have forever; if I'm lucky I have a few years left to become a mother.

Are you sure you're ready?

The question taunts me from the screen. Who wrote this ad copy? If the goal was to scare the ever-loving pee out of someone, then mission accomplished. If they were hoping to attract clients, then frightening the bejesus out of people maybe wasn't the best way to go. Am I sure I'm ready? No, but how can I know when I'm ready? And what if being completely ready means never actually doing this? Can I see myself without a husband? Sure. But lately when I picture myself in five years it's with a little curly-haired preschooler. It's with a swing set in the backyard and one of those little plastic swimming pools in the summer. Everyone always says you're never ready. My limited friends and family with babies have all said this. And I'd trust them over this website any day.

I go back to my search results and choose another link. An artsy photo fills my screen and I gasp. It's a sleeping baby swaddled tight, surrounded by syringes in the shape of a heart. Her little pink mouth winks out from her chubby cheeks and I can almost imagine what the top of her head smells like—that combination of fresh-baked bread and baby sweetness that has me swooning lately. There are thousands of needles—so many that they are five and six deep— and the caption tells me these are the injections it took to have this baby. They're part of the fertility treatments that were endured to get to this point. To have the end result of a baby. And this isn't the only one of these on the Internet. I scroll through the images, looking at babies in onesies that say "worth the wait." Pregnancy announcements fill my screen, testaments to how difficult this might be. It should scare me away. I hate needles but I look at these photos and think *I could do that.* I wipe the tears that have settled on my cheeks away with the back of my hand and save the pictures to my desktop.

Now I'm addicted to the clicking. I keep scrolling, choosing another website. This time I ignore the helpful advice and dive straight into the terminology. I'm a smart girl, always at the top of my class and known for thinking outside the box, but this has me feeling like the dumbest person in the room. I know maybe one word out of the fifty on this list. I scroll through them getting more and more confused. Assisted hatching? Zygote intra-fallopian transfer? I read through each description, taking notes on the yellow legal pad on my lap. After an hour I'm ready for more than a cup of coffee and there's only one thing that I have circled in bright red ink on my notepad.

Fertility Workup

Step one according to all my new Internet besties. My doctor had mentioned the same thing when I'd tentatively broached the subject of a baby at my last appointment. Just checking to make sure everything's running smoothly, especially since already on the older side. I stretch and work the kinks out of my back. It's already noon and I'm still in my pajamas. I can call my doctor Monday morning and put things in motion. A fertility workup doesn't sound too scary. It feels more like stepping out into the sunshine, like taking control of this situation in the way I normally do. I'm moving toward my goal and that puts a smile on my face. It's like a checkup only with more on the line. Or less if I decide this isn't for me. *Which I can still do*, I remind myself. I haven't crossed any line that can't be uncrossed. Not yet, anyway.

6

Michael

I put my truck in park once I pull into the little slip of driveway. Houses in this neighborhood don't usually have much room to park, but I can't exactly put the truck on the street and then lug the ladder back up to the house. I block the silver Lexus that's already parked there completely in. Hopefully, whoever drives this car won't need to get out in the next few minutes. Since this is an emergency call, I'm pretty sure no one will mind me inconveniencing them a little.

Taking a call on a Saturday is supposed to be an inconvenience for me, actually. That's why we have a surcharge for the visit. People hate to pay extra; I've learned this the hard way over the past few months. Even if the more expensive way would be better or cheaper in the long run, people want to think they're getting a deal. It's the most frustrating part of trying to run this business. People would listen to my grandfather and take his recommendations but when I rock up with my estimate, I get questions. *How long have you been*

doing this? Are you sure? Should we check with your boss first?
My blood pressure rises just thinking about it. But an "emergency"? People will pay for that. They don't really have a choice.

This emergency is actually one of the more reasonable ones I've had recently. It's on the way home and I've got nothing left to do tonight. Well, nothing but hunkering down with my shoebox full of receipts and then hopefully sending out some invoices. No excuse not to make a little extra money before I commit to a long night of more work.

A stack of cardboard boxes is wedged between the recycling bin and the side of the house. There's got to be thirty of them there, all flattened, ready for pick up. If these are new tenants, they'll be annoyed there's a problem with the roof. If they've just bought this house, they'll be even less happy. I prepare myself for dour faces and angry questions as I climb the steps to the front porch. I ring the bell and wait.

And wait.

I ring it again and hear the sounds of someone rustling around on the other side. There's a muffled curse and then the sound of something clattering to the floor. Not good signs. I put my hands on my hips and tap the toe of my work boot, looking up at the underside of the porch roof. It's in good condition, no visible cracks or leaks. The ceiling's painted blue like so many Southern porches and there are two hooks where it looks like a swing used to hang. There's no welcome mat, no pot of flowers, no chairs to sit in—only the railing stretching along the side. I think about leaning there while I wait for whatever is going on inside the house to calm down but before I can make a move the front door bursts open.

And there's Kat.

"Hey there, Thumbs," I drawl out before I can stop myself.

Her hair's wet from what I assume is a recent shower. Extremely recent considering she's wearing nothing but a towel. Her eyes narrow as she takes me in, raking from my boots to the top of my ball cap before settling back down on my face. She scowls. "Do you always show up unannounced on women's porches?"

"Do you always answer the door in a towel? Because if the answer's yes then I'm going to start showing up here all the time." I wink because I've apparently gone into full on asshole mode. I'm here about the roof but instead I find myself extremely concerned with what Kat's got going on underneath that towel. The swell of her breasts rises and falls with every irritated breath she takes. The towel doesn't cover much and what I can see I like more than I should admit. If this is what forty looks like then I have been focusing on all the wrong women.

"Eyes up here, buddy," she snaps and my gaze jumps back up to her face. "I thought you were someone else."

"Sorry," I lie. I am not at all sorry to have her stuck here with me like this. "I'm actually here about the roof." I wave the work order in between us. Kat reaches for it, changing hands gripping the towel. The shift is enough to give me a good look at the top of her right thigh. I look at the porch roof again. Yep, sturdy construction.

"You're actually the roof guy?" Kat asks exasperated.

"Yes, ma'am."

"Of course you are," Kat sighs. "And don't call me ma'am." She glares at me. "Give me a second." And then she slams the door in my face.

I hang out on the porch, eventually leaning against the railing. How long am I supposed to wait out here while she does whatever it is she's doing in there? I consider, for a second, the possibility she might not be alone. *Please don't let there be some recently showered dude in there with her.* Hopefully the universe won't make me witness that, especially since now I've seen her in a towel. I'd still like the chance to soap her up, although she's made it pretty clear that's not going to happen. I could kick myself for calling her ma'am. It's reflexive; I use it with everyone when I'm working. But knowing how Kat feels about our age difference, I'm sure she took it the wrong way.

When the door flies open Kat's dressed in yoga pants and a T-shirt, her wet hair piled on top of her head. This outfit's almost as good as the towel because when she turns around and throws a "Come on in" over her shoulder, I realize that the only thing I'm focused on is the way the fabric of those pants hugs her ass. God bless yoga pants. I remind myself I'm supposed to be working and I try looking around the house as she leads me through the living room but I barely manage to give anything else any attention. Until we get to the fireplace, that is. Then I'm all business as I take in the spectacular mess of wet plaster.

"It was like this when I woke up. Well, there was still water coming in, too, but that's stopped now." Kat stops and folds her arms across her chest. Even under her T-shirt I can see her breasts press up against the fabric. Now that I have an inkling what they look like out of her clothes I'm not going to be able to let that idea go, apparently.

"Yeah, we're going to need to figure out what's going wrong over there," I say, sounding like I know absolutely nothing.

"Do you think?" Kat juts her hip out. "Is that your professional opinion?"

I smile. "Yes, in fact, it is." I try not to sound too sarcastic, but Kat's face tells me I've failed. "We need to drain this water. Do you have a bucket?"

"I think so." Kat moves through the house to find it. The place definitely looks like she's just moved in. There's nothing on the walls yet and the couch and other furniture are still placed haphazardly in the middle of the room.

"How long have you lived here?' I call out after her as I inspect the plaster bubble protruding from the side of her fireplace.

"Like a week?" Kat yells back. "Nothing's organized yet. Sorry about the mess."

"I wasn't..." I don't bother finishing my thought. I wasn't criticizing. Already I can tell that Kat's got her life more together than I do. Her furniture's expensive and her house is more decorated than mine even with most of her stuff in boxes. I'm guessing that's her Lexus in the driveway.

"Here's a bucket. You aren't going to pop that thing, are you?" Kat eyes me suspiciously. "My brother specifically told me not to touch it."

"And then he called *me* to come and fix it," I respond a little more irritated than I'd planned. Her brother had actually called my grandfather. Either way I'm the guy here now. I'm the one who knows what they're doing. I'm the boss. I take my multitool out of my back pocket and look for the best place to slide it in. There are already towels on the floor and I kick them over closer to the place where I'm about to hopefully save the day.

"Can I help?" Kat asks. She's still not convinced I know what I'm doing.

"Nope. I've got it under control. We need to get the moisture out from under here so it can dry out as much as possible. You don't want mold even if this plaster's going to have to be redone."

Kat nods but still stands there watching me like a hawk. I stuff down the feeling of being a kid with a babysitter as deep as I can. Kat would hate that comparison almost as much as I do. I slide the blade against the smooth plaster underneath the bubble and try to catch as much water as I can with the bucket. A steady stream of rainwater pours from the small hole I've made. The towels easily catch what the bucket misses and in two minutes I've smoothed most of the liquid from the blister on the wall.

"I should apologize for the other night." There's no way I'm keeping this job if Kat's angry about that kiss. "I was out of line to kiss you like that."

"Probably shouldn't make a habit of it." Kat's mouth presses into a hard line. She's not going to let me off the hook.

"With you or in general?"

"I'll let you figure that out on your own." She moves closer to the wall to get a better look.

"Your boyfriend couldn't take care of this?" I ask, fishing for information. As far as I can tell there's no one else here, no boxes labeled with some man's name, no trace of steady male companionship. Probably should have tried to figure that out before I kissed her, but that ship's already sailed.

"I don't have a boyfriend," Kat tells me, putting her arms back across her chest. She knows exactly why I'm asking.

"Huh, interesting," I say, letting myself enjoy getting under her skin. "So now just let it dry out a bit. If you have a fan you can aim over here that'd be great. The plaster's still going to need to be redone and there'll be painting, too, but it's better not to have the water sitting there." I wipe my damp hands on the front of my jeans. "I can dump this in the yard." I hold the handle of the bucket as Kat stares at me.

"Oh, okay," she finally spits out, shaking her head. "Thanks for fixing that. Do you bill me or how does this work?"

"I'm not done," I explain. "I haven't even looked at the roof. When it rains again more water'll come in if I don't find the source of the leak."

Kat blinks. "Oh, right. That makes sense. Do you have a ladder or something?"

"Or something. I have a drone I send up there first to take a look. Then I'll get the ladder."

Kat nods. "I have no idea about all this house stuff," she confesses and gives me a little shrug.

"Lucky for you I do," I tell her, not even trying to hide the pride in my voice. If there's one thing I know how to do it's fix a goddamned roof. "Give me a minute."

Kat follows me out onto the front porch and tags along behind me into the yard.

"How does the drone work?" she asks. For someone who doesn't want to spend any time with me she's going about this the wrong way.

"Like a drone," I snap, but regret it when Kat's lower lip juts out. Great, now I'm thinking about her lips and how they taste. The way they opened just a bit when I'd kissed her at Smitty's. If I'd had more than a minute to kiss her, I could have done a more thorough job. Especially if I'd known it would be my only chance to do it.

I fish the drone out of the case I keep it in and hold it up for Kat to see. "It's basically a remote control helicopter with a camera. I can use this instead of getting a guy up on the roof. Better first step than having somebody walking around up there."

Kat looks at the drone and I flip it over so she can see the bottom. She comes closer to get a better look and I get a whiff of her hair, the scent of her shampoo still strong on the wet strands. One of them comes dangerously close to my fingers when she leans down to inspect the machine. I keep my hands where they are, resisting the urge to tuck the errant strand back behind her ear. She smells like the beach —coconuts—and I wonder if she always smells like this and if I'll ever get the chance to find out.

"So, send it up," she tells me and gives me that eyebrow again. It hints at something way more mischievous than roof repair, so I do what I can to keep her standing here—I use the controller and send the drone up and over the house.

"See, just like a video game," I say as I keep my eye on the drone. I don't want to run it into a tree or something. That wouldn't help me look competent, and for some reason looking competent in front of this woman is all that matters in this instant. Looking like I know what I'm doing is pretty much consuming me.

"I'm guessing you play a lot of those," Kat says and I roll my eyes.

"Video games? Not really. I don't like being cooped up inside." I don't look at her. I focus on taking pictures and looking at the roof through the eyes of the drone. I'm pretty sure I know the main problem already, but older houses can sometimes trick you. There can be unexpected issues and I don't want any surprises with Kat's house. I pride myself on estimates that are as close to the final bill as possible. If I can come in under budget and under the time I've estimated, everyone will become repeat clients. They'll tell their friends and neighbors. Right now, word of mouth is all I've got. I inherited this business with my grandfather's stellar reputation and work ethic. I'm not about to fuck that up because a beautiful woman is standing next to me.

I bring the drone back down and land it on the grass. Kat's already moving toward it before I can say a word.

"Do you mind if I take a look at this?" she asks me over her shoulder even though I'm betting she'd still do what she wanted even if I said no.

"You can touch it if you want," I tell her and her surprised face tells me that came out differently than I intended. Everything I say to her becomes sexual innuendo, somehow. I should take it back before I lose this job, but instead I decide to roll with it. "Just try to be gentle with him." I watch her eyes flame. "I need to get the ladder," I call over my shoulder, already walking away. I need to get away from Kat and the way she's looking at me like she's not sure if I need slapping.

I take my time at the truck, pulling the ladder down off the rack and hauling it back to the house. I've only got the small ladder so I'm limited in what I can do with it. That's another reason for the drone. That, and, apparently, chicks dig it. Kat's still holding the stupid thing when I get all the way through the yard and back to the house. It's the kind of one-story home with older trees standing all around. There's a tire swing hanging from one of them, the rope around it tethered to a thick branch up in the leaves.

"Does anybody actually use this thing?" I ask as I pass it. It could use a new rope and probably someone should check the knots up there.

"My nephews do sometimes," Kat tells me offhandedly, still absorbed in her investigation of the drone. The sunlight coming through the leaves puts a dappled pattern on her back that I'd like to trace with my fingers. I could easily run one up the entire length of her spine just following the outline of the shadows flickering there. I tighten my grip on the ladder and lean it up against the house.

"Do you need me to hold that for you?" Kat asks from entirely too close behind me. I jump and end up almost up against her.

"Jesus! You're like a cat. You should give people a warning when you're moving around."

A slow smile works its way across Kat's face. "What would be the fun in that?" she asks and the urge to kiss her becomes almost overwhelming. She's so close, looking from my eyes to my mouth, telegraphing all the right things to my brain. But I'm reading things wrong, obviously, because if she wanted something other than roof repair she'd come right out and say so. She'd have called me and there'd be no ambiguity. She doesn't seem like the type not to know what she wants and she doesn't want me.

She called for a repair job, not to give a—

I clear my throat. "I'm not sure I can trust you to hold the ladder."

"Worried I'll strand you up there?" she teases but I feel like that isn't something too far outside the realm of possibility. She'd probably make me spend the night up there, too.

"I'd figure out how to get down," I tell her, hoping she doesn't take that as a challenge. "But then you'd need to find someone else to fix your roof."

Kat considers this. "Probably not worth it, then." And when I don't scamper up the ladder with that slight admission she follows up with, "I promise I won't strand you on the roof." Her grin says something else entirely. God, this woman. I'd almost be enjoying this torture if I thought it might lead to something other than blue balls.

I sigh as I climb the rungs one by one until I'm all the way out of her sight. That lets me relax a little, but not much because this roof is steep. I run my hands over the chimney, inspecting the bricks and the mortar. The few cracks are nothing that would have let in that much water. Then I confirm what the drone's already told me: the base of the chimney's the real problem. I take a look at the gutters and the rest of the shingles just in case I'm missing something and then I look over the edge of the roof to see Kat looking back up at me.

"How's it look?"

"I'm coming down," I warn her before putting the soles of my work boots back on the rungs. True to her word she hasn't messed with the ladder and she's holding it steady for me even if I don't really need it. When my feet hit the ground, she shifts so we're standing face-to-face again. Kat really needs someone to explain the concept of personal space to her before I decide to ignore my better judgement.

"Did you figure it out?"

"Yeah, it's the flashing. The sealant's old and it dries out after a while. I need to replace some shingles and get it all sealed up again. Nothing major. The chimney looks fine but you'll want to have some of those cracks repaired eventually." I shove my hands in my pockets and take a step back to put some space between us.

"So now you go back to your boss and then he sends me the estimate?" Kat cocks her head to the side and the bun on top of her head flops over.

"No, now I go home and write up your estimate and email it to you. I am the boss." And I'll be fucked if Kat doesn't laugh. She barks out one of those surprised laughs that infuriates me. "Something funny?" I ask because I'm not laughing. Not at all.

"Oh, I thought you were joking." The smile slides off Kat's face. "You're the boss?" She doesn't look convinced.

I reach in my back pocket and pull out one of my business cards. It's the same logo my grandfather used only now my name's the one next to the word *owner* underneath *Cruz and Sons*.

"Oh." Kat inspects the card. She runs her fingers over the lettering on the front as she reads it. "You work for your dad?" she asks and my hackles rise again.

"No." I collect the ladder and start my walk back to my truck. "I'll email the estimate to your brother tonight. Tell him to let me know if he wants me to schedule the work. I'm pretty full right now but I can probably get some guys over here end of the week. You'll want to get this fixed before it rains again." I don't look back at her, don't even pause as I swing the ladder back on the rack and secure it. I return to her only to retrieve the drone. "I'll let you get back to your Saturday. Don't want to take up too much of your time."

Kat's mouth opens slightly like she's about to say something, but she closes it quickly when she makes eye contact with me. I can't seem to get the irritation under control. I march back to my truck like a stubborn toddler and pack the drone back up without another word. I can feel Kat still watching me, probably deciding if she should make a run for it.

I've gone from thinking about flirting with her to furious in about sixty seconds. She thinks I'm too young to spend time with, too young to run a business, too young for pretty much anything worthwhile, I guess. It's been a long time since anyone other than my father treated me like a kid. There's a reason why I don't spend as much time with him as he'd like. I'm a grown ass man. And now I've spent a good chunk of my Saturday being treated like a baby by a woman I barely know.

As I back out of the driveway, away from her expensive car, I catch sight of Kat still standing in the yard holding my business card in her hand. Her other hand comes up in a little half wave and I can't stop myself from giving her a little nod.

But that's all I'm giving her.

7

Kat

"Hello? I'm just letting myself in!"

Nothing.

"Julia?" I push the front door open and peek inside. My sister-in-law is nowhere to be found. I go ahead and make myself at home in the living room, hoping that silence doesn't mean that I'm going to get an unexpected sighting of my brother naked. That's happened more than a few times now that he and Julia have had to get more creative with their sexy times. At least today Julia knows I'm coming. She's the one who called me begging me to take the twins while she runs out on some emergency photo shoot.

Most people wouldn't understand how a photo shoot could qualify as an "emergency," but Julia's done enough work with me at my public relations firm for us to under-stand each other. I've called her plenty of times and asked her to drop everything and come double time to some mystery location with her camera. Regardless of what she's got going on today, I'm more than happy to help her out if it means she can keep growing her photography business.

And I'm happy to help out if it means I can sneak in some baby practice.

I'm usually pretty far down the list when it comes to babysitters for my nieces. They're still pretty small and between Julia's parents and mine they have two sets of overeager grandparents who basically fight over babysitting rights. I even think Cassie and Graham are more likely to get an emergency babysitter ask before Julia would call me—and until a few months ago I was more than happy to avoid being put in charge of the twins. But if Cassie's down with morning sickness and the grandparent brigade is otherwise occupied then Julia's probably had to call in the C team.

I pull out my phone and text Julia. Maybe she's putting babies down for naps and I don't feel comfortable going hunting for her through the rooms of her house. I've accidentally caught her and Zach in the laundry room before. No place is really safe around here.

I'm sitting on your couch wondering if I've stepped into a hostage situation.

The little bubbles start almost immediately.

Be right down! I've got one sleeping and the other one on the boob about to be lights out.

Breastfeeding. I'll have to put that down on my research list eventually. Maybe by the time I need that information I'll have gotten around to telling everyone. Julia would think random questions about her boobs today were a little weird. She's been trying to wean my nieces, but neither of them have fully given up bellying up to the milk bar. Still, even if she talks about her breastfeeding woes every so often it isn't like I can use that as a conversation starter.

Julia tiptoes down the stairs into the living room like she's sneaking away from the scene of a crime. I cringe, thinking of how I'd basically yelled when I came in the front door. I probably cost her a few extra minutes with all my bellowing.

"Thank you so much for doing this!" she tells me as she gives me an awkward hug. I'm still sitting on the couch so she has to lean over while I stretch my arms up. "Zach's got the boys and all the grandparents were already booked. Lucky for me I've got a deep bench when it comes to childcare."

"No problem, really. I was just avoiding all the unpacking I have to do. I feel less guilty if I do it over here at your house."

"Did that leak derail you too much? Zach seemed to think there's going to be some big repair." Julia's packing her camera bag, her head leaning over as she checks her equipment. Thankfully she can't see my cheeks heat because yesterday's little roof issue derailed me for the entire day.

"It wasn't too bad," I lie. "But thank my brother for that little surprise he sent over." I try to muster some indignation. I'd been annoyed when Michael had shown up on my porch. That annoyance had burned off pretty quickly until I'd somehow insulted him in the end. "If he doesn't like me getting kissed by strangers then he shouldn't let them know where I live."

"What?" Julia's head snaps up from her bag.

"Tell Zach it was really funny to send Michael over, but payback is going to be hell." I probably shouldn't say this right before Julia leaves me with her helpless children, but I figure she was in on the joke.

"What are you talking about?" she asks, genuinely confused.

"The roof guy?" Still nothing. "He's the guy from the bar the other night. Don't tell me you didn't know this."

"The guy who kissed you is the same guy fixing the

roof?" Julia's brown eyes widen. "Ohhh... how did you handle that?"

I ogled him within an inch of his life and then gave him a bunch of mixed signals.

"Kat, I had no idea. I'm pretty sure Zach didn't know either. He's been complaining about that guy kissing you since it happened. You know how he is about guys taking advantage. I don't think he'd have sent him over to your house on purpose."

"It was fine." I leave out the part about how watching him work left me thinking about every badly produced porno ever made about the horny housewife and the handyman. While Michael was fixated on doing his job, I was fixated on how the muscles in his arms flexed. "He left in a huff though."

"He got angry? That doesn't sound very professional." Julia's brow furrows. "He didn't try to kiss you again, did he?"

"No, no. Nothing like that. He was super professional." I don't admit the times when he wasn't it was usually me who started it. "I think I just said something he took the wrong way."

"What did you say?" Julia's pulling on her sneakers, still trying to get out the door and on to her appointment.

"I might have laughed when I found out he owns the roofing company. I guess I hit a nerve or something."

Julia stops and looks at me the way my mother does when she's disappointed. I'm going to have to get to work perfecting that look too if I'm going to be a successful parent. Julia's got it down pat because I feel her reproach down to my toes.

"Well, I can see why he'd get mad at that. You rejected him at the bar because he's too young and then you laughed like you couldn't believe he had his own business? You're acting like he's a baby."

"Well, if he can't take a little criticism then he is a baby." *Take that, Julia.*

"What is he supposed to be taking criticism for again? The year he was born? And we both know he's far from a baby. I don't think he was hoping you'd give him a bottle and put him down for a nap." Julia smirks at her own joke. "But then again I don't know what you're into."

"Speaking of babies..." I change the subject because there's no way I'm having a discussion about what I'm "into" with Julia right now. "What should I know about yours since you're probably already late."

"Well, they're both sleeping and if you're lucky they'll stay that way for a little while. Claire's getting a cold or something so I'm hoping they both rest for a bit, but Jane will probably decide she doesn't need a long nap. When they wake up you can give them the snacks I left on the counter. There's a note if you need instructions. And if you want to get adventurous you can take them out in the stroller. I packed the diaper bag and it's by the door. Hopefully this won't take long, but you never know."

"Have you got a diva client?" I ask, hoping Julia's got some great story to make me forget about how crappy I've been to Michael. Julia's criticism from earlier's just starting to sink in.

"Worse. This is an engagement shoot that I was supposed to do last week but then the couple called it off—called off the whole wedding. Now they're back together so I'm not sure if I'm walking into the euphoria of make-up sex or World War III. Could go either way." Julia hoists her bag over her shoulder. "Keep your fingers crossed no one gets hurt."

I raise my crossed fingers and give her a wink. "But you know what would make the better story, right?'

"Sure—if you and your roofer hook up. Keep me posted on *that*. That's the only story I want to hear."

I toss a throw pillow at her as she leaves.

"Have fun with the girls!" Julia calls and then I'm left sitting alone on the couch. For this part of parenting I'm already a pro. I've got plenty of things to occupy my time until the girls wake up. If I were really the mom, I'd need to do laundry or something, but when you're the fun aunt you get to read a book.

Or Internet stalk the cute guy who's going to fix your roof. Especially if he's the same guy whose kiss is keeping you up at night. Despite my need to act like I have no interest in Michael, I'm spending an awful lot of my time this weekend trying to find out more about him.

I've only made it through some light detective work before I hear one of the girls making noise in their bedroom. While Cruz and Sons' website could use an overhaul, their work gets stellar reviews. I'm sure Michael's face has something to do with the large number of housewives willing to put their comments up on the Internet. His body probably doesn't hurt either, although none of them come out and say this unless you count the multiple mentions of him being "a dream to work with" and "aiming to satisfy the customer."

I bet.

∽

After the girls finish some dry Cheerios and sliced bananas, I make the executive decision to attempt a walk to the park. I wipe them both down and try to get them into the stroller without scarring anyone either physically or mentally. I've already wrestled them both into clean diapers and found the hats my brother makes them wear. Neither one wants to wear those, of course, and once I get a hat on Jane, I have to reattach the one that should be on Claire but is now on the floor. We do this a few more times, the girls squealing as the floppy cotton hats hit the carpet again and again. How does Julia do this? How did my mother do this? I make a mental note to try my hardest to have only one baby at a time. If I'm lucky enough to ever have one.

I get both babies buckled into the stroller and reposition the sun shade so it at least keeps most of the glare off their faces. Getting them out to the stroller required carrying them, one under each arm like squirming footballs, onto the front lawn and then doing a little dance between the one in the stroller and the one waiting on the grass. There must be a trick to doing everything double, but no one's taught it to me. When I've been places with Zach and Julia and their kids, I've never paid attention to how the nitty gritty gets accomplished. On the few occasions I've been in charge it's usually been with the boys. It's easier to trust the fun aunt with elementary schoolers, I guess.

"Here we go," I tell the girls as I try to push the stroller down the driveway and out to the sidewalk. They both babble to each other as I push against the bar in front of me. We go nowhere. Their twin talk bubbles up through the rough navy canvas of the stroller as I try again.

"Okay, ladies, Auntie Kat will get this all figured out. Give me just a second." By the time I realize the brake's on we've been standing out in front of the house for at least five more minutes. I shove the pedal up. It's surprisingly difficult and leaves me rubbing the top of my foot where the plastic has dug into my skin. Who knew strollers had so many hidden hazards?

Since there's no one here to see us get off to a rocky start I straighten the diaper bag on my shoulder and push Jane and Claire in front of me like we do this every day. I'm already sweating before we get half way down the block. These girls are turning into chunky monkeys. Their chubby little legs bounce as we move down the sidewalk. Should I have slathered them in sunscreen before we left the house? The thought of making Jane and Claire even more slippery feels dangerous but not as dangerous as being the one responsible for giving them skin cancer before their second birthday. We'll just have to find a shady spot once we get to the park.

The afternoon's still cool enough to be pleasant—one of my mother's favorite words—and who doesn't love a day that hasn't gotten so warm it makes you want to melt right on the sidewalk? I wave to Zach and Julia's neighbors, enjoying the chance to pretend that I'm out walking my own kids through this happy suburban neighborhood.

"Aunt Kat can handle this, right ladies?" I ask my two little practice cherubs. "And I bet you'd like having a cousin. Then the two of you wouldn't be the littlest anymore."

The girls don't answer me. They're too busy pulling at their hats and their shoes to listen to whatever I'm talking about. "You guys need to team up and start doing that for each other," I tell them conspiratorially. "There are two of you. You should take advantage of that while you can."

Amy and I used to get in more trouble that way. "Helping" each other out with problems, though usually causing more in the process. What was the issue with using the fact no one could tell us apart? We never switched places on dates, but changing places so only one of us had to study for a Math test while the other one worried about Science? That might have happened a few times. I'm sure Jane and Claire will figure out all that on their own, but if they need pointers at least they have some experts to consult.

When we round the corner and the park comes into view, I realize I've had the same fabulous idea as every other kid-saddled adult in Julia's neighborhood. The place is swarming with children, every swing and bar on the jungle gym already taken by a sweaty, possibly sugar-addled kid. I glance down at the fuzzy heads of my nieces and think about turning around. We could just go for a walk and call it a day, spend the rest of the afternoon trying to shove those blocks into that shape sorter thing in the comfort of the air-conditioned house.

Wait? Why are they hatless?

I put the brake on the stroller and come around to confront the two cutest little weasels on the planet. Two sets of brown eyes light up when I squat down to their level. "Girls, where are your hats? When I suggested you work together, I meant against other people, not when Aunt Kat is in charge."

Neither baby answers me, of course, they just keep laughing and kicking their legs, especially once I have to start digging around their little bodies—with plenty of tickles—to find where they've stuffed their sun hats. Once I locate them and do the whole wrestling them back on routine, I'm even more convinced that we should just start our walk back home.

But then I see him.

I'd know that back anywhere, unfortunately. Maybe if I hadn't spent so much time yesterday memorizing the exact way his shoulders look under a T-shirt or the way he holds his head to the side just the tiniest bit when he's thinking, then I wouldn't even have noticed Michael standing in the line for the ice cream truck. But there he is, reading the menu and holding the hands of two small dark-haired boys, one on each side of him. Their little hands are dwarfed in his and they both have the same little tilt of their heads as they listen to him recite all the choices from the list painted on the side of the truck.

"Can we get more than one thing?" one of them asks, and Michael turns his head to look down at the little boy.

"What do you think?" he asks, and I'm pretty sure I know the answer just from the tone of his voice.

"Yes?" the kid asks again, his voice hopeful in that way only small children can effectively pull off.

"No," Michael answers. "Do you need me to keep reading? I think you guys might be able to read the rest yourself."

"What does the last one say?" the other mini-Michael asks and I almost fall over once the realization of what I'm looking at hits me.

Cruz and *Sons*. *Michael's* sons. Two of them.

"Mom would let us get two, I think."

"Your mom would kill me if she found out I filled you guys with sugar before dinner. One is pushing it." They're almost up to the front of the line, neither boy letting go of his hand for even a second.

Claire chooses this moment to let out an ear-piercing shriek. Not to be outdone, Jane follows this with a scream of her own that has heads turning in our direction. I shush them, but that only makes them yell louder and I can't fault them, really. Outside voices are for outside, after all, and I've been crouched down beside them with my mouth hanging open for more time than is strictly necessary.

There's no place to hide when Michael turns and

catches sight of me. His eyes land on my face and then skitter over to the stroller, before landing back on me. He looks at the girls again and I watch his brow furrow before he whispers something to his boys and then comes trotting over. They follow, two smaller versions of him on either side like matching bookends.

"I thought that was you," Michael says, still looking at the babies. "Didn't expect to see you in the park today."

"Didn't expect to see you, either," I counter, straightening up and wiping the dust from my palms on the fabric of my pants. His kids look up at me, their brown eyes questioning why they're no longer standing in the ice cream line and are now standing in front of this stranger.

"Your babies are loud," one of them finally says. I'd almost forgotten about the screeching coming from the stroller. "Is something wrong with them?" He peers under the canvas top just as Jane belts out another squeal.

"Oh, they just do that sometimes, I guess," I tell him once he recovers. "They think it's funny or something."

Michael takes a good look at Jane and Claire and then back at me. "They look like you," he says, taking in their dark hair. "But they must have their dad's eyes."

I blink. "Oh, these aren't ... I don't ..." I stumble over my words. "These are my nieces, Jane and Claire. And I'm Kat." I put out my hand for one and then the other tiny Michael to shake. They do so like they've done this a million times.

"Nice to meet you," they say in unison. They're kids with manners. Way to go, Michael. And their mother. Who it occurs to me still might be attached to their father.

"How do you tell which one is which?" the smaller boy asks. "They look exactly alike." He screws his face up as he looks at the girls again. One of Jane's screams surprises him and he steps back.

"After a while you start to notice little differences," I tell him, handing Jane a toy from the diaper bag. Maybe that will stop some of the yelling. "Like Claire's face is a little fuller and Jane's nose is just a little bit pointier. When they get older it will be a little easier if you spend lots of time with them. Only strangers will have a hard time." Not that Michael's sons will be spending tons of time with my nieces. They'll probably never be able to reliably tell them apart. They'll probably never see them again.

"They're your nieces," Michael repeats back to me and I think I detect a hint of relief in his voice. Is he relieved that he didn't start something with a woman with twins? Of course he's not interested in a woman with children.

"Yep," I say. "I think you're seeing the family resemblance, but they aren't mine."

Michael nods. "They're still pretty cute."

"Can't deny that," I joke. "What are your boys' names? They're pretty cute, too. Or handsome? I guess I should say they're handsome." *Like their father.*

"My boys?" Michael asks like he's forgotten that the two kids are standing here. I point to his two little doppelgängers and he gives me a confused look. "These guys?" he asks like he has no idea what I'm talking about.

"Unless you've got two other sons stashed away in a different area of the park," I say, keeping my fingers crossed that this isn't the case. How many kids can a twenty-eight-year-old man have? Millions maybe.

"Sons?" Michael's mouth quirks up. "No, no, no. These are my brothers. This one's Will and this one's... what's your name again?" he asks the smaller one.

"Andrew!" he answers as Michael ruffles his hair.

"Andrew, right. I forgot there for a second."

"Are we still getting ice cream?" Will asks and Michael

seems to come to his senses. "Oh, yeah, of course, buddy. We have to get back in line though." They all turn to walk back toward the truck. "Can they have ice cream?" he asks, pointing to the now quiet stroller.

"I think so." Have I seen the girls eat that before? Is there some magic age when babies are allowed to have ice cream?

Michael seems to sense my hesitation. "What about if I buy one for you and you give them a few bites?"

"Okay," I say before I realize I've just agreed to let him buy my ice cream. "Or I could buy you guys ice cream. To apologize for yesterday. I didn't mean to—"

"No way, Thumbs. I offered first. And how about we just forget about yesterday?"

Julia's disappointed expression from earlier reminds me that he's probably not going to really forget about yesterday anytime soon. "I was just surprised you have your own company. At your age."

Michael raises an eyebrow. "Were you expecting a paper route? Come on, let's get in line." He puts his hands out again and his brothers attach themselves immediately. Andrew gives me a side glance but goes back to looking at the menu once we're close enough to see the list.

I wheel the double stroller along behind them, admiring the way Michael's legs eat up the space in front of him. He's tall, I realize, so tall he has to squat down when one of his brothers asks him a question. The boys are young, maybe the same age as my nephews Charlie and Noah. How can Michael have brothers in elementary school? I try to ignore the relief that washed over me when Michael told me they weren't his children. Kids aren't a deal breaker for me, but a baby mama or ex-wife? Having him unattached shouldn't be putting this smile on my face. His personal life is none of my business and I have no right feeling the rush of warmth that comes when he turns his head and looks at me over his shoulder.

"What do you think, Kat? What's reasonable for the girls to eat?"

Anyone else would think we were here together, maybe might even mistake us for a family. Out for the afternoon with our kids here at the park. Buying ice cream before we walk back to our house. We'd make dinner. Put the kids to bed. Snuggle on the couch.

"Kat?"

"Oh, um, the vanilla cup. They can help me eat that." I try to keep my eyes on the menu, but Michael's smile is hypnotic. I remember the way his lips pressed against mine when he kissed me, and I'm lucky there's no more talking required right now because I'm not sure I can trust what might come out of my mouth.

"Vanilla cup. Got it." He gives me a wink before he turns back around to talk to the ice cream man, quickly delivering the cones and cups to waiting hands. When he hands me mine our fingers brush and I wonder how the ice cream doesn't melt from the electricity I feel.

"Let's find some place to sit," Michael says as he starts herding Will and Andrew toward a set of empty picnic tables. He's unhurried, patient with them as he helps them carry their cones without dropping them. He takes a lick of the cone he's gotten for himself and I nearly faint at the sight of his tongue darting out to grab the melting ice cream. And now I get to sit and watch him do that over and over again.

Lord have mercy.

8

Michael

"You scared me there for a second, Thumbs."

"I scared you?" Kat spoons a little bite of vanilla ice cream into one of the open mouths in front of her. The girls have been like ravenous baby birds ever since they got their first taste of what Kat has in that cup. I should have bought two of those because the few times I've seen Kat slide that spoon between her lips would be worth the extra two dollars and then some. I'd like more of that. The babies are cute, but nothing beats watching Kat's mouth work.

"Yeah, I thought you'd been hiding a secret family from me." I take another lick of my ice cream cone and watch Kat get extremely interested in putting another bite together for the girls.

"How exactly was I doing that? We barely know each other."

She's right. We're virtual strangers. I've figured out a few things from the times I've been able to get a glimpse into her life, but I know next to nothing about her.

"Well, let's change that. Tell me everything I need to know."

"Why would I do that?" Kat looks at me with a raised eyebrow. "You bought me dessert, not a Ferrari."

"Okay, then why don't you agree to give me the chance to figure things out on my own. Let me take you to dinner." I shift on the picnic bench so I can see Kat and my brothers at the same time. They're on the swings, pumping their legs to go higher and higher.

"I don't think you really want to do that," Kat says, her hands busy wiping two little puckered mouths with paper napkins.

"Why wouldn't I?" I'm sure she's got a reason why we shouldn't see where this goes, but I've got a whole bunch of reasons why we should. Even more now that we've run into each other again. That's the universe talking right there, and I try not to let opportunities pass me by when they fall into my lap.

"Because this can't go anywhere."

"Why does it have to go anywhere?"

Kat rolls her eyes. "Only a twenty-eight-year-old would ask that question."

"You know what I think? I think you're using that as an excuse not to give me a chance here."

"You don't seem like the kind of guy who needs other people to give him chances. You seem like you want to make your own luck."

I consider this, taking a bite of my cone as I think. Kat's eyes focus on my mouth. She's interested. At her house she'd tried to seem like there wasn't this attraction between us but even here at the park surrounded by kids I can't keep from thinking about touching her.

"Here's the thing," I start with as much confidence as I can muster. "I know you're attracted to me."

Kat's eyebrows shoot up. "Wow. Ego much?"

"You told me at the bar you thought I was cute and you keep looking at me like you'd rather be licking me than that spoon." Kat's face flames and I know I've hit a nerve. "And I'd much rather be licking you than this ice cream cone so why don't we see what happens when we admit that and quit fighting it."

Kat looks at me like she's got no idea how to answer. Her mouth opens, then closes and her brows knit together. From the swing set Will yells for me to watch him and I have to take my eyes off Kat's for a second even if I'd rather keep looking at her until she has to say something. Will jumps from the swing when it hits its highest point and I cringe as he comes back down to Earth with a thud. Andrew starts prepping to do the same. "Hold that thought," I say before I jog over to the boys.

I can see the hesitation in Andrew's eyes before I give him the warning he knows is coming. "Only climb as far as you're willing to fall," I call up toward the bottom of his sneakers. My father says it all the time so I know it isn't the first time Will and Andrew have heard it. "You don't have to jump just because Will did it."

When I was growing up there was only me. I didn't have the pressure of an older brother to help me or hurt me. Now, I'm less of a brother to these guys and more of an uncle since my dad's started over again in the family department. But even fun uncles need to make sure no one breaks their neck while he's supposed to be watching them. Andrew decides not to jump and instead lets his feet start to drag along the ground until he comes to a stop.

"Baby," Will taunts and I have to get in the middle so

Andrew can at least pretend to want to scuffle over the insult. We walk back toward the picnic bench with both boys staring daggers at each other.

"Don't call him a baby," I admonish. It won't do much good. As soon as they're home, they'll be right back to it. "It was smart not to jump if you didn't feel ready. You could hurt yourself." I give Andrew a pat on the back. "When you're ready to jump then you do it, okay?"

Andrew nods, but still shoots an angry look at Will. They're competitive and neither one wants to back down. When we get back to Kat and the stroller, she's packing up her things and pulling the strap of her giant bag over one shoulder.

"You're leaving?" I ask.

"I should get them back home," Kat says, letting me know she's serious by picking up the paper napkins and collecting the rest of our trash.

"We were in the middle of something." I keep my voice low and move closer to her. I reach a hand out to touch the skin along the underside of her arm. She shudders.

"I think I'm not quite ready to jump yet," she says, giving me back a small dose of my own life lesson. "Thank you for the ice cream. Nice to meet you, boys." She gives my brothers a wave that lets her move out of my reach and I curse the limitations of this kid-friendly environment. "Say 'bye, bye,' girls." Two chubby hands wave to us from under the canopy.

I let her turn and walk out of the park and back onto the sidewalk. When she turns her head to see if I'm still looking, I give her a smile. *Of course I'm still watching you, baby*. She starts to smile back, the edges of her mouth twitching just enough for me to see it but I'm sure she thinks she'd be encouraging me and that's not something she wants to do.

Except I already know I have her on the hook.

Yet. She said she wasn't ready *yet*.

"Is that lady a friend of yours?" Will asks. I never gave them any explanation about us sitting in the park with some stranger.

"No," I answer. "But she's gonna be."

9

Kat

It's Thursday before I realize I haven't talked to my sister in days. With moving, work, and now my inability to stop thinking about Michael, I've gone for over a week without calling or texting Amy. She hasn't called or texted me, either, which gets my wonder twin powers on high alert. We're not attached at the hip the way we used to be, growing up, but we still talk almost every day. She's usually pretty concerned when I fall off the face of the Earth. Her life during the school year is a flurry of stuff I can barely understand. Amy goes through craft sticks and glitter the way most women go through lipstick. She's a great teacher—funny and patient with just enough kid left in her to relate to a room full of kindergarteners—but it consumes her from August until June. But here we are in the first weeks of June and my sister hasn't checked in even just to remind me that couches need vacuuming.

Naturally, Amy's the person I ask when I need to be told not to have a pot of coffee ready tomorrow when Michael shows up to work on the roof. When Michael's *crew* shows up to work on the roof, I should say. Because this isn't all about Michael, obviously. I'm not thinking of him when I buy four different kinds of coffee at the supermarket, one of them decaf even though he doesn't seem like the kind of man to drink decaffeinated coffee. I'm especially not thinking of him when I consider making muffins—from a mix because I'm a little challenged in the kitchen, especially under pressure—to have here in the morning. I'm doing this to be a good host. Not because I'm hoping Michael will end up leaning against my kitchen counter and saying something that makes my panties melt.

I'd much rather be licking you than this ice cream cone.

Gah. I was lucky to be able to walk away after that. Taking him up on that offer in front of scores of impressionable kids would have been a bad move. Who knew all I needed was just the slightest hint of dirty and I could be sent fleeing from a public park rather than find myself arrested for public indecency? For all my brave words, I'm having a hard time remembering why Michael isn't a great choice right now. I most certainly need a wake-up call from my two-minutes-older sister.

I pull Amy up in my contacts and wait for her to answer the phone. She's usually Johnny on the spot with a cheery hello—two rings maximum—but the phone rings and rings until it pushes me to voicemail. I stare at the screen for a minute. I don't think I've ever heard Amy's voicemail message much less left her any kind of a request to call me back. I hang up and consider driving over to her house. Amy Winston not answering her phone? Something's definitely off about this situation.

Before I can grab my keys and rush out the door my phone begins to vibrate in my hand. Amy's face appears on the screen. It's a photo she hates. She's wearing her glasses and glaring with that I told you so look she always gives me. I breathe a sigh of relief. No need to go over and rescue her just yet.

"Hey, were you in the shower or something?" I ask without even bothering with a hello.

"No," Amy answers, breathless.

"Did you have to run to get to the phone? You sound like you're dying over there." Amy does not run unless something is chasing her and even then it's more like a serious walk. She's panting pretty hard though, struggling to get a deep breath. "Are you having an asthma attack or something?"

"I don't have asthma," Amy quips. "You know that."

"Fine, then can I run something by you while you try to recover from whatever's got you wheezing?"

"Sure," Amy stops gasping so much, letting out a big breath. "Shoot."

"When you have guys come over to do work on your house do you make them coffee?" I ask, already grimacing a little.

"Do I make them coffee?" Amy asks. "Of course not."

"Then you wouldn't make them muffins, either, right?" Muffins would most certainly be off the table if I'm not supposed to be making them coffee.

"It's not a dinner party, Kat. They're supposed to be working. You really are clueless about this homeownership stuff, aren't you?" There's rustling in the background and the muffled sound of what I think is a man's voice. "Hold on a second."

I wait while Amy does whatever it is she's doing on the other end. When she comes back, she's breathless again. "Is that all you needed to know?" she asks, impatiently.

"I guess," I hedge. Where is my helpful, sunny-side-up

sister? I really need Amy's no-nonsense practicality here, but now I'm disappointed she's nixed the coffee and muffins. If Michael comes over and just works then there'll be no chance for the flirting I'm planning—the flirting I've told him is off-limits along with everything else. I really am a mess.

"Spill the rest," Amy orders and I don't even wait two seconds before I start to pour it all out.

"Zach's roof leaked and the guy who's coming to fix it is the guy from the bar." I blurt it out like it's been burning a hole inside me.

"The kissing guy? From Smitty's?"

"The very one."

"And now *you* want to make muffins?" I can already hear the hint of disbelief in her voice.

"From a mix!" I argue like that changes anything. "But, yes."

"How can you manage to conquer corporate America but need to ask me about this? I thought you weren't interested in him." Amy's right. This is why I called her. I need her to set me straight. "But he is kind of sex on a stick."

A decidedly male voice in the background voices its displeasure.

"Is there someone over there?" It's not even eight o'clock.

"The cable guy," Amy answers. "They start pretty early." I hear another muffled chuckle.

"You don't have cable."

"They're trying to convince me to get it. You know, with those deals and stuff." My sister is a terrible liar.

"Amy, do you have a man in your house at eight a.m.?"

"Yes, I just told you. The cable guy." Amy tries to be evasive, but we've been together our entire lives.

"I see. So instead of calling you like they do everybody

else, they sent a guy over to convince you to get a cable package. Is it working? Is he *convincing*?" I stifle the laugh I'm dying to let out. Amy would rather die than give me any ammunition for teasing her, but there's no way I'm buying her excuses.

"Yes, he's extremely convincing," she tells me and I hear more muffled talking on her end. "I need to go. Make the sexy man some muffins if you want. Just know he's going to realize they're more than just muffins." And then Amy hangs up on me.

Cable guy, my ass.

I've gone overboard on the muffins. And burned two batches trying to figure out the timer on the oven. They're from a mix, sure, but I've baked three kinds just in case there are preferences. I'm not sure how many guys are coming over this morning so I've used that as an excuse to bake more than necessary. Maybe one of them will prefer lemon or have an allergy to pecans. Maybe one of them will hate chocolate.

An image of Michael's tongue darting out to lick the chocolate ice cream from the side of Sunday's waffle cone has me clenching my thighs together. The more I think about him the less resolve I have. Even in the face of my possible baby plans I'm starting to see the benefit in all this sexual tension. And after a long night of trying not to let Michael become the dominant character in my dirty fantasies, I had an epiphany.

I can have both.

I'm not looking to marry him. If I keep working on my plan to have a baby on my own, then by the time he's out of my system, I'll still be on track. I can still get the family I want even if it isn't the most traditional one around. It's not like I'm going to find someone who's daddy material in time for my biological shortcomings. The last man I dated looked like he would have been perfect for the job of husband and father, but our shared work addiction was the only thing we had in common. He was solidly in my age group and solidly boring once we spent more time together. No spark. But with Michael there's more than a spark. With barely any fanning we'd have a wildfire going. And Michael's not even thirty; he'll lose interest long before I get my ducks in a row for the baby stuff. No sense in fighting this attraction in the name of decorum.

A truck pulls into my drive at exactly 7:30 a.m. Can't complain about Michael not being prompt. I find something to complain about two seconds later when the guys spill out of the truck and he's nowhere to be found. One, two, three big bodies amble onto the lawn and Michael's not one of them. I squint to see if there's anyone in the cab of that truck but—nope—it's empty.

One of the guys I recognize from Smitty's saunters up to the front door while the others start to unload things from the truck bed. A ladder comes off and a few packs of shingles. Other tools and equipment I don't recognize all get hauled off into the yard. I duck behind my recently hung curtains before the doorbell rings. I don't want to look like I've been sitting here like a puppy waiting for them to arrive.

When I swing the door open, I'm met with a mop of brown hair and a grin that looks more mischievous than professional. "Ah, Ms. Winston?" the man asks. "We're here to get started on the roof. I'm Dan." He extends his hand and I shake it. "We'll try to get the work done without bothering you. Let me know if you need us to move the truck or anything like that."

"Thanks, and you can call me Kat."

Dan nods.

"No Michael this morning?" I ask, trying to sound nonchalant. It shouldn't matter to me who shows up to do the work so I try to act like it isn't the huge disappointment it suddenly is.

"He'll probably come to check in a little later. Why? You need him for something?" Dan's mouth quirks up and I blush, remembering that he witnessed the kiss at the bar.

"No. Just wondering."

"I can call him if you need to talk to him," Dan offers with a smirk.

Rein it in, Kat. "No, that's not necessary."

He turns to return to the truck and I remember the million pastries I've got littering my kitchen counter. "Oh, I made coffee."

Dan turns, adjusting his tool belt. "You made coffee? For us?" He looks at me quizzically.

"And muffins. I also made muffins."

"Muffins?" Dan's head cocks to the side.

"Three kinds. If you guys want some before you get started." I die a little inside at my admission.

"Um, let us get set up and I'll tell the guys. If you don't mind us in your kitchen, we'd love coffee and muffins."

"Just whenever," I answer and close the door as he walks away. I pour myself a cup of coffee and go back out to sit on the front porch with my laptop.

Less than five minutes later Michael's truck pulls up in front of my house and he jumps out like his hair's on fire. He glances at me as he rushes over to Dan and the other guys, now up on the roof of my house, clomping around. Michael looks over the pile of things on the ground and then stands with his hands on his hips.

"What the hell, Dan?"

Dan looks down at Michael from the edge of the roof. "What?" he asks as the other guys snicker.

"You texted me 9-1-1. What's the emergency?" Michael pulls off the baseball cap he's wearing and runs an exasperated hand through his dark hair.

Dan smiles wide, revealing the gap between his front teeth. "Kat made coffee and muffins. *Three kinds.*"

10

Michael

I'm going to kill Danny.

He's pulled me from another job just so he and the other guys can witness me fall on my face with Kat. They're all up on the roof when I get to her house, laughing their asses off at the way I basically ran over here... for muffins. But come on. A 9-1-1 text? For all I knew one of them was headed to the hospital. Which is where they'll be going if I get my hands on them anytime soon.

All that irritation and anger dissipates, burning off like morning fog when I get a good look at Kat. Someone's found the porch swing but hasn't managed to hang the damn thing up, so she's on the front steps, laptop balanced on her lap. Her mouth's worked itself into a little pucker as she stares at the scene in her front yard. All that dark hair spills over one shoulder and when my eyes lock with hers I swear I can hear a little gasp. Shouldn't she be at work? There's no need for her to be here. I told her brother this over the phone and he seemed more than happy to not have me crossing paths with his sister today. But there she is with a cup of coffee in her hand.

Coffee she made for me.

Dan's an idiot but he may be onto something. Kat's missed a day of work. She's made muffins, for fuck's sake, even though I would have doubted she knew how to boil water. And she's looking at me like I'm the best thing she's seen in a long time. I stride across the lawn and up the stairs to where Kat's sipping from her mug like she doesn't have a care in the world. But I catch the hint of a smile playing over the rim of her cup. She's not fooling me.

"Three kinds of muffins, Thumbs?" I ask.

"From a mix," she clarifies.

"You make breakfast for the electrician when he comes over, too?"

Kat raises an eyebrow. "He hasn't been over here yet. Maybe. I'm new to this whole home repair thing."

"Well, I'll tell Dan you'll make them waffles next time they come back."

"I wouldn't count on that," she says and takes another sip of her drink. "Do you want to come in for a cup of coffee?"

And there's my chance.

"Please." I give her just enough space to get past me but I'm right behind her when she opens the door and breezes back into the house. I catch a glimpse of Dan out of the corner of my eye back down at the bottom of the ladder. He's giving me a thumbs up and I shoot the bird back at him. Totally unprofessional and I'm hoping it only goes downhill from here.

Kat cuts through the living room and rounds the kitchen counter. When she stretches up to grab a mug from one of the cabinets her shirt rides up just enough to let me see a sliver of taut belly. I fist my hands at my sides. As much as I'd like to run my fingertips along that little stretch of skin, I wait to make sure I'm reading this situation right. No touching. Not yet.

"Do you want any cream or sugar?" Kat asks me while she pours the steaming hot liquid into a cup.

"I always like a little sugar," I tell her, my voice rough. I watch her falter a bit as she reaches for a spoon. "Not too sweet though. Just a little."

She hands me the cup, watches me spoon the sugar into it, and give it a stir. I take a sip, careful not to burn my tongue, and settle myself against the counter. Kat stays on her side of the room, but her green eyes stay locked on mine, glittering with heat. It might look like we're just having coffee, but we're deep in negotiations. Obviously the rules have changed in the past few days and even though I'm not sure why, I'm not complaining.

I push off the counter and close the space between us. Kat's eyes get wide but she doesn't move. Once I'm in front of her I can see her pulse drumming at the base of her throat, her chest rising and falling as she waits.

"You want something?" I'm not stealing another kiss until she makes things perfectly clear.

"Yes," she answers and rises up on her tiptoes to brush her lips over mine. When she lowers herself back down, she stays well within reach. There's the tiniest bit of gloss on her lips and they shimmer a little when she takes in another breath. I want to kiss that lip gloss right off her so that's what I do.

I pull her against me and she comes willingly, molding her body to mine while I take her mouth. I don't ease into it; I start dirty from the get go. Kat whimpers and I slide one hand down the length of her side until it comes to rest on the curve of her ass. I back her up against the counter and then haul her up against me. Dragging my lips from hers, I explore her jaw, her neck, the bit of her collarbone that her T-shirt isn't covering. She makes a noise of contentment that has me smiling against her skin.

"You like that?" I ask as I pull her up against the bulge in my jeans. I'm hard as a rock and I don't care who knows it. I've been hard for her since the night we met and that isn't going to change.

Kat's hands make their way across the expanse of my back, feeling along my shoulders. Her fingers thread through my hair as our tongues tangle and our bodies grind up against each other.

"They could walk in here and catch us, you know," Kat says once I move my lips back down to her neck again. It takes me a second to remember that I'm actually here for work, that she's talking about Danny and the other guys stomping around on the roof above us.

"They won't," I tell her, barely taking a break from nipping at her. If they know what's good for them, those boys'll stay right where they are, coffee and muffins be damned.

"But they *could*." Kat moves her face to look at me and those green eyes tell me I'd be better off slowing things down a bit here.

"They could," I concede and put a little space between us. Her bottom lip comes out in a slight pout and I celebrate that tiniest of reactions. I run my hands along her shoulders but keep my lips to myself. "I should probably get back to work anyway. Why aren't you doing whatever you do for a living?"

"Had to stay home to make sure the workmen didn't ruin my brother's house." She leans toward me, letting her breasts rub against me for just long enough to make me stupid. "I can take a day here and there."

Kat's nipples straining against her T-shirt make it difficult for me to focus. "Lawyer?" I manage to ask while the rest of my brain tries to keep my fingers from sliding across Kat's chest.

"PR," she answers as she lets her hands run along the edge of my chin. The stubble there nearly ignites under her fingertips.

"You can tell me all about it when I come back tonight," I tell her, stealing a few more tastes of her now that she's so close.

"Tonight?" Kat asks, startled.

"Yeah, tonight. I'll come over around seven," I say against the shell of her ear and she shivers against me. Then I pull away before I let myself get in over my head. The urge to set her on the countertop and spend the rest of the day here is becoming harder and harder to ignore. Before Kat can protest, I grab three of the muffins from the platter beside her and plant one last kiss on her questioning lips. "For the road," I say before I leave the kitchen.

When I turn back to look at her, she's still leaning against the counter, hair slightly mussed, lips swollen, a few tell-tale red blotches coloring her neck. I could be back over against her in two seconds. Instead I keep my hand on the doorknob. "See you tonight," I say and give her a wink before I let myself out onto the porch.

11

Kat

I've brought this on myself, of course. I've gone from pretending to have no interest in Michael to spending the day in panic mode over exactly what he's expecting tonight. When he'd announced he'd be back my brain hadn't had time to recover from the onslaught of his kisses. It was like I was surprised he could use his mouth for something other than making me almost burst into flames. When he actually tried to talk none of that registered.

Until the front door slammed behind him.

If I had any sense I would have chased after him, insisted that I wasn't available tonight, made up some elaborate plans I had no way of canceling. But I'm not fooling anybody here anymore. Not Michael. And not even myself if this afternoon is any indication. I've cleaned the house like the Queen of England will be visiting, not exactly sure where we'll end up. I've changed the sheets on the bed even though it made me feel more than a little presumptuous as I pulled the corners tight. There's a good chance I'm overestimating my odds here, but what else does a twenty-eight-year-old man expect when he invites himself over to an almost forty-year-old woman's house? I'm guessing the same thing most of my forty-and-over aged dates have expected, only with less recovery time between rounds. I'm doubting Michael's coming over for conversation.

Which just barely explains the hour and a half I've spent trying to figure out what to wear. Do I stay casual and act like it's almost a surprise when we tumble into bed, or should I just go ahead and answer the door in my underwear? It's like I've never done this before and my own nervousness surprises me almost as much as the firmness of Michael's mouth on mine did this morning. He hadn't wasted any time once he figured out my breakfast ploy was just an excuse to get him into the house. And he left me breathless, wiping my brain clean of all those excuses I'd so neatly catalogued as to why this fling is a bad idea. But what's the harm in one last ill-advised hook up before I turn myself into the ideal mother? None at all, I convince myself as I scoot my boobs into my favorite push-up bra. That plus the quick maintenance on my most recent bikini wax has me ready once the doorbell rings.

"Here we go," I say to the empty space of the living room before I open the door.

Michael's there on the porch, dark jeans and a plain white T-shirt. The work boots are gone, replaced by some soft brown boots that make him look like he's trying for casual but not too casual. He smiles when he sees me, only lingering for a second too long on the cleavage I've worked so hard to showcase before finally letting his gaze rest on my face.

"Hi," he says. "You actually opened the door."

"I wouldn't leave you standing on the porch," I tell him, noticing the bags he's holding. "What's all that?" I point at the reusable shopping bags he's got dangling from each hand. I've never had anyone come prepared with props before.

"Ingredients," Michael says.

"For what?" I let my forehead wrinkle in a way that might accidentally accentuate the real wrinkles I've got going on there. I try to relax my face so he can't see the beginnings of my frown lines.

"For dinner. You haven't eaten, have you?"

"Dinner?" I say it like it's the craziest thing I've ever heard. "You brought groceries?"

"Sure. I thought I'd cook. If you ever let me come in off the porch, I can show you the choices."

"Oh, of course." My face heats as I move out of the doorway and let Michael into the living room. Dinner was not on my agenda for this evening. As he squeezes by me, he drops a kiss on my cheek and I get a second of that delicious stubble against the side of my face.

"I wasn't sure what you liked," Michael says without a hint of innuendo. "So I brought a few things. You aren't allergic to anything, are you?"

"No," I stammer. *Not unless you count not getting my way. Or waiting.* I keep that to myself as Michael makes himself at home in my kitchen, unpacking the bags and spreading things out all over the counter.

"What are you hungry for, chicken piccata or steak? You aren't a vegetarian, are you? I didn't even think about that. If you are, I can come up with something." Michael sorts through the vegetables he has on the counter. "Yeah, I can make this work." When he looks up at me, I'm sure my mouth is hanging open.

"You're going to cook? You can cook?"

"Of course I can cook. It's not rocket science. It's way easier than fixing a car or, I don't know, putting a roof on somebody's house." He grins at me. "Speaking of which, the guys think they can be finished up with one more day."

"That's good to know," I manage, still baffled at the scene playing out in front of me.

"What are you hungry for?"

I try to keep the dirty, dirty thoughts running through my brain to myself, really I do, but I've been told I have no poker face, so when Michael looks up again from sliding things around on the kitchen counter I'm pretty sure it's obvious what I'm hungry for isn't anything he's suggested so far. His face completely changes as he looks at me, the heat from this morning returning to his eyes.

"You're going to make it very hard to stick to my plan, aren't you?" His fingers flex against the edge of the countertop.

"That depends," I say as I move into the kitchen. "What exactly was your plan?"

"Dinner," Michael tells me, watching me with a mix of interest and caution as I get closer. "I wasn't assuming anything else."

"You don't have to cook dinner."

"What'd you think I was comin' over to do?"

I stop. There's only the island between us now, Michael on one side and me on the other, with the contents of what looks like the entire produce department from Whole Foods between us. I tilt my head, considering. "Why would you bother making dinner when it's obvious you don't have to put in the effort?"

Michael's brown eyes glint from the other side of the island. "Is it obvious?" He lets his eyes scan the parts of my body he can see and I feel the slow perusal burn through me. "Because I'm gonna let you in on a little secret, Thumbs. I'd love to pick up where we left off, but I think it's better when you have to wait." The last part comes out in a gruff whisper. He's torturing us both and I find it harder and harder to breathe. "Plus, everybody needs to eat so you need to decide what you want for dinner or else I'll decide for us."

When he isn't looking at me, I can at least pretend to be the mature adult I am. "Fine. I'm interested in seeing you try to make chicken piccata." I slide onto one of the kitchen stools. "Dazzle me."

He smirks. "I'll see what I can do."

"Fine. You can cook."

"Not sure why I'd lie about that. Wouldn't exactly have looked good to act like I was going to feed you and then show myself to be a liar."

Michael takes another swig from the bottle of beer in front of him. He's somehow made dinner while simultaneously cleaning up after himself. The plates in front of us are all that remain of the impressive meal he made. Technically I guess there is one cutting board in the sink, but if I'd tried to make anything more complicated than grilled cheese you can bet this entire kitchen would be a grease-splattered mess. And I probably would have burned the sandwich. I swirl the wine around in my glass.

"Where'd you learn to cook like that?"

"My mom taught me, mostly, when she lived with us." I catch the slightest tic of Michael's jaw before he hoists the bottle again. "Before my parents divorced."

"Does she still live close by?"

"No, she moved to Reno about fifteen years ago."

"Do you see her much?" A million other questions flit through my head. *Do you miss her? What's it like to be raised by one parent? Do you have some sort of mommy issue?*

"Not as much as I'd like. I think living close to my dad was hard for her. She stuck around as long as she could. Can't fault her for that."

"Is this how you impress all the girls?"

"With my cooking?" He leans back in his chair. "Nah. I impress them with a different set of skills."

He's cocky—almost arrogant—in a way that usually would have me showing him the door. But for some reason instead of irritating me Michael's boasts only make me laugh.

"Really?" I ask, taking another sip of wine. The sauvignon blanc is cold and crisp and I've probably already had too much of it tonight to be able to decide what's charming and what's annoying. It's making me far too interested in these other skills Michael's got. Him showing up with more in mind than just sex has me off-kilter, unsure of my next move. This is not how this evening had played out in my imagination.

"You want a demonstration?" he asks and I sit up straighter in my chair.

"Please." It's breathier than I intend and tells him exactly what I think he's about to show me. I ignore his smirk and wait for him to make a move. I picture Michael moving from his side of the table over to mine, maybe knocking the plates to the floor and just propelling himself across the top. He's probably pretty agile. He does spend all day climbing around on people's roofs.

"Do you have a deck of cards?"

"What?" *Are you kidding me?* "Cards?"

"If you want me to show you how I used to impress girls in college, I need a deck of cards." His hands come behind his head as he waits, his smile slowly spreading across his face.

"You're serious."

"As a heart attack."

We stare at each other across the table and I wait for him to admit he's joking. He's not, of course, and he has the gift of endless patience, apparently. Not only can he wait me out for this vital deck of cards, but he can keep stringing me along. He hasn't even so much as kissed me tonight and still I'm willing to play. Sucker.

"I might have some in one of these boxes over here." I get up from the table and start fishing around in one of my unpacked boxes.

"While you look I'll just clean this up." He's clearing the plates and I'm not sure if I should be thankful or get ready to shove him out the door. I hear the water running and the dishwasher door clanging open and then shut again while I hunt unsuccessfully for the useless pack of cards.

"Found them!" They're bound together with a rubber band and probably a million years old. Still, I deliver them to the kitchen and Michael's waiting hands with a flourish. He runs his fingers along the edge of the stack. "Please tell me that this isn't the start of some middle school magic show. You aren't about to do your top five card tricks or something, are you?" I don't know if I'll be able to stand it.

"No," he tells me, letting his fingers move from the cards to the space on the inside of my wrist. He slides his thumb over the skin and goosebumps rise all along my arm. "I don't actually know how to do any card tricks."

"You don't?"

"Not a one."

"Then why did you ask me—"

The rest of my question gets lost as Michael leans forward and presses his mouth on mine.

12

Michael

I lied about the card tricks.

I do know a couple. They're all the kind anyone can do, the kind that prove anybody can be an elementary school talent show magician. I really only asked for the cards to give myself a few more minutes to think. From the moment Kat opened the door it's been clear she expected one thing and one thing only from me. Not that I'm complaining exactly—that's pretty much all I've been thinking about since I left this morning with a raging hard on. The temptation to kiss her the second I got through the door was hard to fight off. But I get the feeling Kat usually gets what she wants, so I've made it my mission to make her wait as long as possible.

I'm punishing myself too, unfortunately, and the small talk is killing me. We skirted the issue of my mother, thankfully, since I'm not sure Kat really wanted to hear that story. The way she's been looking at me all night makes me think she'd be happier if I quit talking. The way she ground up against me this morning has me thinking I wouldn't mind it either. But I run the risk of having Kat show me the door as soon as she's through with me, so stalling's a little bit about saving my own skin right now.

Because the more time I spend with Kat the more I think I'd like to stick around.

When I kiss her things go from zero to sixty faster than I anticipate. We've been dancing around the obvious all night here and once my chest ends up pressed against hers there's no reason to pretend anymore. From the get go our kisses are frantic, messy. My hands tangle in Kat's hair and we careen across the room like two drunken sailors until we bump into the couch and nearly fall over. Kat slides her hand under the fabric of my shirt and we're off to the races. She's got that thing up and over my head before I have time to blink. As much as I like cutting to the chase, that's not how this is going to go down tonight.

"Whoa, whoa," I protest once I manage to get a little oxygen to my brain. "Slow down. You trying to make the midnight movie?"

Kat stares at me with glassy eyes, her gaze flitting between my bare chest and my mouth. "What?" she asks, panting.

"Is there some reason we need to get this taken care of in five minutes, or would it be possible to take our time here?"

Again Kat looks confused. Her brow furrows and she looks at me like I'm some sort of exotic animal she's found on her front porch. "You want to take your time? Why?" She's already working to shimmy out of the top she's got on.

I fight against the very vocal parts of me that are asking the same question. *You've got a gorgeous woman here who really wants to ride your cock. Why the hell are you fucking that up?* "Why wouldn't I?"

Kat pauses, her hands still holding the hem of her shirt.

"You've already fed me. That was above and beyond the call of duty. We don't have to pretend this is something it isn't."

I pull my head back to get a good look at her. "What does that mean?"

"It means I'm not expecting anything from you. I'm fine with just this." Kat goes back to yanking on her shirt and I have to put my hands over hers to stop her from pulling the silky thing all the way off. Once she does that, I know I'll be a goner; there'll be no more talking.

"Why are you so convinced this is the only reason I came over here?"

Kat rolls her eyes, clearly annoyed that I won't just get with the program and start ripping her clothes off. "Michael, you really want to talk about this? Right now?"

"Yes." *And no.* I look at her pout and curse myself for not just kissing her again.

"You're not even thirty years old. I'm not thinking of this as step one to us settling down with a picket fence and a house full of kids, and you can't be thinking that either."

She's right, I guess, but I'll be damned if I let her just dismiss me as some sort of fuck boy especially even before I've had the chance to actually fuck her. Kat seems to sense I'm rethinking things because she gives me a shove that lands my ass on the couch. She slides into my lap before I can get my bearings enough to think twice about it.

"Why are you getting so serious? Dinner was fun. This could be fun too." She moves to straddle me and I forget all those earlier reservations I was having. She gives me a little grind and I'm almost back in this. Almost.

"So, what you're saying is you're only interested in a fuck buddy." I try to play it off as a joke, but it doesn't come out that way. If this is how it feels to be reduced to nothing but a body, then it turns out I don't like it very much. She's offering me sex without the looming threat of a relationship. This should be an any easy choice. Even if we're only talking about tonight I should be jumping at the chance. Instead of turning me on, it's leaving me cold.

"I'm not looking for anything else right now," Kat says, pulling back a little. "I thought we were on the same page. You didn't come over here tonight hoping to find more than that, did you?"

I knew good and well what I was coming over here for tonight. "It just doesn't seem very optimistic. That's all."

Kat laughs. "And you're an optimist?"

I shrug. "I should go ahead and leave." The rest of this night's dead in the water anyway. I deposit Kat on the couch next to me and start to get up.

"The sex probably wouldn't have been that great anyway."

"What did you say?" My mouth falls open.

"I was just saying that after all that build up it would probably have been disappointing."

I turn to face Kat and, sure enough, there's that glimmer in those green eyes that has me suspecting she knows exactly what she's doing. "Are you saying that you think I wouldn't ruin you for anyone else? Because you know I would."

Now it's Kat's turn to shrug. "I guess we'll never know now, will we?"

I've got her on her back in two seconds flat, my body covering hers. She looks up at me with wide eyes and I scowl down at her. She juts her chin up at me and I know it's a challenge but I refuse to kiss her and instead let one hand do a slow meander down the side of her body. I graze the side of her breast and she murmurs, turning into my touch until I'm millimeters away from her nipple. I could slide my hand over just a hair and be palming her. I don't. She's pinned underneath me and I let her squirm a little, enjoying the feeling of having her writhe up against me. I sit up and Kat frowns, her hair fanned out over the couch cushions.

"Stand up," I tell her, but she doesn't move.

"What?" she asks, disappointment tingeing the question.

"Stand up. Do it right now, Kat."

She sits up and slides to the end of the couch, looking at me with more of that earlier confusion. "I don't understand."

"I think you do. Now are you going to be a good girl and stand up? Don't keep me waiting."

Kat stands, her legs a little wobbly and her forehead still crinkled.

"Come over here in front of me. There. That's better." I lean back into the couch cushions and put my hands behind my head. Kat's hair's falling around her shoulders, her lips still swollen from earlier. She shifts a little as she stares at me, waiting to see what I'm up to.

"Michael?"

"Shh. No talking." Kat closes her mouth but keeps looking at me from underneath lowered lashes. "Now strip. Slowly." I stretch the word out and watch Kat weigh her options. She knows she can tell me no, but from the way her eyes flash with heat I'm betting she won't.

"I beg your pardon?"

"Is that what you're begging for?" I smirk. She's not offended, not angry, but Kat's obviously used to getting her way. "Go on and let me see what's under that top you've got on."

She cocks her head to the side, eyes locked with mine. If she does what I ask she gives me the reins and I'm not sure that's something she usually does. "Why don't you help me?" she asks as she lets her hips just barely shimmy.

"Because right now I'd rather watch." I keep my eyes trained on Kat's face and when her lips tilt up into that almost smile she sometimes gives me, I give her back one of my own. "Come on." My fingers twitch behind my head but I resist putting them anywhere near Kat's body.

She goes for the bottom of that tiny top she's got on and starts to lift it up over her head. My breathing damn near stops when I get a glimpse of the lacy black thing she's got on underneath. I said slow and that's how she's moving, keeping her eyes on mine until the fabric covers her face for a split second. Her hair's a little wild once the shirt comes off but that only makes Kat look even more appealing. I'm already picturing that hair wrapped around my hand and she's not even close to naked.

Kat pauses and I grunt. "Keep going."

She slides her hand down her belly until it hits the top of her jeans. She pops the button and slides the zipper down until I can see a hint of the matching panties underneath. There's no pretending this isn't how she wanted things to end up tonight. I'd be willing to bet there's clean sheets on the bed. Sheets that I fully intend to dirty up after I enjoy the rest of this strip tease. My fingers itch to help Kat out once she starts to slide the denim down her legs, but I don't move. She holds onto the arm of the couch as she pulls the material free of her feet and her hair nearly lands in my lap. The silky strands move along my thighs for a second until she straightens back up again, now only in her underwear.

Kat makes a move to close the distance between us and I put a stop to that real quick. "Don't you dare." A cocked brow is all I get in response as she stops moving. "Naked, please." It comes out less like a request and more like a command even though inside I'm basically begging. Kat stands still while I look her over, nothing between us but the tiniest thong and a bra sheer enough to make my mouth water.

She goes for the bra first, reaching behind her to unhook it and then letting it trail down her arms before it hits the floor. Kat tortures me with the panties next, guiding them down her thighs and to the hardwood floor so slowly that I almost think I'm imagining the whole thing. And then she's completely naked in the middle of the living room, her skin glowing under the light of the lamp.

"Your turn," she whispers as I stare at how she's put together.

"Not just yet," I tell her, my voice gruff with the anticipation of what's to come.

Kat's body rivals her face and I could look at Kat's pert little nose and wide green eyes all day long so that's saying something. Her chestnut hair falls around the skin of her shoulders, the ends brushing against the dusty rose of her nipples. They pebble as I rake my eyes over them, imagining what I'll get to do with my hands and my mouth once we get moving. She's turned just enough for me to see the generous curve of her backside. Kat's not stick thin like so many women think they should be. Her curves are impossible to miss even when she's got them covered up. Now I want to run my hands all over every inch of them, sliding my palms over all that exposed skin.

"Come here." I spread my legs and Kat walks in between them. "Look at you. Perfect."

Kat's pulse drums just under the skin and I take my index finger and put it there, letting it drag down the length of her neck and along her collarbone. She's close enough for me to hear her breathing, watch the rise and fall of her chest as she inhales and exhales. I barely have to move to slide my nose along the top of her breasts and find a nipple with my teeth. My hands find her hips as I give her enough of a tug to pull her closer. Kat groans and falls forward, her hands flexing as she holds onto my shoulders. I lick my way to the other side, using my teeth before laving her with my tongue. The little whimper she lets out has me wishing I'd taken her up on her offer of losing these jeans. But right now, keeping my pants on is the only thing making sure I take this slow.

"Michael."

"What, baby?" I keep my mouth where it is, forming the words around her nipple. Kat shivers. "You okay?"

I take the groan she gives me as a yes and let one hand move from her hip down the outside of her thigh. I massage the skin there, keeping my hands moving while my mouth is occupied with the rest of her. When I tilt my head up to look at her, Kat's face is just inches from mine, eyes squeezed shut.

"Open your eyes."

Kat looks down at me, her gaze slightly out of focus. I slide a hand between her legs and she takes in a sharp breath that she holds for a second, letting it out once my fingers start their slip and slide along her pussy.

"This for me?" I ask her as she starts to grind against my hand. I circle my thumb over her clit and her eyes flutter shut again. "Give me your mouth." I don't ask because right now Kat's going to do what I tell her. She angles her head so our lips meet and I nip her bottom lip, grazing my teeth over it. I work her with my hand until she's panting, her head falling onto my shoulder, her breath hot against my neck.

"There you go. Just like that."

Kat mewls as I pop a nipple back in my mouth, testing it with my teeth again before sucking hard. She bucks against my hand, tensing around my fingers. I keep circling her clit as her legs start to shake and she presses against me to keep from falling. When she cries out it's my name on her lips. She shudders and I gather her onto my lap, licking at the sheen of sweat that's gathered over the pink marks I've left with my teeth.

Kat lets out a muffled curse against the side of my neck, trying to steady her breathing. I smile against the crown of her head.

"Haven't even taken my pants off yet," I whisper in her ear. I feel her lips pull into a smile before I haul her over my shoulder and carry her off into the bedroom.

13

Kat

How we end up in my bedroom is anyone's guess. Did he carry me in here? My knees are still weak when Michael slides my naked body down the front of his still fairly clothed one. I waste no time putting my hands on him.

"Somebody knows what she wants," Michael teases, but lets me explore.

I run my hands over his chest, greedy to touch every inch of him. There's so much muscle there, ridges for my fingers to slide over in places where I didn't think ridges could exist. I make a noise that can only be described as a *purr* and Michael laughs, the movement in his chest not slowing me down one bit.

His hands move to pull me back up against him, sliding down until he's gripping my ass and I'm flush against an erection I can't wait one second more to get my hands on. I fumble with his belt buckle, trying desperately to get to what I want. There's no reason to be coy. I just came all over his fingers not five minutes ago and I'm more than ready to come again as soon as I get these jeans off his body and on the floor where they belong.

"Just a second there, Thumbs," Michael drawls and pulls away a fraction.

The impatient sound that comes out of my mouth surprises us both.

"You that needy, baby? You can't wait?" His mouth's back against my ear, his breath warm as he taunts me.

I wiggle with anticipation, going again for the waistband of his jeans.

"Nope."

I'm not used to giving up this much power, unaccustomed to having any man not want to get right to the main event. When Michael moves away, I let out a frustrated sigh.

"Go turn on the lamp," he orders. "I like to be able to see what I'm doing."

I do it without hesitating, but stay on the opposite side of the bed once I flick on the light.

"Come on back over here." Michael's voice is a gruff whisper.

I think about saying no, about staying where I am and making him come to me, but I find that's not what I want to do. I *want* to let his eyes wander all over me as I cut the distance between us and put my body back up against his. He brings his hands up to cup my face and kisses me. "That's a good girl."

I melt, letting my nipples press against his bare chest. Wanting more skin-to-skin. Just wanting, period. Wanting his hands on me. Wanting his mouth on mine. One hand moves from my face down between my legs and Michael's grunt confirms what I already know. There's no disguising how my body's reacting to him.

"Get on the bed."

Again, I go willingly. I muster up a bit of bossy Kat and try to give an order of my own. "Take off your pants." It still sounds like a request when met with Michael's stern face.

"That what you want right now?"

I nod.

"Do something for me first." His hand rests on his fly. He locks eyes with me, giving me the slightest tilt of his head. "Show me."

"What?" I've propped myself up against the pillows at the head of the bed. Already my naked body's on display for him and has been for a while. My chest heaves.

"Show me what I want." He gives me the slightest nod of encouragement.

The air grows thick between us. I'm already at his mercy, already letting him have control. He knows this but he pushes for more, keeps testing how far I'll let him go. I spread my legs and lift my chin. "Pants, please."

He lets a puff of air out and toes off his boots. He peels off his socks, never breaking eye contact. Before he unbuttons his jeans, he stops. "Touch yourself. I want you warmed up."

I take my time sliding a hand down my body. I start at my breasts, glide along my stomach, and finally find my way to my clit. Michael's eyes follow my hand and he swallows before his eyes come back to my face. Only then does he pop that button and slide his zipper down. The pants hit the ground with a thud and I don't have to ask about the boxer briefs. He's out of those and crawling up the bed to me two seconds later. I've barely gotten a chance to get a good look at him before I'm flat on my back, my hands pinned above my head in one of his.

I try not to squirm as his body covers mine. "I said I wasn't in a rush, but this first time I might have to make an exception," he murmurs as his mouth moves along my collar bone.

"Please." It's the only thing I can say. I arch up against him, trying to get my hips flush with his.

"You want this cock, baby?" He grinds his hips against mine and I groan.

"Please," I say again.

"Well, I do like to reward good manners." I can feel his smile against my skin. There's some fumbling for the condom and then he's rising up over me, pinning my hands above my head again before he thrusts into me. My entire body arches up to meet his, my hands fighting against his grasp. It feels like I've been waiting forever for this moment and I can't get him close enough.

"God, you feel good, Kat," Michael says into the crook of my neck. He's leisurely with his thrusting now, sliding in and out of me at an agonizingly slow pace. Already I'm starting to shake, feeling my orgasm build. "Not yet, baby," he cautions and I squeeze my eyes shut, certain I can't possibly hold the tingling that's threatening to overtake me at bay.

He releases my hands and I frantically slide them down to his ass to urge him deeper. As if reading my mind Michael begins to move faster. Everything starts to loosen inside me as my release coils tight and then washes over me. There's no stopping it now and the noises I make leave little to the imagination.

"I can feel you—" Michael groans and then stiffens against me. He utters a string of curses, panting against the side of my face. I try to catch my breath, my body slick against his. When he rolls onto his side, I reach out for him.

"Sorry that was so fast." Michael has the audacity to look sheepish. "Give me five minutes and we can go again."

The laughter that pours out of me has him propping himself up on one elbow. "What?" he asks, confused.

Five minutes. Heaven help me.

14

Kat

"Hey, I've got to go."

The bed sags as Michael sits. He reaches out and pushes a strand of hair from my forehead. "Mrmph," I tell him because this morning I am far from articulate.

"I made coffee." He plants a kiss on my forehead and I open one eye and stretch out a bit. I'm sore in some very interesting places.

"What time is it?"

"Early. I didn't mean to stay over. I've got stuff to take care of this morning."

"On Saturday?" Why am I even asking? I'm not supposed to care what Michael's got going on this weekend. He's not even supposed to be here, but after multiple rounds last night of some of the most acrobatic sex I've had in recent memory, I wasn't going to argue when he fell asleep next to me. But I hadn't planned on him getting up at the ass crack of dawn and running out. I'm supposed to be kicking him out, not wondering where he's going.

"Especially on Saturday. I'm sure you've got things to do

today too." He runs a finger between my shoulder blades down to where the sheet bunches around my hips. I'm instantly awake and wishing he wasn't already dressed with one foot out the door.

"You could stay a little longer though," I say. "I could make you breakfast." *What in the hell am I saying? Breakfast? Ply me with multiple orgasms and I'm promising omelets I don't even know how to make instead of being happy he's not trying to stay.*

"Nah, I'm good." Michael stands, not even tempted by my offer. "I'll grab something while I'm out." He saunters over to the bedroom door. When he turns around, I find myself hoping he's going to tell me he's changed his mind.

"The guys should be finished with the roof on Monday. Then they'll be out of your hair." And so will he, really, because there won't be any convenient excuse to see each other again unless I admit that's what I might want.

"How long do I need to wait until I can get that plaster fixed in the living room?" *And how can I fabricate another roof emergency?* Good Lord, Kat. It was only sex. Exceedingly great sex. But still. *Let the man leave.*

"Probably should wait a week at least, make sure it's dry. Keep the fan on it. When you have your guy come out he can tell you if it's still too wet to fix."

Just the word wet has me licking my lips. If Michael notices he doesn't show it. "Can you recommend someone? I don't have a guy." *Or the ability to stop thinking about you naked.*

"Your brother doesn't have somebody who does work like that for him? He can't do it himself?" Michael leans in the doorway, arms crossed over his chest. His T-shirt pulls tight.

"I don't know. I'd like to take care of it myself. Not bother him." I flip over and slide up against the headboard, bringing the sheet with me. Michael's seen me without a stitch of clothing on so covering my breasts seems unnecessary, but he's not interested in coming back to bed so I pull the sheet up under my armpits. His eyes stay focused on my face, never even shifting lower than my neck. Apparently, in the light of day I've lost my appeal.

Michael scratches his chin, pulling his thumb over the stubble there. Stubble I can still feel between my legs. "I could do it for you."

"You could?"

"I could."

"Would you just add that to the other bill?" Here we are talking about my home repairs like we didn't just fuck each other's brains out. Like I'm not still sitting here completely naked under this cotton sheet.

"No. It'd have to be off the books."

"Oh."

Michael grins at my confusion, the corners of his mouth tilting up and the edges of his eyes crinkling. "That's not the kind of work I usually do. It'd be a favor."

"A favor?"

"Uh huh. I couldn't charge you the regular way."

"How would you charge me?" Already parts of me that shouldn't be interested in this conversation are getting way too invested.

"We could trade." He runs his tongue over his bottom lip and my mind dives directly into the gutter.

"What do you mean 'trade'?"

"Work for work. The good old barter system. I fix that mess in the living room and you do something for me in return." Michael's brown eyes gleam and I swear I see an eyebrow lift just a fraction.

"What would I give you in return?" I ask, my voice too breathy, not even close to playing it cool. My nipples tighten.

"You're some kind of marketing genius, right?"

I blink. That is not what I was expecting to come out of that delicious mouth. "Not a genius, exactly."

"If I fix the plaster then you can help me come up with a better plan for my business. Give me suggestions for my website. Things like that."

"You want me to help you with a marketing plan?"

"Unless you had something else in mind," he says, the picture of innocence. I have definitely been played.

"No." I tighten my grip on the sheet and smooth down my unruly hair. "That sounds fair. You fix the plaster and I'll help you come up with some ideas for Cruz and Sons." I shrug.

"It's a deal then? I've really got to get going." Michael pushes himself off the doorframe and moves back toward the bed. "Give me a call in a few days and we'll set something up."

I nod and watch as he comes closer, cutting the distance between us in three long steps. The bed dips again as he sits back down. He gives me a smirk and runs his index finger along the top of the sheet, dipping it down between my breasts. Gives the sheet a tug that brings my mouth against his. I don't resist, letting him slide his tongue against mine. When his hand finds the back of my head, I whimper a little and feel him smile a bit against the corner of my mouth. When he pulls away my body follows his. I sway enough that his hands move to my shoulders.

"See you later, Thumbs. Don't stay in bed all day," he tells me, hands still holding me in place and then he's up and walking out before I have a chance for a snappy comeback. Not that I have anything at all sassy to say. The steam from that kiss has completely fogged my brain.

I'm still reeling later as I sit at my desk. How did last night get away from me like that? How did Michael—the twenty-eight-year-old man child—somehow become the boss of me? And why is it bothering me so much that I liked it?

"Should have known you'd be up here."

I look up from my laptop to see the smiling face of my business partner rounding the corner. He's dressed in a pair of track pants and a sweatshirt with the local high school's mascot on the front.

"And I'm pretty sure you aren't supposed to be up here, Mark Miller. Saturday's family day, right? Isn't there a lacrosse tournament today? A cheerleading competition?"

"Soccer. If Rachel texts you don't tell her you saw me. I'm only grabbing a file I left on my desk. The game isn't until noon, anyway." He ducks his silver head into one of the glass cubicles further down the hall. "See, less than two minutes. No one will even have time to miss me."

I'm not sure if I believe him, but I don't argue. Mark's been my colleague and friend since I started as an intern fresh out of college. Back then he was making his way up in an old Nashville firm and I was a few years behind him just trying not to lose my job. But he saw something in me and took me under his wing. When he floated the idea of going out on our own, I jumped at the chance. We've clawed our way to a reasonable level of success in an industry that's more than competitive. I've spent my thirties nurturing Miller and Winston Public Relations and when I look around our offices, I only feel pride.

"You don't think your kids will notice the deafening silence? I've been told you yell louder than the coaches."

Mark pokes his head back through the door of my office. "Who told you that? I'm going to have to have a word with my people. I can't help it if I get invested in the game."

"Invested. Got it." I smile at him. Mark's a workaholic like me but he makes time for his family. Even when we were starting out and there was no such thing as an eight-hour day, he still made it to his kids' school events and home for dinner. He usually came right back to the office once they were all tucked into bed, but he made it work.

"Should I bother asking what you're doing here on a Saturday? It isn't even ten o'clock, Kat." He doesn't mention family day because I've forgotten to have one.

"I was up early and wanted to get a jump on next week. I needed to get caught up." I wait to see if Mark will mention the time I took off.

"Did you sort out the roof issue?" he asks. "Different from just calling the landlord, I'm betting."

"It's all worked out," I say, looking back down at my screen. I've got Cruz and Sons' web page pulled up in one of my open windows. So much for concentrating on my company accounts.

"That guy you found any good?" he asks, shuffling the file folder from one hand to another.

My eyes fly up from the screen to meet his. "What?"

"The roof guy. Does he do good work?"

Does he ever.

"Yes. Very professional." I try to think about the unsexy topic of roof repair but can't get the image of Michael's back flexing as he hammers down a shingle out of my brain. Now I've seen the muscles on the rest of him, I'm making that scene much more X-rated.

"Are they finished already? He's fast."

When he needs to be.

"They'll be done on Monday and then there's just the inside repair work to fix that place where the water came in. It's a mess right now."

"Do you need a recommendation for that? Rachel had some painters at our house. I could get that number for you." Mark reaches in his pocket for his phone. "Do you want me to text her before I forget?"

"No. I've got that covered. Michael's going to do that for me." As soon as it's out of my mouth I regret it.

"Michael?"

"The roof guy."

"Ah. Should I expect to see him at the next company happy hour?" Mark tries to hide a smile.

"No!" I protest too fiercely. "It's not like that. He's helping me with the painting and I'm helping him with some marketing for his company. We're trading work." Even if I'd rather be trading something else, truth be told. Michael's gotten under my skin in a way that's making me a little crazy.

"Sure," Mark says, not entirely convinced.

"He's too young anyway." Again, too much information.

"Too young? Is he in high school?" Mark moves to the little conference table I have in my office and settles into one of the chairs.

"Oh, no you don't!" I threaten. "You're not going to sit there and grill me about this when you have somewhere to be."

Mark doesn't look frightened. "Is he old enough to drink or does he have a fake ID?"

"You're hilarious."

"I notice you aren't denying any of this."

"Isn't your wife going to wonder where you are?"

"I'll text her to tell her I'm here finding out all about your teenage boyfriend. She'll understand."

"He's doing some work on my roof. Don't go making it into something it isn't." I scowl at Mark and try to go back to my computer, but he doesn't budge.

"Well, if you said my name the way you just said his I'd be worried we couldn't work together anymore."

I roll my eyes. There's never been even a spark between Mark and I. Not even when we were here in the office at all hours of the night. Not even before he had a wife and kids and it wouldn't have seemed unreasonable to find out if we were good at more than just putting a marketing plan together.

"Is the roof the only thing of yours he's working on?" Mark means it as a joke, but my cheeks pink up. "You didn't!" He throws his head back, laughing. "You've been in that house five minutes and already you're acting out the storyline to some 1970's porno."

"Shut up!" Like I hadn't already thought of the porn angle. Maybe I should pay more attention to the neighborhood delivery guy next time I order a pizza.

"Now you definitely have to tell me how old he is." Mark leans back in his chair. "This is prime blackmail material."

"Please. Like you'd run around telling anyone my business." Mark's a vault, always has been. "And he's twenty-eight." I brace myself for some sort of exaggerated reaction from Mark, but he doesn't so much as smile.

"That's not too bad. You made it seem like he was still in diapers."

"Not bad? That's a twelve-year difference, Mark."

Mark's face clouds a little. "I hadn't done the math, but who cares? Rachel's younger than me."

"Sure, like five years younger and you're a man. Everyone expects you to go after younger. Twelve years makes me a cradle robber. A cougar." I make a face.

"I should be high-fiving you."

"Hardly. You can congratulate me once I finish the work for the Baylor account. That'll be worthy of a high five." I try to steer the conversation back to work. I don't need to spend any more time thinking about Michael's hands on my body or his twenty-eight-year-old dick in my mouth. I most certainly don't want to hash out this morning with Mark here in the office.

"Fine," he says, finally moving from the conference table. "But I'll be living vicariously through you. Maybe he can convince you to start doing something other than work on the weekends."

"Don't get your hopes up. I don't think it's a regular thing."

"Too bad. I was looking forward to hearing all about all the emojis he was going to text you. Isn't that what the kids do these days? Send each other emojis?"

"Very funny. You'd better leave before I come up with an excuse to text Rachel with a few emojis of my own."

Mark laughs. "Seriously, Kat, don't stay here and work all day."

"I won't. Now go. Watch some soccer. Kiss your wife."

Mark shuffles down the hall and I hear the elevator ding. Once the office is back to nothing but the hum of the air conditioner I go back to staring at the screen of my laptop. More glowing reviews of Michael's work assault me from the Cruz and Sons webpage. I should be able to flip the switch back to professional mode here, look at this assignment like I would any other client. But all that swagger has me off-balance. That's something I usually hate, but I can't stop thinking about Michael's dirty mouth and the confident way he took charge last night. I certainly wasn't complaining then and I wouldn't be complaining if he waltzed in here and offered to do it again. *Focus on work, Kat.*

My phone pings, reminding me that I have an appointment on Monday. My fertility workup is all systems go for eight in the morning. I get a little flutter in my belly. I'm sure this will fine; women have babies at my age all the time. There's no reason for the nervousness that settles over me. If I needed something to get Michael off my mind this is it. He's a good distraction, but not a long-term prospect. He's said so himself. I'm back to the plan, hashing out the steps I need to take to get this baby train moving. Alone. No man necessary, swagger or no swagger.

15

Michael

"What about that one over there?"

"Um hum."

"She's been looking over here for the past twenty minutes."

"Um hum."

"Are you even gonna look? The one in the red with the blonde hair. She's got a friend too."

"Um hum."

Danny slams his fist down on the bar top and everyone around us jumps. The bartender gives us both a look and I shrug. "Sorry. My friend here's got anger management issues."

"Anger management issues, my ass. I've pointed out at least three possible ladies and you won't even bother looking. Why'd we even come out tonight if you don't want to be my wingman?" He takes an angry sip of his beer. "Might as well have stayed home."

I'm wishing I *had* stayed home. Being here at Smitty's with Danny has me regretting ever leaving the house. He's wearing his "handsome shirt"—the only one he's got with buttons—and looking to cozy up to any and all available women in the bar. Danny's never been picky and a few beers in he's already lowering his standards. Truth is, for me it wouldn't matter who was in this bar tonight. There's only one woman on my mind and it's looking more and more like she's not coming out tonight to get a drink at the local watering hole.

The sound of the door opening has me turning to look. I'm disappointed again as another group of women push through the glass doors, none of them a particular brunette with green eyes and the sweetest pussy I've ever tasted. I go back to my beer, thinking about how tough it'd been to make myself leave this morning. I'd acted like I had some-place to be but, in reality, I'd just headed home to my cold and empty bed instead of staying with Kat in hers. I couldn't stand the thought of her kicking me out once she woke up, couldn't imagine the blow my ego would take if she looked at me with regret in the morning. I'd hoped that by fleeing the scene I could keep a little bit of an upper hand. Not that I've got any if the way I keep looking at the door is any indi-cation. Danny's pointed out more than a few girls who would normally have me interested but tonight they're doing nothing for me.

"Why do you keep looking at the door like that? You expecting someone?" Danny asks before the reality of the situation hits him over the head. "You hoping she's gonna come walking through those doors? You have got to be kidding me."

"Don't know what you're talking about." I signal the bartender for another round. Maybe a fresh beer will make Dan forget he's caught me pining over a woman.

"God, it is so obvious. Her house is basically down the

street. You were thinking she might, what? Just happen to come in here for a drink? And she's going to want to hang out with you? Keep dreaming, Mike. That ain't gonna happen." He has the nerve to shake his head at me before reaching for the new drink that's appeared in front of him.

"She might." It is Saturday night and this is where I saw her the first time. There's always the possibility that lightning will strike twice.

"At least we're admitting that you were looking for her. Great." Danny's mouth twists. "A lot of help you're gonna be tonight." He lets out a sigh.

"You don't have to get all pissy, Dan." I turn a little to look at the girls he thinks have been checking him out. "Those two look pretty enough. Go on down there and talk to them." They're both approachable in that bland way that could be any girl around here. Blonde hair, tight jeans, and low-cut T-shirts. They are, in fact, looking this way and when one of them catches me staring she gives me a smile.

"You'd have to come down there with me and now I know your heart's not in it." He puts his elbows on the bar, settling in.

"What's my heart got to do with any of this?" I ask, watching Dan pout. "It's my dick that needs to be interested to pick up some chick at Smitty's. And you're the one looking to get something out of it. Go on down there and offer to buy them a drink. I'll back you up."

"But they'll be able to tell you aren't into it. You can't keep your eyes off the door. I get it, Mike, I saw her in those yoga pants. Her ass is the reason they use that peach emoji."

"Hey now." I don't like the idea of Dan or anyone else taking an interest in Kat's ass. Not that I have a right to get angry about it; I don't have any kind of a claim. But the fact that Dan was looking at all has me gritting my teeth.

"But, she's not exactly the type to start joining you for beer pong and pizza."

"I don't play beer pong."

"I didn't mean that literally. You know what I mean." Danny goes back to nursing his beer, the *girls* at the end of the bar not even a getting a glance.

"I'm not sure I do know what you mean," I hedge. I'm getting a bad feeling about this conversation. Even the fact Danny just used the word "literally" has me feeling anxious.

"Kat isn't exactly our crowd. She's got her shit together."

"I've got my shit together," I protest. Even if the pile of receipts stuck in the glove compartment of my truck says otherwise.

"You *will* have your shit together. But you don't yet. She's not going to put up with that. She's a grown up, man. An actual grown woman. She's not gonna wait around while you figure out how to be an adult."

I glare at Danny. "I am an adult."

"Tell that to all that shit you've got piled on your kitchen table."

"I'm working on that. The business stuff's coming together. That's got nothing to do with Kat." I don't tell Danny that having Kat help me is a big part of what I'm trying to organize.

"Just manage your expectations. That's all. She's hot. She seems nice, but you need to remember she's probably not looking for anything more than fun with you."

"Who said *I* was looking for something more than that? You think those girls down there are looking for something serious?" I point down to the blondes still waiting patiently for some dudes to come and buy their next round. "And since when have you been worried about finding something long-term? I thought we were out tonight to find you Missus Right Now not Missus Right."

"I'm not looking for anything more than tonight, man. It's you I'm worried about. You're looking all lovesick, trying to send her some telepathic signal to get her ass down here. Just call her if you're that into her. If you're just fucking her then fine, but if you're gonna start spending your Saturday nights hoping you're gonna accidentally run into her then there's a problem."

"Shut the fuck up, Dan," I growl and he raises an eyebrow.

"See? She's got you all twisted up already and she's probably out right now with some guy who knows how to balance a checkbook, not even thinking about you. He's probably wearing a tie and shit. I never should have called you to come over to her house. Should've let this thing you two have going on fizzle out. Now I can't even enjoy my beer and you can't see all the perfectly attractive females in this bar." Danny sighs again.

"I'm not all twisted up," I argue.

"You mean to tell me if she walked in this bar tonight you wouldn't run straight over? You'd leave me in a second if she showed up."

I can't deny Danny's right. If Kat walked in tonight, I'd forget he was even here. But she isn't coming to Smitty's and I promised Dan I'd help him out. "Come on. Get your lazy ass up."

"What? Now we're leaving?" Danny protests but starts to stand all the same. "I wasted my handsome shirt on this, you know."

"We aren't leaving, asshole." I grab our beers off the bar. "We're moving to another location." I start the long walk down to the opposite end of the bar, turning to hurry Danny along. "Are you coming or not?"

Danny scurries off his stool and catches up to me. "That's more like it," he says as he gives the girls a nod. They're already turning toward us, big smiles on their faces. I prepare to turn on the Southern boy charm if only to keep myself from thinking about Kat a few short blocks down the street.

But I make sure I can see the door. Just in case. Because there's only one person I'll go home with tonight and I don't want to miss her if she walks in.

16

Kat

Is there some sort of rule that says a doctor's office has to be twenty degrees colder than any other place on the planet? I'm thinking there must be as I shiver in my flimsy paper gown, waiting for the fertility specialist to arrive. I've been waiting long enough to get good and comfortable here on the edge of the exam table, which is to say, I'm extremely uncomfortable. I try to reposition the paper sheet over my knees so I'm better covered, but that's a lost cause. The gown's open in the front so there's a steady breeze no matter how I sit. I've already endured the discussion of my health and every possible question about my family history. The nurse who took down my information wasn't as impressed with my answers as I thought she'd be, but that's the over-achiever in me. I've been good about getting checkups and haven't had any medical issues so I'm expecting smooth sailing other than the obvious discomfort of having my feet in the stirrups. There's no way to avoid that.

A knock on the door has me sitting up straighter. I start to tell whoever's on the other side of the door to come on in, but before I can even open my mouth it swings open and in walks someone much too handsome to be seeing me in this gown.

"Ms. Winston?" he asks, head still bent over the manilla file folder he's holding. When he looks up and stretches out a hand to shake mine, I notice a cleft in his chin. There's no way this man is the fertility doctor. He looks more like someone you'd find starring in the next Hollywood block-buster. "I'm Dr. Sharpe. Sorry to keep you waiting. I was looking over some of the information Dr. Singer sent over." He releases my hand and moves over to the stool across from me.

"Hopefully everything you need is there. And I did spend a chunk of time with the nurse so you should know everything there is to know about me and then some."

He smiles at me and I wonder how in the world I'm going to be able to let him poke and prod around under this sheet. Dr. Sharpe is supposed to be the best. Dr. Singer said so and she knows I'm not interested in wasting time. I could have tried to take a more natural approach to this whole thing, but I'm working at a bit of a disadvantage here. No partner and on the bullet train to forty means I'm going to need some help with the baby making. Still, the handsome Dr. Sharpe is making me think his success rate has less to do with science and more to do with the power of suggestion.

It is a true testament to the level of sex on the brain I'm currently suffering from that I'm thinking this now. Since Friday night I've had nothing but dirty memories running through my head. I could blame Michael, but he's got no control over my imagination. He's only given it some very interesting things to work with. And some beard burn on my thighs that I hope Dr. Sharpe won't mention.

"Tell me a bit about why you're here today." Dr. Sharpe

puts the folder down on the counter next to him and opens a laptop. He balances it on his knees.

"Well," I begin, trying not to focus on that dimple in his chin. "I'm hoping to have a baby, but I'm getting older." I smooth out the paper sheet the way I'd like to smooth the crease I'm developing on my forehead.

"Ah," Dr. Sharpe says. "You're..." He shuffles through the folder. "Almost forty."

"Yes. And I'm going to be doing this alone, so Dr. Singer suggested I get serious sooner rather than later."

"No partner?" Dr. Sharpe asks, head bent over the laptop, fingers clicking the keys.

"No."

"Are you planning on using a donor you know or going through a sperm bank?"

"A donor I know?"

Dr. Sharpe's blond head tilts up from the screen. "Some people ask a friend first. I'll need to know because we'll want to be sure the sperm we're using will get the job done." He looks at me like he expects me to laugh. When I don't, he goes back to the screen. "I'd have health questions for them, things like that."

"I had planned on using the sperm bank." Asking around for sperm had not occurred to me.

"It ups the ante a little when there's an added expense, but today we're only doing your exam, and a few other tests, and drawing some blood. When we get the results back then we can have a longer discussion about what you want. I can give you some literature to look at in the meantime."

"Okay," I say, already feeling a little overwhelmed despite the research I've done on my own.

"No previous pregnancies? No miscarriages? No abortions?"

"No," I answer as Dr. Sharpe keeps typing.

"Alright then. Your advanced age does give us a few extra hurdles, but that doesn't mean you can't have a successful outcome. I don't see anything in your file about frozen eggs so I'm going to assume that we're working with the ones you've got left."

I swallow. The ones I have left? "I never froze any eggs."

"Then we'll just have to see what we've got to work with, won't we?" He clicks the laptop shut and stands at the sink, washing his hands. "This shouldn't take long."

When I finally make it to my car after enduring Dr. Sharpe's lack of bedside manner and the addition of the vaginal ultrasound, I'm ready to call it a day. Unfortunately, I've got an entire morning of meetings and it isn't even ten o'clock. I call my assistant and ask him to get the materials I'll need ready. I can sell ice to Eskimos, but not after having to deal with the reality of my limited fertility. Honestly, I'd known I was teetering on the edge when my baby fever hit, but I had no idea I'd be considered geriatric in the eyes of anyone with any medical knowledge. What I'd thought was going to be a little bit of a rough patch on my way to getting what I want is maybe better characterized as weathering a major storm. Not that we'll know until we get the results back from all the lab work I need to have done, but there is definitely a hurricane warning where I thought there were going to be a few blustery days.

I've got so much more research to do. I'm just at the beginning of this journey—a journey I should have started years ago, according to Dr. Sharpe, preferably with a partner with viable sperm—and I've got a steep learning curve. I thought I knew nothing about raising babies but I actually know nothing about making one. Not if it involves co-pays and office visits. Dr. Sharpe was nice enough in his delivery of the fact that I shouldn't start decorating the nursery just yet but he got less handsome by the minute with his gloom and doom predictions for my uterus.

I try to shake off my melancholy as I drive to the office. There hasn't been an obstacle in my life that I haven't been able to bulldoze over. Getting into the college of my dreams? Check. Landing an internship with the hottest firm in town? Check. Starting my own firm when everyone else thought I should wait? Check. And making that firm successful against all odds? Double check. This little hiccup will be no different. I'll attack this problem like I would any other. Except this problem involves squishy little baby feet and tiny little fingers. I get that wistful feeling in my belly when I imagine what the future will be like with a baby. I'm ready for midnight feedings and first steps, for all those toddler kisses, for watching my son or daughter in the preschool play. This problem isn't the same as most of the ones I've dealt with lately. This one's got the potential to really hurt if I can't figure out a way to make it work.

And there's a chance I won't be able to.

17

Michael

Things still wet over there?

I know I'm going to catch hell for sending a text like that, but after waiting longer than I can stand I've decided to go ahead and make a fool of myself. Again. Kat doesn't respond right away like I'd hoped she would, but like Danny so helpfully pointed out, she's a grown up with a job. She isn't sitting around waiting for me to hit her with a slightly sexual text message that I'm going to pretend is actually about repair work.

Excuse me?

When she responds I've almost forgotten what I'd asked her. I'm in the middle of finishing up some bids and luckily, I'm alone. The smile that spreads over my face would land me in some serious shit if any of the guys saw it. I told her to give me a call, and I should have waited her out, but I started to think maybe she wasn't going to take me up on my offer to trade my repair skills for her marketing ones. I'm kind of counting on Kat's expertise to make things easier from a business perspective. And I was counting on having an excuse to see her again that didn't make me look desperate. But desperate's what I've become now that I've heard the sounds she makes when she comes. I'm hoping to get to hear that again. Repeatedly.

Still wet?

Those bubbles that let me know she's typing keep popping up and then disappearing again on my screen. Then they stop completely and I'm left staring at my phone. Nothing. I can't text her again without looking like I'm sitting here waiting. Even though I am, and will be for the rest of the evening, if I'm being honest with myself.

When my phone vibrates in my hand and Kat's name flashes on the screen, I answer it before it can even ring twice. So much for playing it cool.

"Hey," I say like it's the most casual thing for her to be calling me. Like she does it all the time.

"You cannot send me texts like that during the workday." Kat sounds pissed.

"What do you mean?" I act innocent.

"You can't text me to ask me things like that. I was in the middle of a meeting."

"I can't send you texts to ask about our little project?" I lean back in my chair, listening to her huff and puff on the other end of the line.

"Our little project?"

"Yeah, your plaster and my marketing plan."

"Oh," Kat says before treating me to ten full seconds of silence. "That's what you were asking?"

"I was asking if the plaster seemed dry." I give her a few seconds to let that sink in. "What'd you think I was talking about?" I grin to myself, happy that I've caught her on her heels.

"Nothing." I hear Kat shuffling around. "I'll have to check on the plaster when I get home. I'm still at the office."

"It's after seven. How much longer are you staying at work?" At her grown up job that makes me a kid in comparison.

"Not much longer."

"You want me to come over in a bit and check the wall myself?"

"You don't have to do that."

"What if I want to?" I hold my breath while Kat thinks.

"Then that's up to you, I guess. I'll be home in an hour if you want to stop by."

And I'm back in. Under false pretenses maybe, but I'll take my invitations any way I can get them.

My palms are sweating as I climb the steps to Kat's house. I shouldn't be this nervous to see her again, but I can't seem to avoid the feeling that I might be about to have my ass handed to me and not in a good way. I've brought takeout because I'm sure Kat hasn't eaten and since I've seen the inside of her refrigerator, I know unless she plans on making herself dinner out of ketchup and expired milk, she's going hungry. Showing up with dinner will take away any chance I have of pretending to be here only to check the plaster. I'm hoping it's dry so I can start the work and drag it out for as long as possible. Then I'll have legitimate excuses for inserting myself into Kat's day.

When the door swings open, I nearly drop the bag I'm holding. Kat's still dressed in what I assume are her work clothes—a tight pencil skirt and a silky shirt with buttons I'm already itching to undo. She's at least four inches taller in high heels that make her legs go on for days. How does anyone get anything done in her office if she's walking around looking like *this?* I can barely concentrate on breathing; if you asked me to do anything more than that I'd be showing my stupid for sure.

"Hi," she says and I blink like an idiot. When she turns to walk into the living room I stand there, watching her ass sway in that skirt. "Are you coming or not?"

I scramble off the porch and into the house before she changes her mind. I swallow the urge to tell her that all I can think about now is coming. This naughty librarian fantasy I've got lodged in my brain is going to be hard to shake. Her heels click and clack against the hardwood floor as she goes to the spot on the wall where the water came in and I imagine peeling everything off her except for those shoes. Already I'm hard and she hasn't said ten words to me.

"I can't tell if it's dry or not. The outside looks fine to me, but maybe there's some super-secret trick you know to tell if it's still wet." Kat turns to look at me and I try to remember how to form a coherent thought. I'd taunted her with *wet* earlier, but now the sound of that word sliding between her lips has me thinking some filthy things. She notices the bulge in my jeans but brings her eyes back up to my face.

I clear my throat and try to get control of myself. I can't even be in the same room with Kat without losing my mind. "Let me take a look." I set the paper bag down on the coffee table as I come closer and hurry up and put my hands on the wall so I don't put them on her. The wall feels dry enough. I can definitely start taking the ruined exterior off. It'll be the world's slowest fix, but Kat doesn't have to know that. I can stretch it out long enough to spend plenty of time with her.

"What's in the bag?" Kat asks.

"Dinner." I'm sure she can smell the Thai food I've brought her. "I figured you wouldn't have had time to eat and that you'd probably be hungry." I keep running my hands over the wall, steadying myself. When I turn to look at Kat, she's staring at me like I'm the main course. "Are you hungry, baby?" I ask.

"Starving." She licks her lips. "Just let me change out of these clothes."

"I wish you wouldn't." I move close enough to touch her but keep my hands at my sides.

"You like this outfit?" Kat stands a little straighter, letting me look her over again.

"More than you can possibly know."

Kat's eyes flick back down to my erection. "You want to come help me get out of it? I might need some help with this zipper." She turns her back toward me and I get to see her sashay out of the room, calves flexing with each step. I'm running after her before she even makes it to the bedroom, already panting at the thought of getting my hands on her again.

18

Kat

"Are you sure you want to do this in here? It could get messy."

"Positive."

Michael slides out of bed, giving me a look as he goes. "Fine, but you're the one who wanted to eat in here. Remember that when you're complaining about how we ruined the sheets."

He walks through the bedroom and out the door. He's completely naked and I don't even bother pretending not to stare at the way his back tapers down to the firm globes of his ass. There is absolutely nothing about him that isn't physically perfect. It's unfair that all that has to come with the label that should be pasted across his chest.

Warning: Way too young to be a good idea.

But while I've got him here, I might as well enjoy him. And I'm trying to keep him here as long as possible tonight. I know he's got a tendency to bolt so I've slipped his T-shirt over my head to keep him from pulling on his clothes and walking out the front door. I've insisted that we eat dinner here in bed even though I hate crumbs on the sheets. If I keep him naked and close, I have a better chance of keeping him here all night.

"Do you want plates?" I can hear him banging around the kitchen. The fact that he knows where to find everything shouldn't give me the thrill that it does. This isn't supposed to be getting domestic; this is supposed to be fun in the most temporary kind of way.

"You tell me. You know what's in the bag."

Plates clank and cabinet doors open and close. "Drinks?"

"There's wine in the fridge and that beer from before is still in there." Before. The last time he was here. It's been taunting me every time I open the refrigerator door. Winking at me. I try to tame my hair a little bit. It's tangled in the back and probably looks like I've been in a wind tunnel. I run my fingers through it and plump up the pillows. I need to make this bed as inviting as possible.

"I'm not sure I can carry all this," Michael calls from the kitchen. "Do you want to come and help me or do you want me to make two trips?"

"Hmmm. So my choice is either getting out of this comfy bed and helping you or staying here and watching you walk in and out twice? I think you know the answer to that question."

"What if I want to watch *you* walk in *here*?" he calls out and I get an all over shiver. "Come help me, Thumbs."

I throw back the covers and let my feet hit the rug. I step over my skirt from earlier, the rest of my clothes are scattered all over the bedroom. Michael's T-shirt brushes against my thighs as I move and the fabric rubs against my nipples, making them pebble. By the time I make it into the kitchen they're standing at attention underneath the softness of the cotton.

Michael's eyes shift from my face to my chest and back again. I'm covered up, but under his gaze I feel naked and these porn star nipples aren't helping.

"I like you in my shirt," he says. It comes out slow with the tiniest little lick of his lips. He might as well have put his tongue directly on me the way my body lights up. We've literally just left the bedroom and already I'm hoping we'll be back there ASAP.

"Come over here." There's nothing demanding in the way he says it, but I don't even pause. What is it that has me deciding whatever he wants he's going to get? And how does he already know this?

I stifle the part of me that wants to run back into his arms, and force myself to walk. He reaches a hand out and one of mine meets it without me even giving permission. It's like my body has a mind of its own when it comes to Michael. There's no red light, only green.

He picks me up and sets me on the counter with more strength than I'd have thought he had. He's bigger than me, sure, but every time he hoists me over his shoulder like I'm nothing I remember that he's using this body to make a living. He's using his brain some too, obviously, but Michael's been spending his days carrying around more than a pencil. The countertop's colder than I expect and I jump as the backs of my thighs hit it. The thin material of the shirt's covering my ass, but not by much.

Michael leans in and softly presses his lips to mine. I open my legs to let him get closer and I can feel the smile he gives me against my mouth. When he pulls back to look at my face, he's wearing a smirk.

"Arms up."

My arms automatically raise and Michael eases the T-shirt up and over my head, pitching it into the living room.

Now we're both naked in the kitchen—something I'll have to remember never to blab to my brother or his wife. I don't think this is what Zach had in mind when he was deciding between granite or quartz.

"Hmmm." That sound, not quite a growl, not quite a hum, goes straight to my clit and I feel my nipples tighten even more. Michael moves back into the space between my knees and brings a hand to the back of my head. There's nothing sweet about this kiss, nothing timid.

"Stay right there. Just like that," Michael says. Again I don't fight him, just watch as he takes that firm ass back into the bedroom and rummages around. He comes back with a handful of condoms and opens the drawer closest to my left leg. It's full of random kitchen utensils I don't know how to use: a candy thermometer, something called a zester, and a motley collection of measuring spoons. Michael drops most of the condoms inside and shuts the drawer, leaving a few on the counter next to me. "At least now that drawer'll be useful," he tells me before coming back between my legs again. "Now where was I? Oh yeah, I was about to fuck you on this counter."

My breath hitches and the slow smile that spreads across Michael's face tells me he heard it. Or felt it because he's close enough now I can feel the heat coming off his chest, feel him exhale against my neck, feel his cock line up with my center. I'm instantly wet, like he's flipped a switch that has me willing and ready.

"I thought you wanted to eat," I whisper into his ear. His mouth's gliding along my collarbone, making its way down to my breasts. I lift my chest higher to give him better access to my aching nipples.

"I'm about to," he murmurs into the divot between my breasts, licking his way lower until I can feel his breath on my belly. He slips his tongue into my navel and I squirm. "You have to hold still, baby," he says, and I try to keep myself from wiggling around, even though it's killing me. Even though his teasing has me buzzing with anticipation that I'm having a hard time containing. He drags his tongue lower, hands splaying out on the tops of my thighs and I let him push my legs open wider as he licks and nuzzles a trail down, down, down until I'm panting.

"My favorite place in the entire fucking world, this goddamn pussy right here."

Michael's a filthy, filthy dirty talker. Normally the words he uses would make me cringe, but with him somehow it makes me burn even hotter. Begging him to do the things he threatens, loving it when he does. He bites along the insides of my thighs, teasing me until I'm a mess of quivering nerves, ready to fall over the edge and he hasn't even really touched me yet.

"Michael, please." I sound as desperate as I feel.

"Please what, baby?"

"You know what."

"I don't know unless you tell me." His brown eyes look up from between my thighs. A wicked grin on the lips I need to be just a fraction lower. "You'd better tell me, to be sure you get what you want."

"I need you to…"

Michael nuzzles me and my hips shoot off the counter. "Need me to what?"

"God." I squeeze my eyes shut. I know what he wants to hear, but I'm not a natural with the dirty talk, not even close. I can ask for what I want; I've never had a problem with that. But Michael wants me to ask the way he wants, and teasing it out of me is part of the game for him.

"Just tell me and I'll help you out, Thumbs." He's evil,

waiting there close enough that I can feel every puff of air he lets out directly on my clit. He knows I'll give in long before he gets tired of waiting.

I gulp down any sliver of a good girl fantasy I've been holding onto, because whenever Michael's here I am definitely not that. Not at all. "I need you to eat my pussy." There.

The noise he makes is worth any embarrassment I might have felt. "I'd be happy to."

And then he doesn't waste any time making it happen. The second his mouth is on me I let out a groan I'm sure they can hear down the street. One long lick up my center has me leaning back on my elbows to keep from falling over. I let my head fall back, fully aware of every sensation: the edge of the counter under my thighs, the warm wet of Michael's tongue, and the pressure of his hands as they snake around to cup my ass. He gives me a tug that puts me more firmly against him as he sucks on my clit.

I raise myself back up and fist my hands in his hair. It's like I can't get him close enough. I want more of his tongue, more of the stubble that scratches along the inside of my thighs, more of the sounds he makes. And with Michael, it's those sounds that make me sure he wasn't lying before about this being his favorite place to be. The little moans and appreciative murmurs that tickle against my pussy make me feel like I'm doing him a favor—never the other way around.

When I look down the length of my body, our eyes lock and the look he gives me is so primal, so animal that I almost come right then. He's squatting down, the muscles along his back flexing as he fucks me with his tongue. When one hand slides up past my stomach and finds my nipple, I know I won't be able to hold out much longer. Already I can feel myself winding tight, my orgasm building until I won't have any choice but to tip over the edge.

Which is exactly what Michael wants, so I squeeze my eyes shut and try to put off the inevitable. It's ridiculous that I'm fighting it, holding my orgasm at bay all because I can't let him have the upper hand. But in this battle for control I know I've conceded more than I usually do and that has me trying to hold out, trying to let him see that what he wants isn't that easy to get. Until he pulls that hand from my nipple back down and replaces his tongue with one long finger. When he slides that finger inside me as he moves that talented mouth back to my clit, I can't even pretend I'm not losing my mind. My entire body goes stiff and I thrash against his mouth like it's the last place I want to be. Michael doesn't lessen his grip, of course, and keeps me tight against his tongue as I ride the waves of my orgasm.

I'm still feeling the aftershocks when Michael rises up to his full height and slides into me. It catches me by surprise, and my eyes widen when his meet mine. He stares at me for a second before angling his mouth against mine, kissing me in a way that makes me forget anything but the feel of his body against mine. His head dips to catch a nipple between his teeth, and as he moves from one breast to the other, I try to remember to breathe. His hands knead my ass, pulling me impossibly close so that I'm grinding up against the base of his cock, facing the impossibility that I'm seconds away from coming. Again.

The glasses in the cabinet clink together with every thrust. I wrap my arms around Michael and his face comes back to mine. We're nose to nose as I shatter apart. He's staring as I arch my back, putting my sweat soaked chest against his. It's the kind of moment that I want to avoid, having him look at me the way he is right now. Like he's seeing more than I'd like to let him. You aren't supposed to have meaningful moments with your boy toy. That's probably rule number one on this list of rules I keep disregarding. But I can't look away and as we come together, I stare right back and we stay that way until we've both caught our breath.

"Shower first or dinner?" Michael asks as he separates from me, taking care of the condom and leaving me still shaking on the counter.

"If we take a shower we'll never get to dinner." Not that I'm complaining.

Michael laughs and his chest rises and falls with the effort. "Probably right about that. I can't promise that I won't want to soap you up." He gives me that slow smile that makes every inch of my body throb.

"I did get pretty dirty." I raise an eyebrow as I lean back on my elbows. Naked in the kitchen has gotten surprisingly comfortable all of a sudden.

"I like dirty," Michael says. "But I should feed you before I clean you up." He reverses course on the way to the take-out, returning to me. He leans over and lets his lips brush against mine. The kiss is soft and unhurried, like he's got all the time in the world to explore my mouth. His palms frame my face, thumbs brushing along my cheekbones as he pulls away. He puts one last kiss on the tip of my nose.

I blink and feel my heart lurch a bit in my chest. That's not the reaction I should be having to two seconds of tenderness from the man I'm no-strings-attached screwing. Not at all. I'm going to need to take another look at that rule book. And fast.

19

Kat

"So, I'll get right to the point here. This isn't looking as promising as I'd like."

"What do you mean?" I let my fingers flex against the fabric of my dress. When I'd picked it out this morning, I hadn't given even two seconds' thought to it. Pulling it off the hanger, sliding it over my head, I hadn't thought that maybe I should have chosen something other than a flimsy cotton dress to meet Dr. Sharpe for the results of my tests. I didn't think the natural choice would have been—no, should have been—full body armor and a healthy cloak of self-esteem. Instead, here I am sitting in his office armed with only the floral pattern of this ridiculous dress.

"Well, after our discussion I'd hoped things would be straightforward, but these results make me think we're going to need to be more aggressive than I'd planned." He steeples his fingers and gives me a thoughtful look. One I imagine he's given to a million women in this office.

"More aggressive?" That doesn't sound like the gauzy pregnancy dream I'd been playing in my head.

"I am glad Dr. Singer referred you. If you'd been trying to get pregnant on your own, I think you would have been wasting time. At least this way we can try some things to boost your fertility to hopefully get a better outcome." Dr. Sharpe fiddles with the laptop on the desk in front of him. "There's still the possibility that it happens quickly, but there's a higher probability that it takes a few cycles and some intervention." He finally lifts his head and makes eye contact with me. "Nothing to worry about yet."

"Yet?" The word lingers between us.

"Ms. Winston, you present as someone much older. Fertility wise, I mean. Your numbers aren't good. Your AMH level is low. That usually means you have fewer follicles that can still be developed. That doesn't mean you can't get pregnant. It just means we may need to try a few things. I'd like for you to get an additional ultrasound with some contrast to be sure we don't have a blocked tube or anything unexpected. I'll have the front desk set you up for that. In the meantime, have you done any research into the sperm bank? Picked a donor?" He says it like it's something I should be excited about. Like I'm picking out a new car or looking at the menu at a restaurant I've been dying to try. But even if I had been feeling any of that before, now I can only focus on the fact that I've somehow failed these tests. I'm not valedictorian of the fertility class.

"I've done a little. I haven't made any decisions." I slide forward a bit in my chair. The fabric scratches against the back of my bare legs. Dr. Sharpe's office has begun to feel more and more like a visit to the principal. Not that I was expecting him to be the most warm and fuzzy bearer of bad news, but he is turning out to be pretty horrible at cushioning the blow. He's the expert here and I need him to shepherd me through this, need him to tell me what to do so

I can get from this moment to the one where I cradle my baby in my arms.

"Well, not to rush you, but I'd like for you to focus on that just so we can get started in the next cycle or two."

"I can do that," I say. "But I'd like a little more information about why you think I might have trouble here. What do you mean when you say I present as 'older'?"

"It isn't uncommon. Your chronological age isn't always an indication of fertility."

"But I'm not forty yet. I thought that was some kind of..." I shrug, struggling for the right word.

"Cut off? No. It isn't. It's individual and you wouldn't necessarily know anything about your own personal fertility unless something like this was happening. If you'd started earlier then maybe we'd never be having this conversation. Or maybe you'd be having the same issues, just as a younger woman. But we can't know that so we go from where we are now. There's no crystal ball. It's prudent we're starting now before you get any more premenopausal."

"I'm premenopausal?" I squeak. I can't be going through menopause. I've just decided to open this baby factory and Dr. Sharpe's already telling me that we're closed for business?

"You have some low numbers. The AMH. And your progesterone isn't as high as I'd like. You aren't in menopause, Ms. Winston, but some of your hormone levels are closer to someone who's headed in that direction. The ultrasound will help me determine some other hurdles we may need to jump. Then we can decide what we do next. How does that sound?" Dr. Sharpe smiles and I want to curse his handsome face.

"Vague. It sounds vague."

Dr. Sharpe laughs, not the kind of laugh I would have

expected from his model perfect face. The sound that comes out of his mouth is far too feminine, far too high-pitched to go with the rest of him. Instead of launching into my tirade about his bedside manner I'm stunned into silence.

"You're witty, Ms. Winston. Let's try and keep some of that humor as we go through this process. It'll help." He stands and offers his hand. "Check with the receptionist on your way out and we'll get that ultrasound scheduled. Look at the donor information and keep taking those prenatal vitamins. I'll see you again once we have the ultrasound results."

Somehow I make it to the car and drive home on autopilot. I've canceled my afternoon appointments and told my assistant I'll be coming in after lunch to give me time to put my game face back on. No one at the office needs to know I'm dealing with a personal problem. They need to think I'm still Superwoman.

When I pull into the driveway, I'm reminded of how perfect this house would be for a family. Perfect to bring a baby home to and sit on the porch swing. A swing that's now hanging from the ceiling of the porch instead of sitting on the floor.

"What the..."

Michael's adjusting the chain so the swing sits even. He turns when he hears my car pull closer to the house. He's dressed for work—faded jeans, T-shirt, and his boots, baseball cap pulled tight over his forehead—but he's here at my house instead. He waves when he sees me, giving me a half smile that tells me he's up to something.

"I didn't expect you home in the middle of the day, Thumbs," he calls out to me, that smile still playing on his lips until he gets a glimpse of my face as I come up the steps. "You okay?"

"I'm fine," I lie and I know from the way he looks at me that he sees right through me.

"Hope you don't mind me putting this up for you. I was driving by and thought I'd fix it for you between jobs."

"And you just happened to have a chain? I'm not sure I believe that."

"You're too smart for your own good," Michael says. "I might have made a stop earlier in the week to pick that up. Just in case I was in the neighborhood. Don't want to waste the rest of the summertime without getting to sit on this swing. Come test it out." He holds out his hand and I take it.

I settle myself on the swing and give a little push with one foot. It moves back a fraction and crookedly skims forward again. "Thank you." I let one toe drag enough to stop the swing's movement. "You want to give it a try?"

"Sure. We'll see if it can hold us both." He's joking but I don't laugh and when Michael sits down next to me his eyes are full of concern. He puts an arm around me and I let my head rest on his shoulder. The sigh that forces its way out of me has him pulling me closer. "You want to talk about it?"

"No." What would I even say? I'm sad because I think I might never get to be a mother? That I've got this new ache that won't go away? That isn't something Michael wants to hear. He'd probably run off this porch so fast he'd leave skid marks.

"You want some cheering up?"

I tilt my head to look into those dark eyes.

"I can cheer you up, if you'll let me."

And since who knows how much more time I'll get with him, I let him.

20

Michael

I'm whistling all the way to the next job site, grinning like an idiot after accidentally running into Kat on her front porch. Even Danny can't piss on my parade with his scowling face when my truck pulls up in front of the massive McMansion his crew is working on.

"What're you smiling about?" he asks and I don't even get bothered by the fact that there's no way he and his guys'll be finished with the roof they're working on today. They'll be behind schedule and fuck my entire week, and I can't keep the corners of my mouth from turning up.

"Nothing. Just having a good day," I tell him as I look over the work order he's handed me.

"Well, you won't be having such a good day once I tell you we made a mistake with the shingles. We're short."

"I'll see what I can do. Did you talk to the client?" I scan the page in my hand. The mistake might not be mine and I'm not even slightly interested in figuring out whose head I should be ripping off. Stupid mistakes make me crazy and this isn't even tweaking me in the least.

"You aren't going to yell? Cuss somebody out?" Danny eyes me curiously.

"No need for that."

"Like there's ever a need. Usually you do it as a matter of course. What the hell'd you eat for lunch? We could all use some of that."

I don't lift my eyes from the paper, afraid that Danny will immediately know why I'm so chipper after my lunch break. I give him a shrug.

"Seriously?" Dan rolls his eyes. "You went over to her house in between jobs?"

"I was hanging her porch swing."

"Is that what you're calling it now?"

"I didn't know she'd be there." Not that I need to defend myself to Danny or anyone else. "I went over there to put up the swing. The rest was just dumb luck. Scout's honor." I smile again. Luckiest lunch break ever.

"I do not need your post-sex face. And you're the furthest thing from a Boy Scout I can imagine, Mike. For the record. Can you focus on the problem at hand or do you need more time for the blood to make its way back to your brain?"

I laugh, which has Dan scowling even more. "I'll fix it. Just let me talk to..." I look over the work order again. "Ms. Larkin, and I'll get us all sorted out."

"She might not fall for that, you know. Not every lady's going to forget about work taking extra time just because you walk up there and smile."

Except she does. I explain the situation and she's inviting me in for lemonade in less than a minute. Praising the crew and the work so far, more than happy to have us come back on Monday to finish up. I ask for a rain check on the lemonade and walk back down to where Dan and his crew are packing up for the day.

"All taken care of," I explain as Dan rolls his eyes. "Come back on Monday with the rest of the shingles. We'll try to finish in the morning and you can move on to the next job by ten or so." I put my hands in my back pockets and rock a bit on my heels, my smile still firmly fixed on my face.

"Fine." Dan does not sound at all fine. "We'll take care of it." He glares at me. "And please don't show up here again with that crazy face."

"It's the only face I've got, Dan." I keep grinning.

"No one needs the weird happy vibe you've got going on right now. We'd appreciate it if you could go back to your normal sullen, angry, pissed off face. It's what we've come to expect."

"Can't help it if I'm having a good day, Dan," I say as my phone vibrates in the front pocket of my jeans. My business is on track, I've gotten some time in with my favorite girl, and the sun's still shining. I might try to swing back by Kat's house tonight under the guise of working on that plaster disaster in her living room. In reality I'm thinking of getting her out on the porch swing with a bottle of wine and a blanket, but no one has to know anything about that just yet. Nothing can spoil the good mood I'm in right now.

Until I look at my phone. My brow furrows and my smile falters.

"That's what I'm talking about," Dan says. "We need more of that face." He pauses when I don't immediately start ribbing him back. "Everything okay?"

"Probably. It's Tracy."

"You gotta take that, right?"

"Yep. You all set for Monday?"

"Sure."

"Good." And we're all back to gruff one-word answers.

I slide my finger over the screen as I walk back to the relative privacy of my truck. My stepmother doesn't make a habit of calling me during the work day unless she's got a good reason, and even if she isn't always my favorite person, she's the mother of my brothers, two people I'm determined not to let down. When Tracy calls, I answer.

"Hey," I say as I reach for the door handle. "Everything okay?" Tracy doesn't call to chat so I cut right to the chase.

"Yes, sorry to call you when you're working. I just needed to give you a heads up."

That doesn't sound good. "A heads up about what?" Already I'm thinking the worst.

"Andrew's birthday's coming up and your father's on the warpath. I need you to promise you'll come to the party, but try not to get into anything with Peter."

Peter. My father.

"When's the party?" I ask, not even wanting to know what's set my father off this time. I'm sure I'll get some raging text message later under the guise of parenting.

"August. On the thirty-first. Please tell me you can come. He's already upset I'm having it at home and that I promised a bounce house. He thinks Andrew's too old for a big party. I could use something to divide his attention."

"Too old for a party? He's only eight."

"Tell that to your father."

No, thank you.

"So you need a sacrificial lamb, do you?" I laugh. Tracy's more than willing to push me out in front of a bus if it means my brothers get spared the brunt of my father's anger. And I'm willing to do it because I know how bad it cuts to have him disappointed, to have him tell you how you'll never measure up. If I can save them from that even for a little while then I'm fine to take the heat.

She sighs on the other end of the line. "I really appreciate it. And Andrew would be thrilled to have you here. Will too. They don't get to see you all that much anymore and at least at a party there'll be other people around."

"Text me what I need to know and I'll make it happen." I wouldn't miss my little brother's birthday even if it means enduring another excruciating afternoon with my father.

"You could bring someone, if you wanted. If you're seeing someone." Now Tracy's just fishing for information. An image of Kat's face pops into my head, but bringing her to my father's house ranks right up there with pulling all my fingernails out with rusty pliers. And we're not seeing each other. Not in the way my stepmother means. There's no reason to subject Kat to my father and his overly apologetic wife, not even if she'd agree to go. And having her witness me being reduced to a child for an entire evening? I'd rather have my balls in a vise, thank you very much.

"Not seeing anyone, but thanks for the invitation," I say, needing to get off the phone and back to work so I can show my father how wrong he is about me.

"Anytime, Michael. I know things aren't great with you and Peter right now, but you're always welcome here. You'll always be his son."

I know Tracy means well, means for her comment to remind me my father loves me—or is supposed to—and that I love him, but it raises my hackles instead of calming me down. My neck stiffens and my free hand tightens on the steering wheel.

"That's just it, Tracy. I'll always be his son, but I'm not a kid. Not anymore. And I don't need him trying to act like I'm not a grown man with a functioning brain."

"He has a hard time not being the boss. You know that."

"That's not an excuse. Stop apologizing for him. He can

either figure out how to be reasonable with me or he can keep on being right. There's no in-between."

"I think we all can see where your stubbornness comes from."

"Then you won't be surprised when I don't give in. He doesn't get to run my business and he doesn't get to run me. You'd better get yourself ready for the day when Will and Andrew decide they don't want him trying to run their lives either. He does a shit job of it anyway."

"I didn't call to fight, Michael."

"I know. Look, I've got to go. Send me the details and I'll be there, but I can't promise I'll be on my best behavior if he isn't."

"Fine," Tracy says. "I'll try to make sure he's in a good mood."

I don't want to know anything about how Tracy tries to ensure my father's mood is sunny. She's younger than my father, but she's not twenty-two anymore. Tracy's already getting herself nipped, tucked, and plucked in an effort to keep my dad from trading her in for a newer model. Which I wouldn't put past him to do, Will and Andrew be damned. Scenes from my parents' marriage dance through my head as I hang up the phone. Times when my father couldn't be relied on or trusted. Times when his anger got the best of him until my mother decided she'd had enough. Times that made me realize being the opposite of my father was usually the way to go.

I start my truck and focus on getting the hell out of this driveway, the house suddenly reminding me too much of my father's with its immaculate landscaping and empty rooms, its pretentious pool house and perfectly decorated interior. I need to get as far away from here as possible, back to something that feels less claustrophobic. Something that feels real. Which means that when I find myself back outside Kat's house, I know I've truly lost it. Because this isn't the place I should be running to. But tonight I need that front porch swing with Kat on it, and I'm ready to sit here until I can make my vision a reality.

You can bet on that.

21

Kat

I'm becoming much more familiar with the interior of doctor's offices than I even would have imagined. And although this isn't technically a doctor's office, it might as well be, with the horrible fluorescent lighting and stiff chairs. And there's no disguising what we're all here for, the majority of those uncomfortable chairs are occupied by happy, hopeful couples and plenty of baby bumps. I'm sure some people come to this office to have an ultrasound for other reasons, but today I'm the lucky childless woman who gets to be surrounded by already pregnant women and their supportive partners. I try not to stare as hands cradle bellies and backs get rubbed.

I'm all checked in and patiently waiting for my turn when a familiar voice comes booming from the back of the office. "I can't sing the *Lion King* for both babies, Cassie! What kind of a dad would I be if I just recycled Connor's theme song? Does that look like your nose? I think this little guy's got your nose, Cass."

I try to make myself as small as possible, but there's

nowhere to hide, and before I can think of a good excuse to explain away my presence in this office, Cassie and Graham burst through the door. Their hands are clasped together, and their excitement is hard to miss. Graham looks down at Cassie like she's the most amazing thing he's ever seen and she slides her free hand over the little bump I can now see plainly under her flowy cotton shirt. They both stop short when they see me, Graham's fingers holding the grainy photo of what I assume is baby number two.

"Kat?" Cassie asks and looks at me like I've dropped from the sky directly into their living room.

"Hi," I manage to squeak out. I was not prepared to have an impromptu chat here in this waiting room and from the looks of it neither were Graham and Cassie. We all stare at each other, no one able to think of a way to make this any less awkward.

"Kat, have you got a bun in the oven?" Graham finally blurts out, earning him an elbow in the gut from Cassie.

"Graham! You can't just ask people that," Cassie chastises.

"Well, that's the only time we ever come here," Graham tells her defensively. "Sorry, Kat. I knocked Cassie up again, in case you were wondering." He puffs his chest out like a peacock, obviously proud of himself and grinning ear-to-ear.

Cassie shoots him a death glare. "Thank you, Graham. I think she's figured it out. We haven't told many people, so if you could keep it to yourself for a little bit we'd appreciate it."

"Of course," I answer. "And congratulations. Another boy?" I cringe. *That's not your business, Kat.*

"I'm thinking maybe Graham can only make boys," Cassie laughs. "So, yes, another boy."

"Next one'll be a girl," Graham says. "Or the one after that." He smiles at Cassie who just shakes her head. He's never made a secret of the fact that he'd like a bunch of kids. Their son is his mini-me and I have no doubt this baby will be the same. They'll end up with a house full of little blond bruisers and Graham'll be in heaven.

The silence that follows is more than awkward. I'm not about to confess to Graham and Cassie that I'm here because I'd love to be in their shoes. I haven't told a soul I'm going to try to get pregnant on my own, not even my sister, and she's the one I usually confide in. Unless I think she might try to talk me out of something. Which would explain why she's still in the dark about my all-consuming need for a baby and, come to think of it, why she knows almost nothing about my most recent other obsession—a tall, dark, and handsome distraction who's becoming a more and more frequent visitor of mine.

But now's the time in the conversation where I'd share my reasons for being here if I was going to. When I don't, Cassie gives me a concerned look and an "out" like the trooper she is. "We've got to get moving. Graham's mom's home with Connor and he's pretty deep in his *Paw Patrol* phase. I don't want to subject Jackie to any more of that than necessary." She hands Graham their ticket from the parking garage. "We need to get this validated. Go see if they can do it at the front desk."

Graham doesn't even blink at the request and trots off in search of someone to validate the ticket. I mentally high five Cassie for keeping me from having to invent some lie that will only make things worse down the road. One that will most certainly get back to my brother. Cassie isn't my closest friend, but that doesn't keep me from tearing up a little when she slides into the seat next to me.

"Everything okay?" The concern in her eyes lets me know she's sure I have cancer, or a brain tumor, or cancer *and* a brain tumor.

"There's nothing wrong." I'm unsure of how much to reveal. "I'm just having some things checked out. Nothing bad. I just..."

Cassie leans in so my whisper doesn't carry through the waiting room.

"I'm thinking about having a baby." I blurt it out before I can change my mind. "On my own. Before I miss my chance."

Cassie's eyes widen in surprise. "I didn't know that. Julia hasn't told me anything about you wanting a baby."

"Julia doesn't know. No one knows. You're the first person I've told, other than my doctor, so I'd appreciate it if you didn't say anything to Julia or my brother. Or to anyone, actually. I'm not sure how things are going to work out and I don't want anyone else's opinions just yet."

"You keep my secret and I'll keep yours," Cassie says, smiling. "But if you need someone to talk to, you can call me. It took longer than expected to get this second pregnancy to stick. Graham doesn't want to tell anyone, but we were getting pretty frustrated."

"But your first one was..."

"A complete accident? I know. You would have thought Graham could get me pregnant just by looking at me, but this one wasn't as easy. So, if you need some advice or someone to commiserate with, I'm available. And I won't let Julia or Zach know I saw you here or what we talked about." She gives my hand a squeeze.

I'm saved from bursting into tears by the sound of the nurse calling my name. "Thanks. I'll keep that in mind." I rise from my chair. "Here goes nothing."

Cassie gives me a thumbs up. "Good luck. No matter what I'm sure everything will be fine."

I hope she's right because for all of my bravado in other areas of my life, this ultrasound has my knees knocking and my heart threatening to pound out of my chest. I give her a smile I hope hides my nerves and trudge off to be poked and prodded, keeping my fingers crossed.

22

Michael

"Damn it!"

Kat doesn't even bother looking up. She's hunkered down over her laptop at the dining room table looking at the changes I've made to my website, every now and then furrowing her brow in a way that's making me sweat. I'm trying to keep busy over here in the living room, taking baby steps with the removal of the plaster on the wall. When this is finally done it's going to be a masterpiece that rivals anything Michelangelo ever attempted. I've been sanding for three times as long as it really needs. You can slide your damn cheek over this wall it's so smooth.

Kat's changed into her yoga pants since I rolled her around in the sheets. As soon as I made my way through the front door, I made short work of getting her out of her pencil skirt. Those skirts are going to be the death of me. Seeing her ass in one of those tight things makes my brain shift immediately to getting her out of it. God help us both if I ever see her out in public in one. That could get indecent fast. The fact that I never see her out of this house will probably keep me from ever embarrassing us both. That thought gets stuck in my head and I wonder if I should ask Kat if she'd like to actually try to make it out one of these days. Even just down the road to Smitty's for a beer would be a change from our usual routine.

The white T-shirt she's got on makes it obvious she isn't wearing a bra. The peaks of her nipples nearly poke through the thin fabric, making it impossible for me to concentrate on work. Not that this part of the repair takes much concentration, not when I'm basically redoing work that should have been finished days ago. I let my eyes wander over to look at Kat's chest, but her business face keeps me from really enjoying the view. Those furrowed eyebrows make me wonder if I'm wasting my time on all this. Maybe I should just stick to the manual labor. I know I'm good at that, even if I don't know how to upgrade my website worth a shit.

Kat's tongue pokes out from between her lips and I forget all about anything business-related. I could just drop all this work pretense and scoop her up off her chair and carry her back into the bedroom. Or I could skip the bedroom altogether and spread her out on the top of the dining room table. Push the papers and laptop out of the way and make better use of that surface. Pull that T-shirt back over those nipples and put my mouth on them. Kat reaches for her wine glass and takes a sip, scribbling on that damn legal pad with the other hand. She's filling page after page and I'm dreading hearing what she has to say. I can't even pretend to be busy later with dinner dishes because those were done hours ago. That's the way our routine has been for the past month. I head here right after work without even stopping by my place. Make Kat dinner so she doesn't starve, and then fuck her so thoroughly she forgets I haven't actually taken her on a real date. Which is something I should probably try to remedy soon. It isn't like me to ignore the basic rules of starting a relationship even if things didn't start out in the most conventional way. Sure, I've liked keeping Kat all to myself and she hasn't been complaining about our set up so far. But women like to leave the house. Which is something we can talk about after I convince her to let me test out that table for more than just dinner.

But Kat doesn't even look up when I clear my throat and make a move to quit work. From the way she's acting, I'm sure she hates everything I've done to the website even if the majority of the changes were her idea. She wrinkles her nose and chews on her bottom lip as she scribbles more notes on the paper in front of her. It's worse than any exam I ever took in college, waiting to see if she approves. But little smiles keep creeping over her features that give me just enough hope not to run for the front door instead of hearing what she has to say.

Kat doesn't pay me any mind, even as I untangle myself from the ladder and readjust the drop cloth I've got covering the floor. I try to keep this workspace clean, mainly by doing as little work as possible, but sanding leaves dust so I go ahead and start the process of finishing up, even though in reality I could forge on ahead and be done with the wall tonight. I could even paint the patch I've been working on and have no reason to come back every night to Kat's house. So obviously, I do the opposite, going for the vacuum and a wet rag to wipe everything down again like even a speck of dust would kill all of us.

"Will the vacuum bother you?"

Kat only shakes her head no. Of course she can work through the hum of the machine as she tears apart my ideas.

Ideas I shouldn't be this worried about her critiquing. I shouldn't be giving two shits about how many spelling mistakes she finds or whether or not she thinks the way I've laid things out is better than before. But I want her to think I listened, and, if I'm being honest, I want her to be impressed. I want her to think I'm the kind of man who can run a business and do a good job of it, not see me as some kid with a lemonade stand.

Once I sit down next to her at the table, I'm convinced she hates everything she's seen so far, sure she's doubting not only why my grandfather gave me this business in the first place but also why she's bothering to spend her precious time with me. In trading work she's probably got the muddy end of the stick here, whipping my half-assed marketing ideas into shape.

After thirty seconds of the longest feeling silence ever, I clear my throat. "So?" The hopeful note in my voice makes me cringe.

Kat chews her lip again, still letting her pencil fly across the paper. "Give me one more second," she tells me, preoccupied.

I wait, my knee bouncing up and down until she shoots me a sideways glance that has me freezing mid-bounce. When she finally opens her mouth to speak, I'm so keyed up you'd think I'd asked her to marry me, not just look at my goddamn website.

"I like it," Kat says. "I'm still thinking the blue should be darker to better contrast with the rest of the colors, but the content is one hundred percent better."

"Really?"

"Really. Don't sound so surprised. I told you just a few changes would make a world of difference."

"Then what were you taking all those notes for?" I cut

my eyes toward the pages and pages of what I assume are criticisms.

"Ideas, mostly. All the other things we could do to drum up business. Other ways to make sure when people need roof repair they come to you first." She smiles at me and I want to kiss her, press my lips to hers and taste the wine she's been sipping on while she helps me take these next steps. Since I've got terrible self-control when it comes to Kat, that's exactly what I do.

"We'll never get through this list if you keep doing that," Kat tells me when we finally come up for air.

"I'd be fine with that." I frown when she pulls her chair away from mine.

"If we want to get you running on all cylinders then we need to focus. You can't distract me," Kat teases.

"Oh, I was distracting you?"

"First I had to watch you over there doing all that manly home repair, and now you're tempting me with those lips instead of letting me tell you the rest of these suggestions." Her eyes glitter. Here's the main reason we're both still having trouble fulfilling our obligations when it comes to our barter deal: We can't keep from getting distracted, ending up naked and in her bed before all the work can be done.

"I think it was you doing the distracting." I pull her chair back flush with mine.

Kat scoffs but lets me kiss her again, slower this time, my hands starting to wander the way they always do when she's within touching distance. I'm getting ready to pull her shirt up and over her head when she stops me, pulling back like I'm the naughtiest kid in her Sunday school class.

"Slow down there, buddy. I'm serious about going over these notes. I think we can come up with a few places for you to think about advertising that would really bring in business. We should talk about some of these ideas so you can get started soon. That way you'll be pulling in jobs before there's any winter weather."

I let out a frustrated sigh. Kat being right doesn't change the way my cock feels about stopping what I was pretty sure we were about to start. I take a deep breath and surrender myself to an hour of business instead of pleasure. "Okay, tell me what you've come up with."

"One question first." Kat shifts in her chair to face me. "If we bring in all this additional business how are you going to handle it?"

"What do you mean? We'll do the work." That seems like a no brainer to me. You get more jobs, you do more work. That's basic.

"I know you're solid..." Kat's eyes shift down to the erection still trying to punch through the fly of my jeans. "On the work part. I'm talking about scheduling and billing, keeping up with the books. How are you going to handle that?"

"The same way I always have," I tell her. "I'll be at the work sites during the day and then do the rest at night."

Kat's mouth twists. "That won't work long-term. You know that, right? You can't do everything yourself. That won't be sustainable as the business grows."

That blast of reality is an instant boner killer. As much as I hate the numbers part of having this company, I can't see myself handing things over to someone else. "Why not?" I already know the answer to this question.

"There aren't enough hours in the day for you to go to the sites and also do the rest of it. You can either do all of the office part yourself and stop working with the crews or you can let someone else do the office part and be out with the guys doing the physical work."

I scowl a bit. "I can do both," I protest.

"Not well," Kat tells me gently. "And not forever."

"My grandfather ran Cruz and Sons out of his kitchen until the day he died," I counter.

"Sure, but he wasn't trying to grow the way you've said you want to. I'm sure he did a great job, but he wasn't thinking about advertising and marketing to make things happen the way you are. You'll burn out trying to do it all."

"I can't give up the time with the crew. Won't be that guy."

"What guy?" Kat asks and I know she doesn't understand why I'm being so stubborn, why I'm digging in my heels.

"The guy who leaves all the dirty work to the other guys, asks people to do the work he won't do himself." I spit it out more forcefully than I should. I'm not angry with Kat, after all, I'm angry at a man who can't ever live up to my expectations and doesn't really care to. I should leave Kat out of this. Instead I wade in deeper. "That's non-negotiable."

"No one's asking you to give anything up, Michael."

"Sounds like it." I fold my arms over my chest.

"Then you aren't listening," Kat says and I'm immediately embarrassed about the tantrum I was getting ready to have.

"I just don't want to be the kind of guy who forgets how the money's made. I don't want to be in the office all day while other people break their backs. I'm not my father."

"Your father?" Kat tentatively pokes around at a wound I never had any intention of even letting her know I have. *Way to go, idiot. Now what? She's going to be your therapist too?*

"Yes, my father." A man I don't want to talk about, especially not with Kat.

"Because he doesn't do the hard work?"

"Not if he can help it."

"And you're not that guy."

"No," I tell her. "Never will be."

"But to make this thing successful you're going to have to see that sometimes you can't be everywhere at once. I get it, believe me I do. I'd like to be the one handling every single account at my firm and for a while there I tried that. But you know what? The accounts suffered and so did everyone who worked for me. You have to be smart about this. Did you call the accountant?"

I nod. "I wish I didn't need you to hold my hand through all of this." It'd be a hundred times easier to take advice from someone I wasn't trying to convince I was more than just some kid. Someone I wasn't thinking about naked all day long.

"But I like holding your hand," Kat says, giving me a wink. "Nobody's born knowing how to run a business or how to promote it. I can help you figure that out. Think of me like a mentor."

"A mentor?" I'd been seconds away from kissing her, but now I stop, leaning back in my chair. "You're not my mentor, Kat."

"Sure I am. Not all the time, but I'm someone with more experience guiding you through some of these decisions. A mentor."

"Pretty sure most people don't fuck their mentor." Or make her dinner, or sleep in her bed every chance they can get. Unless I don't understand this mentoring thing the way I thought I did, those activities should be off limits for this professional relationship.

Kat looks at me like I've killed her cat. "Don't be rude."

"I'm not. I'm saying you're a lot of things but I don't think I'm going to go around telling people you're my mentor."

Kat squirms in her chair. "Well, what have you been going around telling people?" Her mouth turns down and I know this isn't a conversation I want to have.

"I haven't been telling people anything about us because I don't even know what this is. What've you been telling people?"

"I haven't been telling people anything. Just that you're doing some work over here."

I can feel my jaw start to tighten. She's been telling people I'm working for her. That I'm just hanging around. She's not thinking I'm going to be a part of her life for real, not long-term. "So I'm just some guy you've hired? I think we both know it's more than that."

"We're friends, Michael. With benefits, I guess. Do we really need to define it?"

"I guess not," I tell her, pushing my chair away from the table and reaching for my car keys. "I need to get going. I should sleep at my place tonight. Got an early morning."

"Don't be like that," Kat pleads. "Don't leave."

"No reason to stay, right? I finished my work and you had your business discussion with me. Good talk, Thumbs." I stomp over to the front door, pulling my baseball cap back down low on my forehead.

"Michael, you know I'm not looking for anything else right now. I've got... things going on."

"So do I. Glad we're on the same page. You let me know when I can come by and finish that wall. Should take me a few more hours, tops."

Kat frowns but doesn't try to keep me from leaving. "You can finish it this weekend, I guess."

"I'll try to come by on Sunday. Won't bother you until then," I growl before reaching for the doorknob and launching myself out onto the front porch. I hear Kat call after me but I don't stop moving until I'm back in my truck. I reverse out of her driveway with enough force to leave tire marks. There's no way she didn't hear that exit from inside the house. Hell, half the neighborhood probably heard me peel out. That's going to be hard to live down. Right now, I'm angry enough not to give a damn as I drive back to my own apartment and my lonely bed.

Mentor, my ass.

23

Kat

"Is there food in this refrigerator?"

I look up from my seat on the couch. "Where else would I put it?"

"Well, in my experience *you* don't put it anywhere. If I open the pantry is there going to be food in there too? More than just a sleeve of Saltines and the leftovers of that gift basket with the pepper jelly in it?"

"I don't know," I answer. I really have no idea what's in the pantry. I'm not in charge of that. My grocery shopping habits haven't changed. What's changed is the amount of time Michael was spending here supposedly fixing the ruined spot on the living room wall. When I sent my sister to grab the wine from the kitchen, I didn't realize she'd find something much more interesting than the sauvignon blanc I'd put in the freezer earlier. Like I said, I'm not a planner when it comes to what's in the kitchen and I needed it cold for this conversation. And this might be my last glass of wine for a while if I follow Dr. Sharpe's recommendation to cut out alcohol.

I've invited Amy over to talk about my foray into the world of motherhood, but when she comes out of the kitchen holding a growler of beer from the brew pub down the street, I know we'll be spending some time talking about something else—some*one* else—entirely.

"What is this doing in your house?" she asks, a note of disapproval in her voice.

"Chilling?" I answer, knowing my smartass retorts aren't going to save me.

"Since when have you been such a beer drinker?"

I shrug. "I like beer."

"Enough to go and get a *growler*? I don't think so. What is going on here, Kat?" She plunks the oversized bottle down on the dining room table and crosses her arms over her chest. "Beer and groceries in the fridge? What looks like leftovers from multiple home cooked dinners? Where is my sister and what have you done with her?"

I rub my eyes with my fingertips. "You make it seem like having a functioning kitchen is a crime."

"Katherine Winston, I have known you since before birth and never once have I seen you so much as boil an egg. Don't act like you've suddenly gotten an urge to make short ribs. First you call me about muffins and then I come in here..." Her eyes widen. "Do you have a sexy new roommate you've forgotten to tell me about?"

"He's not my roommate."

"Bed buddy? Boyfriend? Emphasis on the boy? It is who I'm thinking it is, right? Sexy, Mr. Fix It."

I groan. "Please never say that again. Michael. His name is Michael. And he isn't my boyfriend."

"He's your personal chef?"

"No. He just likes to cook." And he'd been over here

almost every night for the past three weeks. Until I went and muddled it all up. I zip my lip about that.

"He just comes over to whip up some dinner and then hits the road? That sounds totally believable." Amy raises an eyebrow behind her glasses.

"He also fixes things. He's working on that place where the water ruined the wall, remember?" He'd also changed the knob on the back door, fixed the leaky sink in the guest bathroom, and changed every blown lightbulb in the house. I had come home earlier in the week to him up on the ladder replacing the rope for the tire swing in the front yard. He'd been worrying about Charlie and Noah playing on it with the old, frayed one that's been there for God knows how long. But that doesn't mean I'm special. That's probably how he is with everyone—helpful, thoughtful, protective. And I've made it clear I'm not looking for anything from him.

"That's taking a while, don't you think?" Amy asks.

Nothing comes out when I open my mouth to argue. It is taking longer than it should. I know it and Michael knows it, but I couldn't bring myself to say anything because that would have put an end to my little fantasy of keeping him here forever. It would also eliminate his need to shower here so often after all the "work" he'd been doing. Plaster is messy, after all. I frown, busted by my sister. There are reasons I've been neglecting her all summer and this is one of them.

"I'll let you ponder that while I get the wine," Amy says before basically dancing back into the kitchen. I'm mulling over every possible denial when she lets out a string of curse words so loud and profane, I bolt up from the couch and rush to her, ready to punch whatever's surprised her in the face. I find her standing next to an open drawer, her chin nearly on the floor, and her hands full of condoms.

"That's not where I keep the corkscrew," I whisper.

"Obviously," Amy answers.

"I guess you figured out something you're good at in the kitchen." Amy smirks. "Zach is going to die when he finds out what you've been doing in there."

I give my sister a swat, nearly spilling her wine. "Not a word. I will kill you."

"Not if Zach kills your boyfriend first," Amy tells me, taking another sip of her drink. "Which is a real possibility, especially since you're trying to keep him secret. He'll think that's brotherly love."

"I'm not hiding him. There's nothing to hide."

Amy rolls her eyes. "Kit Kat, who are you trying to fool here? Me? Or yourself?"

"We've never even been on a date, Amy. It's just fooling around. He's too young to want more than that."

"And you do?"

"No," I say although the word feels like sand in my mouth. My half-hearted efforts at keeping Michael at arm's length have failed miserably. "He doesn't fit in with my long-term plans." No matter how fun or sexy he is. No matter how much just seeing him makes my stomach flip and my heart beat faster.

"You mean your long-term plans of working until you drop dead? He seems to have fit in fine with those so far. He's over here every night feeding you and banging your brains out. I noticed you actually have some art hung on the walls, and I'm guessing you didn't get out your trusty hammer for that." Amy settles back into the cushions. "Go ahead. Deny he's been basically taking care of you for the past few weeks."

"Fine. It doesn't change anything, though. It'll end soon and he'll go back to his life and I'll go back to mine. It's a summer fling, that's all." Without warning I find myself tearing up, the sadness welling up in my chest before I can tamp it back down.

"Oh, no!" Amy pulls me in for a protective hug. "I didn't mean to make you cry. If he's a jerk who can't commit then that's his loss."

I blink away my tears. I'm hormonal and I've barely even started the meds Dr. Sharpe put me on. "No, it isn't about him. We haven't even talked about what this is or what we want."

"Then how can you know he doesn't want more? He's acting like he does. He's still hanging around."

I remember his hasty exit the other night and wince. "It doesn't matter what he wants because he can't possibly want what I do, Ames. He's not ready."

"For a relationship?" Amy pulls back to look at me and I have that out of body experience of looking myself in the eye, staring at a carbon copy of my own face.

"No, for a baby."

It's like I've dropped an atomic bomb in the middle of the living room. Amy blinks and blinks, looking at me like I've grown another head.

"A baby? With the boyfriend you've had for five minutes?" Amy's brow knits with confusion.

"No, no. A baby on my own. Michael's not part of that. He doesn't even know."

"Then how are you planning to..."

"I'm looking at sperm donors. I'm going to do this alone,

Amy." I say it with more conviction than I feel. "Before I lose my opportunity."

"You never told me you wanted to have kids, Kat." Amy looks like I've punched her in the stomach. She tilts her head and looks at me like she's never seen me before.

"Maybe I never spelled it out, but I always thought I'd end up with a family. It just never happened. Now I can't stop thinking about it, hoping it isn't too late. You have to have thought about it, too? Missing out on having kids?" I try to cover my lower lip's tremble with my wine glass. I'm not looking for pity from my sister.

"Missing out?" Amy shakes her head emphatically. "No. Never."

"You haven't thought about having children? You can't tell me it's never crossed your mind. You're an elementary school teacher. You love kids!" I would have thought, of all people, Amy would understand my need for a baby. Maybe she'd even been feeling the same thing herself. We've done everything together; getting baby fever at the same time wouldn't be that crazy in the world of super twin powers. When I'd wanted a bike, she'd wanted one too. When I dreamed of eating gelato in Italy, she'd already been planning the same trip. How can she not be counting down the dwindling days of her fertility the same way I am?

"Sure, I love *other people's* kids. Fun aunt? I love being that lady. Awesome kindergarten teacher? I couldn't ask for a better job. But I don't want to come home to a house full of kids. None for me, thanks. Why does everyone keep asking me that?" Amy takes a sip of her wine before giving me a death glare. "What?"

"I'm just wondering who's been asking you about having children." Our parents gave up on that line of questioning ages ago. Amy shrugs and tries to play it off, but my curiosity meter is starting to ping.

"No one," Amy says, far too interested in her wine.

"And I didn't ask you how your vacation's been going. Anything new and exciting I should know about?"

Amy squirms just enough for me to notice. "Nothing worth mentioning."

"Liar." I've been avoiding Amy so I wouldn't have to spill my secrets, but it looks like she's been avoiding me as well.

"We're not talking about me, Kat, we're talking about you and your ticking uterus. You'd better let your boyfriend in on your plan or else he's going to get a nasty surprise. You aren't going to be able to get yourself pregnant without him noticing."

"I know. But at the rate things are going he'll be out of the picture long before I'm anywhere close to pregnant." Even with Dr. Sharpe I'm probably doomed. And Michael stomped out like he was never coming back. Instantly my eyes swim with tears and that ache rises up again.

"Oh, honey." Amy's face crumples to match my own. "I wish you'd let me know sooner. Then you'd have had someone else to talk to." Amy wipes the tears from my soaked cheeks.

"You would have tried to talk me out of it," I whimper into her shoulder.

"Maybe. You should probably come and spend all day with my classroom full of kindergarteners before you fully commit to this, but if this is something you really want then you should go for it. I'll support you no matter what, you know that."

"I know." Amy never lets me down even when she doesn't fully agree with me.

"But I think you really should tell Michael before he gets in too deep."

"You don't need to worry about Michael," I tell her. "He's not as interested as you think. He's having a good time, not planning for the future."

"If you say so," Amy replies in that singsong voice that means she thinks I'm wrong. Michael's been true to his word not to bother me after he walked out, and I'm starting to think I might never hear from him again. Which would make the unpleasant conversation about my failing uterus and his place in that plan unnecessary. No need to include him in something he isn't going to be around to worry about.

24

Michael

When Sunday rolls around I'm angry enough to spit nails. Kat doesn't owe me anything but her dismissal still burns. Sure, I'd been the one to leave, but that doesn't seem to make any difference to my pride. For her to act like there was nothing between us still stings even after I've had time to tell myself I shouldn't care. And I shouldn't. If she's not into more then I should be fine. I should be walking away without a problem. Instead I'm driving to her house to complete the work I'd hoped I'd never actually finish.

Which goes a long way toward explaining the flash of anger I get when I try to pull into her driveway on Sunday morning and find another car parked in my spot. I ease the truck onto the side of the street and watch as Kat's front door opens and the owner of that black BMW comes strutting onto the front porch like he owns the place. He's older with salt and pepper hair and a smirk that makes me want to jump out of my truck and shove my fist into his smug mouth. He's wearing a suit—no tie—one that I'm sure is a holdover from last night because it is way too early for him to just be stopping by this morning. When I'd texted Kat yesterday to set up a time for me to come over I'd suggested early, pretending I had plans for the rest of the day. That lie's come back to bite me in the ass because I didn't think she might have had plans too—ones that would spill over from Saturday night into Sunday morning.

Kat's dark head pokes out the front door and I get to see her smiling face tilt toward his and plant a kiss on his cheek. She's playfully shooing him off the porch, laughing at whatever he's telling her as he basically skips down the steps. I squeeze the steering wheel so hard I hear it crack under my fingers. She's not even bothering to sneak him out, not worried that the neighbors might notice him leaving this morning. Not worried I might show up on time—even though she knows I'm never late—and see last night's sleepover finishing up.

That asshole doesn't even notice me parked here as he backs out and drives down the street. He probably doesn't even know I exist. I doubt Kat's volunteer mentoring program came up last night while they were doing whatever they were doing. And now that's all I can think about—what this guy's been doing with Kat. The thought of someone else's hands on her has me gritting my teeth, yanking the truck door open, and stomping up the front porch steps. I ring the bell like the force of my finger will make it clear to Kat that this is no joke, like my jabbing will bring her to the door ready to apologize for what I've just seen.

She answers the door like she hasn't just made me have an aneurysm. She's got a cautious smile on those full lips of hers and looks like she's been sleeping through the night with no problems since she made it clear I was just visiting over here. Apparently, kicking me out of her bed and getting someone else in it right away leaves her looking like she's been on vacation. I all but snarl at her as she lets me into the living room.

"Well, good morning to you, too," she says as she turns and walks into the kitchen. I follow the movements of her backside, still mesmerized by the sway of her ass even if I'm pretty sure I shouldn't be looking. "I've got coffee if you want a cup."

"No, thanks." I'm not drinking what's left of her new boyfriend's morning joe. I know she didn't make that for me.

Kat looks at me over her shoulder and her forehead crinkles. "Suit yourself."

"I'll just finish the work and get out of your hair. I'm sure you've got things to do today. Probably need a nap."

"What?" Kat asks. "Why would I need a nap?"

"No reason."

"If you have something to say, just say it."

I turn my back, determined to get to work and get out of here. I don't need to start a fight with Kat; that's just a waste of breath. But as I pull out the drop cloth and start to open the can of paint she's so helpfully left out for me, I can't seem to get my irritation under control. I can't tamp down the need to set things straight with her.

"I saw him leaving this morning." I say it to the wall in front of me, not wanting to see the look on her face.

"Who?" Kat asks and I hear her pause in the kitchen.

"The new guy. Or maybe he's an old guy, I don't know. He's older. Better suits your ideal demographic, I suppose."

"I don't know what you're talking about."

Maybe it's the tension of being away from her the last few days or maybe it's my disappointment at having been replaced so soon, but when I spin around to face Kat the fury that comes over me is more than I'm ready for. "You don't have to fucking lie about it. I saw him leaving. Saw you kiss him goodbye. I just want you to know that I know. It isn't a big deal." Except the way I'm raising my voice makes it seem like a big deal. A huge deal. And the shock on Kat's face has me realizing that yelling at her about how quickly she's moved on isn't going to be the best approach.

"I don't know what you think you saw, Michael, but I don't like what you're insinuating." Kat's voice is hard and the way she sets her mouth is even harder.

"Did you or did you not have some other man over here this morning?" The jealousy I'm trying to deny bubbles over and starts to spill out all over the place. Remembering how Kat smiled up at him makes my gut churn. "I guess when you said you weren't looking for anything else you meant you weren't looking for anything else from me." My voice wobbles and I have to look away from Kat's face so she can't see the hurt that's bound to be on mine. When did I get so attached to this woman, and why in the hell am I acting like her telling me no is the end of the world?

"The only person who was here this morning is Mark. He's my business partner. He came by to tell me we landed a big account. He was on his way to church and he wanted to tell me in person." Kat's voice is soft, like she's coaxing a cat out of a tree. "The only man who's been in my bed lately is you."

"Then why're you trying so hard to kick me out of it?" My shoulders slump, but I force myself to look at Kat. I know I'm basically begging here, but unless she gives me a better reason than this age difference, I'm not going to be able to accept it.

"Because you don't know what you're getting yourself into." She smiles a little, but it's more sad than usual. "Trust me. I'm doing you a favor."

"How do you figure? The way I see it all you're doing is

keeping us from having a good time. That, and ending something before it's even close to being finished." She has to know this thing between us is far from over. I'm not done with her and she's not done with me. Not if the past few weeks are any indication.

"We're at different places in our lives, Michael. We should stop things before they get too involved, before they get too complicated."

"How do you know we're at different places? You've never asked me. We've never even had a conversation that would let you know what I want."

"Well, we don't do a lot of talking." Kat gives me that wan smile.

"That doesn't mean I don't want what you want." How can she know the answer to a question she won't even bother to ask?

"Really?" Kat asks, the corners of her mouth twitching up a fraction. "You want to know what I want? You really think it's going to be the same thing you do?"

I know what I want from Kat—more so this morning than I ever have before. I want to be in her bed every night or to have her in mine. I want to take her out and let people see she belongs to me. I want to think about more than the next five minutes with her. I want this to be more than a passing thing.

"Tell me what you want," I dare her. She thinks I don't want more than a fling? She's wrong. "I can guarantee what you want isn't that far off from what I want."

Kat lets out a sigh and I watch her eyes fill up with tears. "I want a baby, Michael. That's what I want."

I stare at her for what feels like an eternity, sure I've heard her wrong.

A baby? What the hell?

25

Kat

Michael's face clouds for a second like he's misunderstood me. He hasn't, but his brain can't seem to process what I've told him. He shakes his head the way a puppy would, clearing out the cobwebs, moving from side to side. But no amount of shaking is going to make what I've said any more reasonable for him to hear.

"A baby?" he asks. "You want to have a baby?"

"Yes," I say although I can tell he isn't really hearing me.

"But we always use a condom. We're religious about the condoms." And here's where the panic sets in. "You've been trying to get pregnant this whole time?" I can almost see the wheels turning in his head.

"No, no, no," I reassure him. "I'm planning on using a sperm donor. I just started getting serious. This doesn't have anything to do with you."

The shock on Michael's face takes me by surprise. "The hell it doesn't. You're going to try to get pregnant and you're my..." He trails off. *My girlfriend. My girl.* He was going to say something that hooks us together as more than two strangers standing in my living room. But all the *sweetheart, honey, darling* in the world won't change the fact I'm not taking him along for this ride. I can't. It wouldn't be fair to him.

"I don't understand," he says and his face really shows it. I've blindsided him.

"I'm older, right? And I don't have much longer to have a baby of my own. Lots of women do it this way."

"Do it what way? By not telling anyone and then just springing it on them?" There's more anger there than I expected. "Why wouldn't you tell me this?"

"Why *would* I tell you anything about this? So I could watch you run? It's not exactly the kind of thing you include with an introduction. Should I have opened with that at the bar? Mentioned it last week over dinner? You know if I'd even hinted at what I'm planning you'd have been out the door."

He can't deny it and I don't blame him. Who in their right mind would start anything with someone so clearly crazy? But so far he isn't running, not yet. Michael's still standing dumbfounded in the living room, staring at me with that gobsmacked look that really just means he hasn't had time to realize he should be fleeing the scene.

"It's okay to admit this isn't what you want, Michael. I won't hold it against you. I've known from the beginning you wouldn't be able to commit to this. I'm giving you an out. You should take it." I try to keep my voice even, make it sound like I won't fall apart once he walks out the door, but trying to have this baby—even if it turns out to just be a pipe dream—has to be more important than trying to hold onto him. I've known since he saw me at the park with my nieces the idea of a woman with kids wasn't one he was going to be excited about.

"How am I supposed to know what I want, Kat, when you spring shit like this on me?" Michael asks. "I can't think in here." And he turns his frustrated face away from me, heading toward the door. He's still shaking his head, balling his hands into fists as he goes. And then, predictably, he opens the front door and leaves me.

An hour later I'm still sitting on the couch staring into space. I'd expected to cry when Michael walked out, but instead I'm numb, too exhausted to even haul myself off to bed. The no alcohol rule Dr. Sharpe's enforced means no wine and really this situation calls for something stronger, anyway. I just keep breathing in and out, letting the minutes pass, hoping I'll be able to pull myself together enough to make my legs work. But I know time won't make any of this better; I'll wake up in the morning and find myself still missing him. The morning after that will be the same and the next one, too.

The sound of the doorbell jerks me out of my trance.

Michael's on the front porch, his hands full of groceries.

26

Kat

"I do *not* understand," my sister says, sipping more of the wine I wish I could have during this conversation. "He just came back? With groceries?" She raises an eyebrow. "I'm going to need more information about what you've been doing in your bedroom, because that is not how I thought that discussion was going to turn out."

"Don't joke."

"Who's joking? You've got some serious mojo working if you dropped the baby bomb on Michael and he decided to make you brunch. You did tell him, right?"

"Yes! I said, 'I want a baby.' I couldn't have been any clearer than that."

"Maybe he thought you wanted more of whatever you've been doing in the kitchen." Amy shudders. "Did you *explain*? Is it possible he misunderstood?"

"I explained! He isn't an idiot, Amy. He freaked out, left, and then came back and made eggs Benedict."

"Did he make hollandaise sauce? I cannot believe he cooks. Plus he's got those other skills in the kitchen." Amy gives me an eyebrow waggle. She cannot let that go. "And he's cool with you having some random guy's baby. I would not have predicted that."

"I'm not having some random guy's baby!" I protest. "I'm starting to regret telling you about this." I take another sip of my cucumber water. That's another Michael specialty that I'm not about to tell my sister about. I hate the taste of regular water so he's been making me different flavors with fruits and things. Apparently, I need to stay hydrated.

"How does it work?" Amy asks. "Because I'd love to get started choosing a not-so-random guy for you to make a baby with."

I groan. "I'm not going to let you help if you keep making it awkward." *More awkward*. Not that Amy will care about that. It's barely been two weeks since I confided in her, but Amy's already extremely gung-ho about my baby project.

"Just get your laptop and let's take a look at the options. Is your private chef coming over tonight? Will it be weird if he walks in on us looking at sperm donors for this baby he's allegedly okay with you having?"

"He'll probably come by later. We have time."

I don't tell Amy Michael will most definitely be by later and he'll stay all night. That after that Sunday morning's blip, Michael's been more reliable than ever. He's even got a drawer full of T-shirts and a spot for his toothbrush by the bathroom sink. All of which feels surprisingly great, except for the elephant in the room. Because if he's my sort-of-boyfriend then is he really okay with me having some random guy's baby?

"Is he working late or something? It's not like he can be out on somebody's roof after dark, right?"

"He usually does the billing and receipts after he leaves

the job site, but I've found him a great assistant who's going to be doing all of that soon."

"Please tell me she's eighty years old."

I give my sister a look. "She is not."

"Well, at least tell me you didn't hire some cute twenty-something to spend hours sitting next to your boy toy. That would not be a smart move."

I stand to grab my computer from the kitchen counter. "He isn't my boy toy."

"Then what is he, exactly? Because from the looks of things it is getting pretty cozy around here. Is he planning on sticking around for a while?"

"We haven't nailed things down, Amy. He's here for now and we're seeing where things go."

"Well, things are going in the direction of you getting extremely fat and cranky. Is he ready for pregnant you and then a baby?"

I glare at Amy. Who knows if Michael's ready for what's about to come barreling toward us? "We'll see, I guess."

Amy shakes her head. "Did you at least hire someone who's going to be able to make your pregnant thighs look skinny in comparison?"

"I hired her based on her brain." Although maybe I should have given a bit more thought to Meghan's appearance. She is pretty cute. "Can we focus on the task at hand, please?"

"Of course." Amy cracks her knuckles. "Time to pick a baby daddy."

"We're picking a *donor*, Ames."

"Right. Because Mike's going to be the baby daddy." Amy looks to me for confirmation. "Maybe?"

"Please do not say that in front of him. Actually, if you could never say anything like that again, I'd appreciate it."

"Fine, fine. No sense of humor. Let's get going. I've got to make sure my little niece or nephew doesn't get hit with the ugly stick."

I load the fertility clinic's web page and click on the link for the donor registry. Once I enter my password, I've got hundreds of potential fathers at my fingertips. *Except they won't be fathers*, I remind myself. I'm not shopping for daddy material as much as for the perfect DNA.

"There aren't pictures?" Amy asks.

"Some of them have photos of themselves as kids." I scroll through the list of possible attributes and physical characteristics on the left-hand side of the page.

"How are you supposed to choose if you don't actually know what the guy looks like?"

"You put in the things you want. It's like shoe shopping." That's a terrible analogy, but I don't bother to correct it. Amy will see soon enough this isn't that much different than looking for a new dress, albeit, there's a lot more riding on this than my usual Internet shopping.

"I was thinking tall. Maybe dark hair and eyes? The baby'd look a little like Zach and Julia's kids." I select six feet and over and check the rest of the boxes to pare down my choices. Thirty-two donors pop up.

Amy snatches the laptop from me, clicking on the first profile. "This isn't a ton of information," she complains, taking another sip of her wine.

"That's why I need another opinion," I tell her and try to be content with my water. "So much of it feels like guessing."

Amy scans the profile, chewing on her bottom lip. "This one's celebrity look-a-likes are Russell Brand and Jared Leto. That'd be a hard no from me." She wrinkles her nose.

"We're not looking for celebrities I'd like to sleep with, that's just to give us a visual."

"But then you'd have a baby who was possibly fifty percent Russell Brand. I'm not going to let you do that to yourself."

"It isn't really Russell Brand's sperm, Amy. And he has good bone structure." I roll my eyes. Where is my practical-to-a-fault sister?

"Do you have a dream daddy in mind? Someone who'd be the perfect man for making cute, smart, successful little babies with you?"

Michael's face pops into my head. *What the hell, subconscious?* That is not a suggestion that's going to help me choose the perfect vial of spunk. Although Michael *is* handsome and seems genetically blessed in more areas than I can count. My face must give me away because when I come back to focus on the profiles in front of us, Amy's smirk is a mile wide.

"Now he's a dream daddy, is he? Oh, Kat, you've got it bad."

"I was thinking of Bradley Cooper."

"Sure you were. Dark hair and dark eyes. Tall. You are a terrible liar."

We've got it down to five possible donors when I hear a key scraping in the lock. Amy tilts her head at me. *He has a key?* she mouths and then sits up a little straighter on the couch. Michael has no idea what he's walking into.

I try to give her my most pleading look, begging her not to be an ass, but this is Amy on summer vacation and two chardonnays in, so all bets are officially off. She gives me a little shimmy that tells me she has no intention of doing anything I ask.

"Hey, babe," he calls from the doorway. "I got you some more of the stuff on that fertility diet. I know you think that's all bullshit but it couldn't hurt." He blinks when he sees Amy with me on the couch. "Sorry, I didn't know you had company. Hey, Amy."

Amy gives him a smile. "Hello, yourself. You always come home with groceries?"

Michael strides across the room to me and plants a kiss on my mouth. He isn't shy, even in front of my prying sister. "I try to. You know Kat can't feed herself." He brushes a thumb over the place where his lips met mine, looking into my eyes like Amy isn't even here. As he goes toward the kitchen, I catch Amy watching him walk away. While I'm appreciating the view, I'm less inclined to let my sister ogle Michael's ass. When she notices me glaring at her she just shrugs. And has the audacity to fan herself.

"We can take a break to go talk to your boyfriend, can't we? He's going to be slaving away in there making you some kind of super special baby-making dinner. I'd hate to seem antisocial by staying in the living room."

"Don't act crazy," I warn. "And please don't say 'baby-making dinner' ever again."

"You're giving me a pretty long list of things never to say again. It is going to be hard for me to remember them all..." Amy gets up from the couch before I can threaten her appropriately. Michael doesn't scare easily, but unfiltered Amy is hard to ignore. I trail along behind her, wishing I'd prepped him a little better for family interactions with my crazy twin sister.

"Soooo..." Amy begins as she settles herself down on a barstool at the kitchen island. "Should I have asked if this was a recently serviced area of the kitchen?" she asks me under her breath. "I'm okay to touch this countertop, right?"

"It's clean," Michael tells her and gives Amy a smirk that rivals hers. "Nothing but cooking going on in here for at least twenty-four hours." I shouldn't have worried. I'd forgotten Michael can handle whatever Amy's trying to dish out.

"I haven't gotten to give you the third degree," Amy tells him as she moves to fill her wine glass with more alcohol she has no business drinking.

"You staying for dinner?"

"Not if we're eating anything that gets me pregnant."

"That's not how it works. You know that, right?" Michael asks, smiling at Amy with that glimmer in his eye she's only going to see as a challenge. "And it turns out the fertility diet is really just Mediterranean, so it's actually going to be delicious."

"Fine then, let's see what's been keeping Kat so satisfied lately."

"Amy!" I do not need my sister almost flirting with my sort-of boyfriend.

"I'm talking about dinner. Get your mind out of the gutter, Kit Kat," Amy says before waving her suddenly empty wine glass in my direction. "I'll just take your word on the rest of it."

Michael refills Amy's glass, clinks his beer bottle against it, and they settle in thick as thieves.

27

Michael

I know I'm taking advantage.

I saw an opportunity and I took it and I'll be damned if anyone out there tries to tell me they wouldn't have done the same thing. Okay, maybe making myself indispensable to Kat at a time when I know she's weak isn't the most honorable thing I've ever done. But if the alternative was walking out for good, I'm happy to choose the path I'm taking. Because if I can stick around long enough to convince Kat she needs me for more than just a good time then I'll be well on my way to showing her how happy we could be.

And I do want Kat to be happy, but I'd be lying if I didn't admit that all this supportive boyfriend shit is taking a toll. We're just a few weeks into something that isn't going to have an easy expiration date. This summer's breezing by but Kat might not get what she wants before the leaves start changing. According to her, this could take months, years even. It might not even work. I love taking care of her, making sure that, for once, she's doing the things she needs to do to keep herself healthy. Eating every now and then and having a damn glass of water shouldn't be things a grown woman forgets to do. But Kat on her own means takeout and white wine, and not necessarily in that order. Hell, sometimes it means only wine from what I've seen of her fridge. I can't have that. Not only because it's something I can easily do for her but also because I'd probably starve to death if I left her in charge of feeding us, and I like hanging around her place as much as possible. Two birds. One stone.

None of that bothers me the way it should—me becoming Kat's live-in caretaker. I'm fine with coming home to her at the end of a long day and making my day even longer. I'm even fine with her talking business with me, trying to keep up her end of the bargain by helping me run Cruz and Sons. What actually has started to get me hot and bothered in a bad way is the fact that there's no way Kat'd be letting me do any of these things if there wasn't an end goal. She's got her eyes on the prize right now, making her body a temple for the one thing that's probably got the best chance of knocking me back out the door and ending this thing once and for all.

The baby.

He's a nebulous little thing right now, but he's getting more and more real by the second. And even though I know sperm donor #646 isn't really my competition, I can't help but wonder what'll happen if those swimmers manage to do what they're supposed to and Kat ends up pregnant. Her sister's been helping her to pick the perfect guy for this situation and I've been taking a few dings to my pride here and there as they whisper on the couch. I know they've been trying to keep their voices low, but my ego still manages to hear every detail about this guy. He's brilliant and handsome, and I have to remind myself that's all on paper. That profile could be full of shit—that guy could be anyone in real life. That's a thought that soothes my competitive nature but does exactly the opposite when I think of how much faith Kat's investing here. She's going to try to make a baby with this guy and all we've got are the answers to a few general questions. Not nearly enough to decide if he's daddy material. Not nearly enough for me to let him get this close to Kat.

But that's not my decision and bringing it up with her is guaranteed to start a fight I don't want to have.

"I thought you were going out?" Kat yells from the living room once she pries her key from the front door lock. "I was expecting you to be at Smitty's."

"I'm going later." I slide the pan out of the oven. "I thought we'd eat first. Don't want to drink on an empty stomach."

"I'm sure that's not what you were worried about." She drops her bag on the counter and comes over to give me a kiss. I press her up against me, letting her feel how much I've missed her. "I could've worked out dinner on my own."

"I know, but I figured you'd be tired and I'm trying to limit the time I have to spend with Dan. Pretty sure he can hold down the fort all by himself for a little while."

"Poor Dan. He's your excuse for waiting here for me? It's almost nine."

"Don't need an excuse." I let my hand slide down the curve of her back. The little grunt she gives me tells me she's not all that tired. "Are you hungry?"

"Very." When Kat starts to nibble on my neck, I know she isn't talking about the lasagna I've got growing cold on the counter. I shove the pan out of the way and hoist her up into my favorite spot for a little pre-dinner warm up.

"You brought your girlfriend to guys night?" Dan leans against the bar and gives me the full force of his frown.

"This isn't guys night."

"The hell it isn't. You see any of the other guys with dates?"

"None of them can get dates, that's why we're all out tonight." I reach forward and take the beer the bartender hands me, watch as he pours a tonic with lime for Kat. "Can I get a glass of water to go with that, actually?" I ask and wait until that glass is in front of me as well.

"Something you want to tell me?" Dan eyes the drinks in my hand.

"Not sure what you're talking about."

"Any reason why your girl, excuse me, your *lady*"—Dan rolls his eyes— "Isn't having a real drink?"

"Doesn't want one." I shrug. Dan needs to forget this line of questioning right about fucking now.

"You brought her out to the bar so she could play darts and hydrate? That's two different kinds of water."

I glance toward the back of the bar where Kat's in the middle of a serious game of darts with the rest of our group. She sucks at darts—can barely manage to hit the board at all much less get near the bullseye—but she tries. She screws up her face and lets the dart fly from her hand as all the guys move back to give her room. It goes in the right direction at least, and Kat does a little dance. She laughs as everyone makes a big deal about her not maiming any of them. I'm too far away to hear her but the sound echoes in my head just the same.

"Hello, Mike? I'm not trying to be nosy. I just want to make sure you haven't gotten in over your head. You haven't managed to get your fling-that-can't-possibly-go-anywhere knocked up, have you?"

Now Dan's got my full attention. "I haven't gotten Kat pregnant," I snap. "And I'd appreciate you not asking any more personal questions."

"Just checking. In my experience, a woman turning down a drink at Smitty's means one of two things: either she's eating for two or she doesn't know how to have any fun. You keep telling me I'm wrong about the last one so you'll forgive me for thinking it might be the first one."

"Why would you think Kat wouldn't be fun?" From the corner of my eye I can still see her whooping it up with the rest of my roofing crew. Not fun? Give me a break.

"Well, you two stay holed up at her place so I haven't had the pleasure of seeing her out."

"We're out now," I argue.

"Congratulations. But since June you've been up to nothing but what I assume would be further evidence in the baby making category." Dan folds his arms over his chest and gives me one of his satisfied looks. "Am I wrong?"

"Fuck yes, you're wrong. You don't know anything about what's going on here." I take a sip of my beer. "And it's none of your business."

"I know she's got you tied up in knots. Runnin' all over the place to keep her happy and now she's not drinking, so thinking she's got you all locked up doesn't seem too far off."

Locked up? I certainly wouldn't mind that. Not one bit. But that's not the kind of thing I'd tell Dan, here, propped against the bar at Smitty's.

"Why're you making that face?"

"What face?"

"That stupid dreamy face. Are you over there thinking about how cute your babies would look? We can get out that app that squishes two faces together." Dan's expression tells me there's nothing he'd rather do less.

"Shut up." I try to school my features into something blank. "And shut up about babies for God's sake. Don't you have somewhere else you can be right now?"

"Sure. But you let me know if you want me to make you a little Mike and Kat mash up. That seems to be where we're headed." Dan pushes away from the bar with a sigh. "You're disappointing me, man."

Not nearly as much as I'm disappointing myself, because now I'm picturing what that imaginary baby would look like. Would he have Kat's eyes? My nose? Those are questions I'm never going to get answered, because Kat's baby isn't going to be mine. I'm not sure when that idea burrowed its way under my skin, but now I can't think about much else. And I'm too chickenshit to do anything about it.

Kat

"You absolutely don't have to come to this."

"Why wouldn't I?" Michael turns to face me.

"Eyes on the road, there, buddy."

"I'm not going to just drop you off. You should have someone else with you at these things. You shouldn't do this alone." Michael goes back to watching the road and I bite my tongue to keep from reminding him that alone was part of the plan. I *expected* to do this by myself. Having him around for even this long has been something I would never have imagined. If I need someone I should be calling my sister or even Cassie to be my appointment buddy, not letting Michael be my doctor's office plus one.

When his hand comes over to take mine, I let him twine our fingers together. "Unless you don't want me to come with you."

"No, it isn't that." Although Michael's about to see a side of me that I'm not sure he's ready for. There is nothing sexy about a visit to the fertility specialist. I'm grateful for his support even if I don't fully understand it. "I just don't want you to feel obligated."

The way Michael's jaw tightens has me bracing for the worst. "Why don't you let me worry about me."

But I am worried. Worried about becoming dependent on all this attention. Worried that any second now, Mr. Not-even-thirty will realize he's wasting his time. Worried about what will happen if this all works out and I get the baby I've been hoping for. Does Michael even want kids of his own one day? Has he even thought about it? And shouldn't he be with someone who can do that on his timetable? I'm too scared to even try to find out.

He holds my hand all the way to the office, opening the door, ushering me into the air conditioning and out of the late July heat, then reaching for my hand again. I'm sure to anyone else it looks like nothing. There are plenty of couples in this waiting room and hand holding in these situations is pretty expected. But to me it feels like so much more and I'm not sure if the knot of feelings I've got tangled in my stomach means I should enjoy it while it lasts, or get ready to fight like hell to keep it.

~

"Here, let me do that." Michael takes the dish I've been rinsing out of my hand. "You've had a long day."

Today has felt like one of the longest ever, but I'm sure he's feeling as exhausted as me. Accompanying your maybe-girlfriend to find out all about how she probably can't get pregnant has probably scarred him for life. He's been quiet since we got back to my house, concentrating on making dinner and giving me these sideways glances that look an awful lot like pity.

"Do you want to pick a movie? We can hang out on the couch and watch something." He tosses it over his shoulder as he finishes with the last of the glasses. "How does that sound?"

Domestic. Boring. Not at all like what a twenty-eight-year-old man should be suggesting for a fun night in. He's never going to want to tear my clothes off again now that he knows I'm not only old but defective. The things Dr. Sharpe had prescribed to get my fertility on track haven't been working the way they should. Now he wants to move on to more serious measures. Michael held my hand through the entire discussion, only flinching a few times as Dr. Sharpe outlined our next plan of attack. I haven't even tried to get pregnant yet mainly because handsome Dr. Sharpe thinks it would be a waste of donor sperm. He'd been careful when I walked in with Michael, unsure of how much I had already told him. I've been adamant about not having a partner in this and then I waltz in with a much hotter version of Florence Nightingale. By the end of the appointment, Dr. Sharpe was showing Michael how to help with my follicle stimulant shots like it was a given he would be around.

I'm well aware that it is not.

"Hey, what's going on?" There he is again, a glass of water in his hand. "Have you had enough water today?"

I scowl and take the glass because, no I haven't. "I can figure out if I'm thirsty."

"Are you? Thirsty?" Michael cocks his head to the side. Maybe all of the playfulness hasn't left yet. But it will.

I gulp down the entire thing and put the empty glass on the coffee table. "You know you don't need to take care of me like that. You've gone above and beyond today. I'll understand if you need some time to yourself." It will kill me to let him walk out the door, but I would understand.

"I'm right where I want to be, Kat. Come here." He slides onto the couch and pulls me into his lap, taps at my temple. "I don't like when you get all in your head about things. Talk to me."

I want to, but I see the danger in that.

"This is just... it's a lot. And I would think you'd need some time to process things."

"Do you want me to leave?" Michael's forehead creases. "If this is your way of sayin' you want to be alone, you don't have to try to make it something it isn't."

"No." But I hesitate.

"What?"

"I don't want to tie you to this. It's not fair to you. This all started out as something fun and now it's..." I don't dare finish that thought. "This could get complicated, you know?"

Michael smiles that lazy smile that always lets him get his way. "It already has, Thumbs."

And he's right because the feelings I'm starting to have for him are already such a tangled, jumbled mess that I'm going to have an impossible time extricating my heart.

"I'm here for more than fun, Kat. I can handle complicated. I want to."

He sounds so sure I decide to believe him, even if it's only for tonight. Maybe Michael will stick around. Maybe he'll be okay with everything that's about to happen. My heart says to put my trust in that even though my head says that's foolish. But I don't pull away. I keep letting him hold me. I put my nose in the crook of his neck and breathe Michael in. He smells of soap and cedar, and just the tiniest hint of lemon from the shrimp he made earlier. It's a smell that's started to comfort me and one that I'm ashamed to admit I've come to crave.

When he angles his head down to nuzzle my cheek, I tilt my face toward his. I close my eyes and let him kiss me, surrender to his hands and the heat of his body. I give in to the thing I want more than anything in this moment.

I let him stay.

29

Michael

"I was thinking about having a housewarming party."

"A whrph?" I spit the rest of the toothpaste into the sink. The sun's not even up and Kat's out of bed. "Sorry. A what?"

"A housewarming party. Or maybe just a party. I haven't had anyone over since I moved in and it might be nice to host now that I've got room."

"Okay."

Kat shifts her weight, putting one hip against the edge of the sink. The strap of her tank top slides a bit down her shoulder. It's loose and gives me a glimpse of the side of her boob when she moves. The skin there—creamy white against the black of the fabric—keeps me from paying any attention to my own reflection in the bathroom mirror.

I rinse and wipe my mouth on the towel that hangs from the hook on the wall. "Is there more?"

Kat hasn't moved, not even to fix the strap that keeps sliding lower and lower. The one that's making my hands itch in a way they shouldn't when I've only got twenty minutes before I need to be at our latest McMansion roof repair to check in with Danny.

"I just wanted to make sure it wasn't inconvenient for you." Kat's eyes flit to my toothbrush as I put it back in the holder. Scan over the shaving gear I've got all over the counter.

"Ah, you need my stuff to be out of here." I ignore the little punch I get in my gut. I have been spending most of my time here when I'm not at work. It would make sense that Kat would start to want a little space.

"No, no. The opposite." Kat fidgets, finally righting that distracting strap. "I don't know why I'm nervous about this."

"You're nervous?" I let my hip join hers. "About having a party?"

"No, about asking you if you'd be sure to be here for the party." She gives me one of those faces that would suit a kindergartener, a slight tilt of her mouth, her nose wrinkled.

"You inviting me to your party, Thumbs?" I drawl it out and she rolls her eyes.

"I'm also inviting other people. My brother. My parents, maybe. People from work. Will you be comfortable with that?" Kat looks at me expectantly and I feel my chest swell just a bit. She wants me here. With her family. With her friends. But there's one little thing I need to hear her say first.

"I'm comfortable with that, but how comfortable are you going to be telling people who I am? I'm not gonna let you tell everyone you're my mentor like this is the Boys and Girls Club over here."

Kat nods. "I know."

"What're you planning on saying when people ask?" One look around this house and people will be able to tell I've been doing more than just working here. Kat'll need to be ready with whatever she's going to tell people, especially since I'm not entirely sure I'm going to like it.

"That you're my boyfriend, I guess?" It comes out soft and shy, and in that second, I don't care at all that I'm about to be late to work.

"You guess? You better damn well know." I growl it into her ear and Kat shivers all over. I'm about to make a mess of that tank top right here against the sink. But she winces when my hand makes contact with her middle and I remind myself that I have to be gentle with her. The bruises I see when I lift the edge of her shirt bring me back to the complicated things that make the idea of being Kat's boyfriend seem ridiculous. Childish. Like we're playing house and this is all make believe. The things that have been keeping her from getting closer to commitment are all still sitting in my way.

"I've got another ultrasound this morning," Kat tells me when she notices my preoccupation with the black and blue marks that mar her skin. "Then we'll know if it's working."

I grunt and run my fingers over the blotches. She's been a champ about the shots, barely flinching when I make myself poke her with the needle. She's determined to have this baby no matter the toll on her body, no matter how much it hurts. I squat down until I'm eye level with her belly button, those bruises just past the tip of my nose. I lean in and kiss the first one, its edges already turning that ugly green color. Kat lets out a little puff of air and I look up. When our eyes lock, I can't read her expression. Her mouth's slightly open and her eyes are wide, peering down at me like it's the first time she's ever seen me. I move to the next mark and put a kiss there too, wishing what she wants wasn't so damn hard for her to get. Wishing I could make it easier for her. I put my lips on every single one of those bruises, not caring that it's past time for me to be in my truck and driving away from her.

"Are these tender?" I stay crouched down there on the bathroom floor.

"That helped. Come here."

I do what I'm told and straighten back up, taking my time getting there, kissing my way along Kat's body until my mouth meets hers. She's like liquid in my arms, wrapping herself around me until I can't tell where she ends and I begin.

"I think I need my boyfriend to tuck me back into bed."

I don't need any more encouragement than that, so I lift Kat's legs up over my hips, bury my face in the crook of her neck, and carry my girlfriend back into the bedroom.

"You tryin' to be fashionably late?"

Danny's eyes meet mine and I know he's annoyed. It isn't like me to be late and I don't tolerate it in other people. Certainly not in Danny or the rest of the crew. Not for work. But for once I don't regret breaking my own rule. Spending extra time with Kat this morning was worth it. Not that I'm required to explain that to Danny. I had even considered going to the ultrasound appointment and now I'm jumping every time my phone buzzes in case she's trying to get in touch.

"Something came up. Should have sent you a text. Sorry about that."

"Oh, I'm sure something came up." Danny moves closer to my truck, pulling the work order out of his back pocket. "The new guy was late this morning." He gives me a pointed look. "Which I would normally have fired him for, although maybe today that's not the serious offense it normally is."

I grit my teeth. "Okay, I hear you. Where is he?"

"I sent him home, because lucky for your hypocrisy he was late *and* still drunk from whatever he got up to last night. That, I have no trouble firing him for."

"Seriously? So we're a man down on this job is what you're telling me." I blow out a frustrated breath.

"That's what I'm telling you. And there's no way we can finish on time this short."

"Well, I'm here now. Let's get to work." I'm dressed for getting up on a roof, even if Kat thinks I should start looking a little more professional. I'm not ready for that yet, and if I'd been wearing a button-down, I wouldn't be able to step in like this without ruining a shirt or losing time going home to change.

"You're gonna get your hands dirty today?" Danny waits for my reaction. He knows better than to imply I can't put in a day's work.

"Dirtier than yours. You up for a little competition?"

"Like it'd be any kind of a competition. I'm willing to bet you'll smack your thumb with a hammer. Been a while since you've handled any shingles." Danny smirks and then yells to the rest of the crew, "Boys, guess who thinks he's still got it?"

They hoot and holler as expected and I take it without complaining because I definitely deserve it.

"Before I forget, we're having a party next Saturday at Kat's."

"*We* are, are *we*?" Danny doesn't look at me.

"Yes, and *we'd* like for you and some of the other guys to stop by, if you're available."

That gets his attention. "Oh, I'm available and I can tell

you every single one of the guys will be too. *We* wouldn't miss it."

"Great. I'll give you the details after I kick your ass today. We'll need something to talk about while we drink the beers you're going to buy me."

"Such confidence. We'll see, boss man. We'll see." But he gives me a smile and one of his head shakes. We're back on solid ground again.

"Let's get to it." I give Dan a slap on the back on my way to the side of the house and the ladder. "I've missed this quality time with you."

Danny snorts. "We'll see if you're still feeling that way at the end of the day. Come on and I'll give you a lesson on how we hammer down a shingle."

30

Kat

"But I thought more eggs was good?"

I sigh and hand Amy another bottle of vodka for her infamous fruit punch—aptly named because it's likely to punch you in the face if you have too many glasses. It's also been known to cause party guests to punch each other in the face, so I'm not sure why I'm letting her make it for what's not supposed to be a frat party. "More eggs is good. But too many eggs at one time is bad."

"But all of them wouldn't have turned into little Kats and Russells, right?"

"I'm not using that donor, Amy." She is never going to let that go. "And we already have a predisposition for twins. Dr. Sharpe was worried about multiples to begin with."

"What does that mean then? It's good that you've got eggs. It's positive, right?" Amy looks unsure as she adds even more alcohol to her concoction.

"It's good that my follicles responded so well to the meds. And maybe all of those wouldn't have actually been viable eggs, but it's bad for this cycle because it means we can't go through with the insemination."

Amy fills a glass, the hot pink of her beverage contrasting with the black of her dress. She's looking suspiciously dressed up for my backyard barbecue. "Perfect. But we need to make sure the kids know this isn't for them." She smacks her lips. "Can you have a glass? It might take the edge off a little bit."

"No, I shouldn't. Michael's got me drinking this fruit water. I should stick with that."

"How's he doing with all this?" Amy shoots a look out the kitchen window at Michael manning the grill. "Is he relieved or... I know you're disappointed, but that's got to be complicated."

"He's been great. He's a saint." More than that. When I'd gotten the news that my body was reacting too well to the stimulants, Michael had been nothing but supportive. If he'd felt any kind of relief, he hadn't shown it. Instead he'd dried my tears, cooked my favorite dinner, and then made love to me like I was the most precious thing in the universe. As demanding as he can be, he can also be gentle when I need it.

"Is he ready for today?"

"He's prepped two kinds of tri tip and smoked what looks like an entire pig, if that's what you mean."

"You know that's not at all what I mean, although I'm sure I'll appreciate him for it." Amy takes another drink from her nearly empty glass. "Mom and Dad are coming today, right? And he hasn't met Mark or anyone from work. Meeting everyone at once might be overwhelming."

"I'm sure he can handle it." I'm sure he can handle just about anything if these past few weeks are any indication. Meeting my parents? That should be nothing for Michael.

Although it's been a long while since I've introduced a man to my family and certainly never one that's this much younger than me. Not one I'm starting to hope sticks around.

"If you say so. Sure you don't want a drink?" Amy shakes the ice in her now empty cup at me.

"No, thanks. And maybe you shouldn't drink all of that before anyone else even gets here."

"I'm done drinking for the afternoon," Amy announces. "I was just sampling. I have to drive out to Leiper's Fork later."

"Why are you doing that?" Amy hates driving. Won't do it unless she has to.

She shrugs. "I have a thing."

"A thing? I've just told you all about my ovaries and you won't give me details about why you, of all people, are voluntarily driving an hour both ways?"

The sound of the doorbell saves Amy from answering my question. "Not important. What is important is answering the door." And off she goes to let the first guests in.

And they keep coming and coming and coming until the house and the yard are full of friends and family. My nephews take turns on the tire swing and the littler kids run around in the grass Michael made sure was trimmed up and looking like a suburban lawn should. He comes up behind me and kisses my neck enough that I feel only the slightest little pang of jealousy when I see people admiring Cassie's baby bump. Everyone eats and drinks and mingles and even Danny looks like he's having a good time.

When my parents meet Michael it's business as usual— none of the awkwardness I had expected. If anything, my mother looks impressed, actually looking him over head to toe and then giving me a suggestive eyebrow raise. Michael even manages to hold his own with Mark, talking over beers about why our hockey team can't possibly beat last season's surprise run to the playoffs. All in all, it's a picture-perfect afternoon, and by the time people start to say their good-byes I can't believe how lucky I am.

"Do you want help in here? I'm pretty good at washing dishes if it means I get to spend a few minutes away from the kids." Zach hands me a few more of the glasses he's collected from the yard.

"If you want." I make room at the sink. "What do you think? Did the kids have a good time?"

"Of course. Nice that they could use the swing again. And the sidewalk chalk and bubbles were a good idea."

"All Michael." I look out the window to see him deep in conversation with Danny and my father. His bicep flexes as he lifts his beer to his lips.

Zach grunts. He's still not Michael's biggest fan after the kiss at Smitty's, but they got along today. "Roof looks good. As long as you're happy, I'm happy."

"That is *so* not true but I appreciate you lying to make me feel better." I hand him a glass to put in the dishwasher. "He's a good guy."

"He'd better be." Even if Zach is the little brother, his protective streak is no joke.

"I'm a big girl."

"That doesn't mean you don't need people looking out for you. I know you can take care of yourself, but it isn't weakness to let other people help." Zach rinses the platter he's been washing and gives it to me.

I dry it and stretch up to put it back into the cabinet.

"What the hell?" Zach's hands grab at the hem of my shirt and lift it up higher on my belly. He stares at the remaining bruises I've got there, his face contorting and eyes blazing. "What did he do to you?"

"No, Zach, he didn't do anything. It's not what it looks like..." But I don't get a chance to explain because Zach goes tearing out of the kitchen and straight to the backyard.

31

Michael

The initial hit's disorienting.

One second I'm laughing with Danny and Kat's dad—he's insisting I call him Frank and I accept this as the win I know it is—and the next I'm sprawled out on my back in the grass. My beer goes flying and I hear it shatter all over the stones of the patio.

"What the fu—" Before I can get my bearings, I've taken two fists to the face. Before whoever this is can land another punch, I roll to the side to try and knock him off me. The sound of people scrambling around us only adds to the confusion. Everyone's yelling as we roll around on the grass. I've been in fights before, but I usually have some idea what we're fighting about—or who I'm fighting. I've got a spike of adrenaline now, but it doesn't help me shake this surprise opponent off me. Who I soon realize is Kat's brother. A guy who basically trains to fight for a living and has, for some reason, decided to beat the shit out of me. Hearing her screaming as we wrestle does nothing to help the situation.

Danny comes to my rescue, along with a few other stragglers at this now officially more-than-over party. He latches onto Zach and pulls him off of me. I have a chance there to land a solid punch while Danny's got Zach occupied but I keep my fists to myself. Hitting him back won't make any of this better.

"What the hell? This is a family function, ya'll." Danny gives Zach a shove and I see some of the reality of what he's done steal over Zach's face, but he doesn't completely back down. Zach lunges at me again and Danny puts himself between us. "I don't know what this is about, but this isn't the time or the place."

"That son of a bitch hit my sister," Zach spits and all eyes turn to me.

My head snaps back like he's hit me again and I ignore the blood I taste in my mouth. "What did you say?"

"You heard me. I saw the bruises. They're all over her."

Danny gives me a look like he's not sure if he should go ahead and let Zach finish what he started.

"I'm not hitting Kat. I would never raise a hand to her." I wipe the blood from my nose with the back of my hand. There's no way to prove I'm innocent here without telling stories that aren't mine to tell. Kat obviously hasn't told everyone in her family all they need to know about what she's been up to. "You can ask her yourself."

Kat appears next to me, her face full of concern. She takes in my bloody face and turns on her brother. "I can't believe you did this. Michael hasn't done anything!"

"Then explain why your stomach looks like you've gone three rounds with Mike Tyson. Has Mom seen those bruises? Has Amy?"

"I have and they're none of your business," Amy interjects as she hands me a wet towel. "This is private and now you've made it a public thing." She looks around and shakes her head. "Winstons in the house! Now!" As they all trudge up the back stairs Amy motions me to follow. "You too. Anybody who just took two to the face probably counts as family."

Once we're all settled in the living room, Kat starts fussing over my nose. "I think this is broken," she says as she runs her fingers over my cheeks and my busted lip. "I should get you some ice."

"In a second, Kat," Amy chastises. "Let's clear the air first. Mike'll be just as pretty if he has to wait a second on that bag of frozen peas. Show Mom and Dad your stomach."

Kat bites her lip, hesitating for a second before lifting the hem of her shirt. Her parents' eyes go wide and when they turn to me, I'm sure the offer of a first name relationship with her father has been officially rescinded.

"See? What's that look like to you?" Zach yells, gesturing to Kat's stomach. He's still a ball of barely contained rage and I regret not trying to say Danny was family too just so I could have a little back up in here.

"I know how it looks, but it isn't anything like what you're thinking." Kat pulls her shirt back down protectively over her stomach and takes my hand. She threads my fingers together with hers and gives me a squeeze. "Michael hasn't been hurting me. He would never, ever do that." Her voice is strong—determined—and I don't even mind the fact that the hand she's holding is the one I'd need the most if Zach came at me again.

"Then you're going to have to explain this to us, honey, because I can see why your brother got... annoyed." Kat's mother furrows her brow.

"It's from the shots. The fertility shots." Kat closes her eyes and lets out a breath. There's five seconds of the loudest silence I've ever heard and then all hell breaks loose.

From that point on it is chaos. Everyone's talking at once and no one's listening. Kat doesn't even try to yell over the chorus of questions.

Finally, Amy's loud whistle breaks through the chatter.

"Kat's trying to have a baby, but she's old so she needs science. Does that answer your questions, because I really need to get on the road." Amy lifts the car keys she's holding in her hand. "I'm already late."

"No, that does not answer our questions. That does not even come close to answering them." Kat's father—Frank, if I'm still allowed to call him that—looks like he's been broadsided.

"You're trying to have a baby? With *him*?" Zach's voice drips with venom. "You barely even know him. Let me guess whose idea that was."

"No, not with Michael." Kat squeezes my hand again.

"If not with him then... I don't understand this." Kat's mother looks at us like we're animals in the zoo. I am probably starting to resemble a baboon right about now. I can feel a bump rising on my cheekbone.

"By myself. I haven't told anyone because I wasn't sure about things, but I'm using donor sperm and I can tell you all about it tomorrow at Sunday dinner, okay? But right now you just need to trust me. I'm fine. I'm more than fine. And Michael hasn't hurt me. He's done the opposite." She gives me a look that's nothing but adoration. Totally worth a broken nose. "But I need everyone to clear out of here and let me clean him up. I promise I'll answer all your questions tomorrow."

Shockingly, they go, grumbling as they gather up their things and make their way to their cars. Zach has to collect his wife and kids and apologize to everyone left waiting in the backyard. I make an appearance just to show everyone

I'm not dead, but have to endure more of the stares of those not privy to our inside conversation. Zach makes a half-hearted attempt at claiming there'd been a misunderstanding, but anyone can tell his heart's not in it.

Kat's parents hover a bit longer by the door as they say their goodbyes. I've got a bag of frozen peas on my mouth, a tampon shoved up my nose, and zero percent of my dignity intact when her mother comes over to me on the couch.

"We'll see you tomorrow, then," she says like it's a given.

"Pardon? Tomorrow?" I ask through the swelling of my lip.

"For dinner."

"I don't know about that, Mrs. Winston. I appreciate the invitation, but I don't think tomorrow's the day for me to come to Sunday dinner."

"It's Lila," she corrects. "And you'd better be there. It's *family* dinner. We'll all want to see how that nose looks tomorrow anyway." And she's up and out the door before I can argue.

32

Michael

"More salad?"

"No, thank you." I try to smile at Kat's mother, but manage only a quick wince instead. My swollen bottom lip's still in no shape to do much more than that. Which is fine because at this dinner we're all sitting stone-faced and nobody's got anything particularly funny to say.

"The roast is good, Mom," Amy says and we all murmur our agreement. Then we're back to silence. The scrape of forks and knives is the only thing louder than all of our chewing. That, and the beating of my heart which seems pretty loud to my own ears, but if there is a God, probably can't be heard by the entire dinner table.

Zach sits across from me, still shooting daggers with his eyes. From that first moment in Smitty's he's been wary of me. Now he's got an actual reason to think Kat should stay away. And this painful family dinner isn't helping to bring him over to seeing my side of things. I try to swallow a few bites of my dinner past the tightening of my throat.

"It's really flavorful. You'll have to show me how you

make it." Zach's wife Julia tries to get the conversation going again, but no one's nearly as interested in the pot roast as they are in the elephant in the room—Kat's bruised middle and how our relationship fits in to all that.

"I'd love to teach you how to make it, but I think you'll be disappointed. It's so easy, really." Lila starts explaining her pot roast recipe as Julia's boys start to fidget in their seats. God only knows what they think's going on here. First their stepdad attacks their aunt's new boyfriend and then we all show up to sit through dinner on Sunday. If last night was confusing at their house tonight's going to be a real treat.

Kat reaches for my hand under the table and I let her soothe me with the small circles her thumb traces along my palm. Ordinarily, just her touch would have me already thinking dirty thoughts completely inappropriate for sitting so close to her parents. As it stands, my brain can only hold the words I need to say to convince them I'm not a monster and the easiest way to defend myself if Zach comes flying across the dinner table. He's got a toddler in his lap, but that doesn't mean anything.

"I've got popsicles in the freezer but people can only have them if they promise to stay out in the yard." Lila says it to the room, but we all know who she's really talking to.

Both Charlie and Noah perk up.

"We can stay in the yard," Charlie promises and he and his brother nearly fall out of their chairs trying to get the hell out of here. I'm feeling pretty jealous about their lucky escape when Kat's father clears his throat and brings me back to this torturous dinner.

"Well, should we hash this out?" Frank asks and we all shift in our seats.

"Okay." Kat squeezes my hand again. "I'm the one who

needs to catch everyone up." She looks over at me and I smile despite my cracked lip. She smiles back and I swear it lights up the whole room. Sometimes the pain's worth it.

"I'm sorry I didn't tell all of you about what's been going on this summer. I was just trying to wait until there was something to tell." Kat scans the room. "And I should have brought Michael over earlier, but there's been so much going on..."

"Just to let everyone know, Kat's been telling me everything." All eyes turn to Amy. "What? I'm not gloating!"

"That sounds like gloating," Zach mumbles. "And would have been nice to know before yesterday."

"I say that mainly because I know this is new for all of you, but I can vouch for the timeline and everyone's whereabouts if need be." Amy folds her arms over her chest and gestures to Kat. "Proceed."

Kat doesn't even try to hide her annoyance. "I'm trying to have a baby. I'm dating Michael. Go ahead. Ask away. I know you have questions."

Silence.

"You two are trying to have a baby?" Kat's father asks, obviously a little surprised.

"No, she isn't having a baby with him. She's having a baby with Russell Brand," Amy interjects and then leans back in her seat.

"Russell who?" Kat's mother asks, even more confused than Frank. "Should we have invited him to dinner?"

"No, Mom, I'm not having a baby with Russell Brand. That's just Amy being silly." Kat tries to get the conversation back on track, silencing her twin with one of her death glares. "I'm using a sperm donor. And I have some fertility issues. That's why I needed the shots. They bruised me up a little. The baby's separate from me and Michael. Well, not from me. From Michael."

"How can that be separate?" Zach asks, exasperated. "He's sitting right there. You're trying to have a baby and acting like your *boy*friend's somehow not going to be part of that?" The emphasis on *boy* isn't lost on me. "I know you've always blazed your own trail, Kat, but in what universe is this going to work?"

"In *my* universe. This is why I kept it to myself. I'm not pregnant yet and I might not even be able to get pregnant, so right now I'd appreciate more support for my hypotheticals."

"Support of your *hypotheticals*?" Zach looks at me. "You're okay with this? With hypotheticals?"

And what am I supposed to say to that? Because I'm not a man who loves hypotheticals. Possibilities? Sure. Hit me up with those any day of the week. The possibility that Kat and I could make this long-term? That this could be permanent? I love those possibilities. That she'll get pregnant and decide to leave me in the dust? That possibility's more likely, but one I'm going to have to face.

"I want Kat to be happy. Hypotheticals or whatever aside. I'll do whatever it takes to make her happy because I..." And then I make the fatal mistake of pausing for a second too long. Just long enough to let everyone in on something that hits me right between the eyes for the first undeniable time.

I want Kat to be happy no matter what because my feelings for her trump my own well-being. They override anything else.

Because I'm in love with her.

And now everyone knows.

33

Kat

"That went well." Amy closes the dishwasher and pushes the button to start the machine.

"Do you really think so?"

"Of course not, Kat! That was the most awkward family dinner I think we've ever had and that includes the time I brought that biker unannounced during my rebellious phase in high school."

I sigh. "I was hoping once everything was out in the open..."

"That they'd all just settle down and let you live your life? Fat chance. Mom's out there right now trying to figure out how the whole sperm donor thing works. Poor Julia's having to show her how to use Google. Do you know what shows up in the image searches when you look for 'sperm donors'? And Zach and Dad are probably grilling Michael some more about his 'intentions.' That can't be going well."

"What? Where are they?" I crane my neck around the kitchen door frame. "I thought they were all in the living room."

"Nope. Backyard. Probably so we can't hear the yelling if another fist fight starts up. Although, I don't think anyone's going to hit your boy today. Not after all those feelings he spilled all over us at the table. They'll take pity on him, I think. What in the world have you done to that kid? He's legitimately crazy about you."

"Can we not call him 'kid,' please? And I haven't done anything to him." I ignore the way my heart starts pounding in my chest when I think of Michael's almost declaration at the dinner table. The energy had immediately shifted and I swear I caught my mother wiping her eyes with the edge of her napkin.

"Is that why you're in here instead of protecting him?" Amy laughs. "Or are you hiding out in here because you don't want to face Michael now that you know?"

"Know what?" Maybe if I can ignore what nearly came out of his mouth earlier, everyone else will too.

"Oh, come on! He didn't come out and say it, but if manly declarations and starry eyes are any indication, Michael's head over heels in love with you." Amy doesn't even wait for my response. "Even with all this baby stuff he's still looking at you like you're the most amazing thing in the universe. He's invested."

"I'm invested."

"Not like that you aren't. If—" Amy catches herself. "*When* this baby thing works out, you're going to have to figure out a way to let him down easy."

"Why would I need to do that?" The thought of losing Michael ushers in a wave of panic I wasn't expecting. I move to the window over the sink, hoping to catch a glimpse of him and hoping he's completely upright.

"Are you thinking this is going to be something more than a fling? Because he sure seems to think things are going that way. Have you thought about how that'll work? It isn't like you not to have a plan." Amy helps herself to the stash of Girl Scout cookies our mother keeps hidden above the refrigerator and offers the box to me. I pull one of the chocolate discs free from the cellophane wrapper.

"I've been trying just to let things happen for once." For the baby I've got a plan. But Amy's right, for Michael I'm suspiciously without one. He keeps surprising me: sticking around when I expect him to bail, responding to every crisis with calm, being vulnerable and emotionally mature and nearly telling my entire family how he feels about me. He's kept me off-balance and for once I haven't minded not always knowing what comes next. For once these surprises feel *good*.

I take a bite of the cookie and take my time chewing. Amy does the same and we're deep in contemplation when Julia comes in from the living room.

"Are those cookies? You guys are holding out on me." Julia reaches out and takes the sleeve. "How does Lila still have boxes of these? We finish them as soon as they're delivered."

"She only has to hide them from Dad," Amy explains. "I think it's harder if you have to keep them away from kids too."

"Speaking of that." Julia gives me a sympathetic look in between bites. "You're going to need to go in there in a minute and explain this all a little better. Your mother's convinced you're not telling us the whole story."

"What else would there be to tell?" I swipe another cookie and crunch down on it.

"She's wondering why you need a sperm donor when you have one out in the yard. Just warning you. And she's got quite a few ideas about how you could spice up your sex life, if you're having trouble in that department. You owe me one weekend night of babysitting for convincing her not to tell you some of the more acrobatic positions." Julia gives me a wink.

I groan. "Thanks, I think. I knew the Michael part would be confusing."

"She's not the only one with questions. He seems great, but..."

"See? No one understands this." Amy takes back the cookies and helps herself to another. "He's too good to be true."

Except he's not. He's as human as the next man, but for some reason he's decided to hang around with me.

"He's..." I don't even know what to say, how to express all the feelings that have started to make their way into my heart.

"Ugh. She's about to do the same thing." Amy looks at Julia and passes her the cookies. "You're going to need more sugar for this."

"What? What am I about to do?" I look from Amy to Julia, hoping one of them will clue me in to whatever they think's happening here.

"Oh, you're right." Julia shakes her head and bites into another chocolate disc. "But I think we just need to let it happen."

"If you two are so confident, why don't you just go ahead and tell me what I was about to do." I put my hands on my hips and lift my chin even though I know this does nothing to protect me from my sister and my sister-in-law.

"You were just about to almost reveal your feelings," Amy says and then goes back to chewing.

"Um hum," Julia confirms. "But then you were going to

pull it back at the last second. You and Michael really need to talk."

"Like yesterday," Amy chimes in and I kind of start to hate the knowing look she gives Julia.

"That's not what I was going to do." My huffing isn't very convincing. "And we do talk."

"About this? About how this is going to work once you're pregnant?" Julia's questions get enthusiastic nods from Amy.

"Well," I stammer. "Actually no." I've been too afraid to bring much of that up. The baby's a day-to-day thing for Michael and me, and looking too far into the future's sure to ruin that.

"Might want to think about that," Julia warns. "Because he's smitten and, by the looks of it, so are you. He's here at Sunday dinner less than twenty-four hours after a fist fight with his would-be brother-in-law. I don't think we need to worry about him running. I think it may be Kat we need to watch on that front."

Amy lifts what's left of her cookie and taps it against Julia's like they're toasting to my stupidity. "Let's hope she wises up before she ruins it all."

34

Michael

The closer we get to my father's house the tighter my shoulders feel. We're not even in the driveway and already I feel suffocated. I've been short-tempered for days and even though Kat hasn't said anything I know she's noticed. Her hand comes over from the passenger side of my truck and lands on the back of my neck. When her fingers start to massage the muscles there, I relax into her touch, wishing we were headed anywhere else.

"We don't have to stay long. I'm fine with leaving early." Kat's voice soothes me a bit, but it can't take away all of the pent-up anger that's sure to come spilling out once I have to spend time making small talk with my dad.

"The party'll only last a few hours. I think I can keep it together until after cake." I try to make it sound like a joke, but it doesn't come out that way. I'm hoping I can make it until Andrew blows out his candles. He's the reason we're coming. Not my father. My little brother's got plenty of people more than willing to let him down. I'm not adding my name to that list.

The gate is open and we start the long drive from the road to the house. Balloons line the entire driveway—my stepmother's obviously ignored my father's request for low key. I can see not one but two bouncy castles in the backyard as we make our way into the circle in front of the house.

"This is lovely," Kat says as her hand slides from my neck and back into her lap.

"Yep, only the best for Peter Cruz. Wait until you see the inside." My father's house is beautiful. Still gleaming and new even if the man living inside is rotten. "Between him and my stepmother I'm surprised there's anything left to buy in the greater Nashville area."

"You told them I was coming?"

"Of course." When Tracy had found out I was bringing a woman she had just about shrieked my ear off.

"Anything I should know in advance? I want to make a good impression." Kat folds her hands in her lap and gives me a look like she's trying to be teacher's pet.

"My dad's an ass, but I already told you that. And you don't need to do anything special. They'll be thrilled you exist. Although, there is one thing you could do."

"What?" Kat asks, still giving me that innocent look that definitely doesn't match the woman I know.

I lean over the center console and slide my hand to the back of her head. She's still got her seatbelt buckled so I can't haul her into my lap the way I want to, but I can bridge the distance with my body and press my lips against hers. I intend to keep things sweet, but because this is Kat, I can't help myself. I'm hungry for her even though I had her before we left the house. Now I'm regretting not pulling over on some back road on our way here to see what we could get up to in this truck. I let my palms glide lower than they should and end up with a handful of ass. Kat whimpers and

I think about putting the truck in drive and just taking her back home. I can think of a million other ways I'd rather spend this Saturday afternoon—most of them naked with this woman.

The sound of another car pulling up behind us makes Kat jerk her mouth away from mine. "We can't be out here screwing around in the driveway at a kids' party." She sounds appalled enough at us to have me laughing.

"If you think that was screwing then I've been doing it wrong. You need me to drive down the road a little bit? This subdivision's got lots of space between the houses. I could give you a little refresher. You know, about screwing."

Kat is not impressed. Her mouth puckers and I'm tempted to kiss her again. "No, thank you," she says primly. "I have a party to attend."

"Fine, but don't be surprised if I take you for a long drive afterward." Maybe having that to look forward to will make this afternoon bearable.

I ease the truck over to the side of the drive and put it in park. I'm surprised my father hadn't insisted on hiring a valet to protect the ridiculous landscaping he's had put in. All these cars touching the grass will be something we all hear about today. I almost feel sorry for Tracy, but she's the one who decided marrying him was a good idea.

Once I'm out the driver's side, I come over to Kat. I open her door and take her hand, trying to keep things as gentle-manly as possible. She lets me open doors for her now instead of insisting she can do it herself, so I try not to ruin it by pawing her too much. She's got on a skirt that shows off her legs and the curve of her ass. I'm sure she doesn't mean to turn me into a walking hard on, but she's done it even in an outfit intended for my little brother's birthday party.

"What?" she asks when she catches me staring.

"Just can't ever get enough of you."

My answer makes her startle, and her cheeks pink up. Being able to make that happen always makes me a little too proud for my own good. I like being able to surprise her almost as much as I like kissing her.

Kat lets out a wobbly breath. "We'd better get inside before you sweet talk me into agreeing to a little more time in the truck."

I mentally give myself a pat on the back. "Come on, then. Brace yourself, though. I'm not sure you've ever dealt with jackassery on this level before."

"I work in PR, buddy. There's no way your family can top the things that have been seen in my office."

My father proves Kat wrong less than five minutes after we get through the front door. I've got my arm around her waist, mentally preparing to introduce her to the man who's basically the blueprint for everything I don't want to be, when he comes tearing down the stairs, my stepmother right behind him.

"Well, just turn them off," my father yells over his shoulder. "Turn them off and let them deflate. Or better yet, call the rental company and tell them to come and get them."

"But the kids are already here. They're already using them. There are kids jumping around in them right now. You can't just decide to shut down the bounce houses because you're angry with me." Tracy sounds desperate but my father barely gives her even a glance.

"I thought I was pretty clear when we talked about it. I didn't want a party at all and I certainly didn't agree to two bounce houses."

Tracy reaches out and manages to get her hand on the fabric of his shirt, giving the seam over the shoulder a tug. "Can't we just let the kids use them? They're already here and paid for. Andrew'll be so disappointed." The pleading note in her voice is something I could have lived my whole life without hearing. Unfortunately, this isn't the first time I've heard my stepmother try to reason with my father. And I'm sure it won't be the last.

"Andrew should get used to it." That has them both stopping on the landing of the stairs, turning to look at me.

Tracy's shocked face takes less than a second to smooth itself out back into hostess mode. "Michael." There's so much relief in her voice I cringe a little bit. "You made it."

"Wouldn't miss it." And I wouldn't, not even if it means I have to do what I'm getting ready to do. "You guys having a party emergency?"

"No," my father answers, brushing Tracy's hand away. "We had a little miscommunication."

"Just making sure you don't need any help. But if it's no big deal then it's probably not worth ruining Andrew's party over." I make eye contact with my father and we stare each other down for a few beats. He's not going to make a scene if there are other people around, not going to escalate this now that I'm in it too. He can push Tracy around, but not me. I stopped letting him control me a long time ago.

"Tracy mentioned you might be bringing someone." My father comes to the bottom of the staircase and extends a hand. "I'm Michael's dad, Peter. I won't try to make you call me Mr. Cruz." He smiles as he takes Kat's hand, waits for the polite chuckling that would normally have come with his attempt at a joke.

But I'm sure Kat's never considered what she'd end up

calling my father and his wife. This isn't high school, even if my father might want to treat me like a sixteen-year-old boy.

"And this is my wife Tracy. Trace come down here and meet Michael's friend. What was your name, honey?"

"Kat—"

"Kat Winston?" my stepmother stops on the last stair, her mouth hanging open. "I haven't seen you... since high school!" She comes down in front of us and pulls Kat into a hug. "Peter, Kat and I went to high school together!"

35

Kat

Tracy Sullivan is Michael's stepmother.

Tracy Sullivan—Tracy Cruz now, I guess—*from high school*, is Michael's stepmother.

I went to high school with Michael's *stepmother*.

I try to process this information as we sit sipping glasses of lemonade on her enormous back porch, watching kids run in and out of the bounce houses her husband has decided to let stay up at least for the moment. She's been talking nonstop about people we both know—who's divorced, who's recently had to return to rehab. Tracy's always been big on gossip which is one of the reasons I steered clear of her when we were teenagers. Even now she's all about keeping up with our old acquaintances, which is why she cannot understand how in the world she's missed what should be an all-points bulletin about me and her stepson.

"How did I not know this?" she asks again, her face scrunching up as she looks at me. In truth there isn't much scrunching because whatever Tracy's been doing to her face doesn't allow for much movement. "You would think I'd put two and two together, but Michael's pretty tight-lipped about his personal life."

I nod, secretly happy Michael isn't big on oversharing with his family.

"Tell me everything. How did you meet? He's always been such a sweet kid." Tracy tilts her head and waits for me to answer, but how can I possibly talk about Michael with a woman who, despite never really knowing him as a child, keeps referring to him as one?

"I thought you'd only known him for ten years? He wasn't really a kid." I've got the quick and dirty version of Michael's father and his younger wife, but I hadn't been paying attention in the way I would have if I'd known I was going to end up here. I've heard all about Tracy's whirlwind romance with Michael's father. The way he swept her off her feet and begged her to become his second wife. Tracy's hazy on the details of the first Mrs. Cruz and glosses over that part. All of Tracy's gauzy declarations of domestic bliss and romantic perfection would be easier to believe if her husband hadn't retreated inside the house, leaving her to host this birthday party alone.

"I guess I've just always thought of him as Peter's child so... I just can't believe you two are a thing." Tracy lets out a little laugh. "You're a cradle robber. No, a *cougar*. Kat Winston, you are definitely a cougar if I've ever seen one."

I try not to let my face show the irritation I'm feeling. I haven't seen this woman in years and yet here we are with her putting all the labels I'd been so afraid of on my relationship. "I'm hardly a cougar, Tracy. And Michael's a grown man." I take another sip of my lemonade.

Tracy's mouth works itself into a smirk. "Oh, I'm sure he is."

She cuts her eyes to the far side of the lawn where Michael's been trapped in the swimming pool for the last hour. He's got a long line of kids waiting for him to hoist them up and toss them into the deep end. With each one we're treated to the rippling muscles in his back and a good deal of water sluicing off his chest. A few of the other moms have found seats in the lounge chairs closer to the action. One of them is actually exaggeratedly fanning herself.

"Aren't you worried about the age difference?"

"Not really." I keep my face neutral. Tracy and I were never really friends so her comfort in asking me a slew of personal questions should be surprising. But if she thinks she's overstepping she doesn't show it.

"I guess for just a casual thing it doesn't matter. If it was something you were hoping would last, maybe you'd be more concerned." Tracy waves to a few late arrivals, her manicured hand barely moving. "I've heard he's a good time. No reason not to enjoy it while it lasts."

A few weeks ago, this would have been my worst nightmare—dealing with someone else's judgement about Michael and I being together. Do I want to be the subject of gossip? No. But do I want to let that stand in the way of spending time with Michael? That's a no far outweighing the first one.

"There's an age difference between you and Peter, isn't there?" I slide the obvious right out there and then put my mouth back on my lemonade glass.

Tracy's nose wrinkles. "Sure, but it's different with a man. They can date younger. Not that you can't date younger, especially looking the way you do. I'm just saying, socially, my age difference with Peter isn't that big of a deal. And he's not much older." Tracy dismissively waves her hand in the air.

"He's twelve years older. Same difference with me and Michael." I stand my ground, refusing to let Tracy make me feel even a sliver of shame or embarrassment.

Tracy considers this for a second before shaking her head. "It's still different."

Before I have a chance to put any more wasted effort into this conversation, I'm saved by an unlikely late arrival.

"Aunt Kat!" Charlie and Noah come running through the grass and nearly tackle me with a group hug. I wrap my arms around their sweaty bodies and squeeze as good as I'm getting.

"Why are you here?" Noah asks as he and Charlie start to wiggle away from me.

"Because Andrew is Michael's little brother. Remember Michael?" I point over to the swimming pool where my boyfriend is now busy with a very enthusiastic game of chicken. Andrew's on Michael's shoulders trying his best to knock his brother William off the shoulders of one of the party-going dads. The man's got a receding hairline and what could only be described as dad bod. Next to Michael he definitely looks his age and once William gets pulled from his shoulders he bows out, wading to the steps and toweling himself off.

"Michael's little brother?" Charlie yells much louder than necessary. "That's crazy."

"It is," I admit and am saved from further explanation by my own brother's sweaty face brushing up against mine.

"Wasn't expecting you here," Zach says as he plants a kiss on my cheek. Then he turns to Tracy to hand off a gift bag I'm sure he had no part in assembling. "Sorry we're late. I had a class to teach at the gym and Julia's got a wedding to shoot today, so I'm the designated party parent."

"No problem," Tracy coos. "There's plenty of food and

drink over there. Beer for the grown-ups, if you're interested. You can all change into your suits in the pool house if you want to swim. And please, please use the bounce houses."

"Can we swim first?" Charlie asks, already pulling on Zach's hand.

"Please, please? Michael's in the pool." Noah takes the other hand and starts yanking as well.

"What's going on over there? Chicken?" Zach raises an eyebrow at me. "I think I'm up for a little healthy competition."

"Keep it reasonable," I warn. The bruises on Michael's face from the last "competition" have barely had time to heal. "No one wants to see two grown men wrestling in that swimming pool."

"Speak for yourself," Tracy stage whispers, giving me a little nudge with her elbow. She's got no idea what this party will devolve into if Zach and Michael really start to get competitive.

"We'll be good. Right, guys?" Zach stands up straighter and gives me a salute.

"Yes." Both boys answer, giving me such practiced salutes I know they've all been working on them. Then they all race down to the pool house, Zach carting their oversized tote bag on his shoulder.

"He's so good with those boys. He's always at school just like he was their real father." Tracy sighs.

I startle. Zach loves Noah and Charlie fiercely. Never has it occurred to me to say anything about him being their stepfather in a way that would lessen that. "He is their real father."

Again, Tracy waves that dismissive hand. "I know he's their father *now*." She adds some annoying air quotes around the word father. "But if their biological father was still alive, things would be different. And now that he has kids of his own... Let's just say those boys are lucky they got sisters and not two more brothers to compete with. That's all." She finishes her lemonade and gives me a smile. "We should put some vodka in this next round."

"No, thank you." I nearly whisper it. I'm still not drinking because we're still trying to have a successful IUI soon. I say "we" but it's really just me. Me and my donor sperm. If my body cooperates.

"Oh, don't go getting all upset!" Tracy gives my shoulder a squeeze. "I'm not saying your brother isn't a fantastic dad. There's just something about men and biology, you know. He's really stepped up, treating those kids the way he has. They're lucky he isn't too hung up on the fact they really aren't his. I'll get us a refill." Tracy walks away from me toward the house, greeting her guests and smiling all the way back to the lemonade.

But I feel like I have a rock in my stomach, one that maybe's been sitting there a long time. One I've been ignoring. I got past the fact Michael's younger than me. I've even come to realize my earlier dismissal of him because of his age says more about me than it does about him. But I haven't had the nerve to ask him more than surface questions about the future, focusing instead on this possible baby and getting to *my* next step.

A baby is undeniably the future—one that I keep seeing Michael in. Me and Michael and this little person who we haven't met yet but who maybe Michael won't actually want to meet. Especially if he's thinking about children of his own someday. He'd been relieved when Claire and Jane were my nieces, not my daughters, surprised when I'd thought Will and Andrew could be his sons. He's just starting his life. He'll probably want to be a father, eventually. He'll want his own children one of these days. Children I won't be able to give him and that he can't possibly be ready for now. He can't adapt to my timeline and I can't wait around for his.

I hear more squealing from the pool as Michael and his brothers are joined by Zach and my nephews. Their exuberant splashing and screaming only increases when the grown-ups ramp up their own tomfoolery. There's more dunking than I'd like to see, but Zach and Michael seem more determined to gang up on the kids than on each other.

Michael chooses that moment to look up at the patio and shoot me a grin. I feel his smile all the way down to my toes. It's not just the fact he's sexy as sin, shirtless in the swimming pool. He's so much more than that. He's kind and smart and takes great care of me. He's oozing so much *goodness* that my heart stumbles in my chest. He's going to make somebody a great partner someday. He's going to be a fabulous and attentive husband, a doting and involved father. There's no denying that.

But he isn't ready for the weight of that life and those obligations now. Things for him are just beginning. And I can't take that opportunity away from him.

36

Michael

Kat begs off early and I don't blame her. She's spent more time than should be legal with my stepmother. I wouldn't begrudge her that Uber ride out of this neighborhood. My father's nowhere in sight for most of the party so I get to avoid having him mention the new and exciting fact we're involved with women the same age. Not that I give a shit but I'm sure he'll think it's something we need to discuss.

Tracy seems to think it needs some sort of big conversation too, so once the candles are blown out and the other guests are on their way home, she tries to bring it up again and again over party clean up. She's never been a motherly figure to me, so why she thinks today's the day to start is beyond me. Still, she pushes. Wanting to know all about Kat and my feelings like that's something I'm going to discuss here in her kitchen as we throw out piles and piles of wrapping paper.

"I've already told you every way I can this is none of your

business." I grab another trash bag and start to fill it with used paper plates.

"I'm just trying to help. Relationships are hard." Tracy gives me a smile. "Especially when the other person is head-strong and a little older."

"If you're talking about my father you can stop, and if you think you're talking about Kat then my advice for you's the same." I make eye contact only to be sure she hears me. This topic isn't one we're delving into.

"I'd think you'd want a little inside information about the woman you're spending time with. I've known her for years. Since before you were born even."

I don't bother disguising my eye roll. "I think I know her pretty well. So, no, thanks, on the middle school gossip."

"*I'm* interested in how well you know her." My father's appearance in the doorway makes Tracy jump.

"There you are! Did you think you could hide out during the clean up?" she asks it like it's all one big playful joke, but I know my father's not one to help with messes. Of any kind.

"Michael, why don't you grab a beer and meet me out on the patio?" It's an order not an invitation, so he turns and walks away, confident I'll follow right behind him. That smugness makes my chest burn.

"I was about to take off," I lie. Although now I'm more than ready to leave and let Tracy deal with the rest of the cake and ice cream piled up on the counters. She's probably got a crew coming in tomorrow to make sure the entire house is pristine so my help's nothing more than a gesture, really. I'm pitching in because she's family and because I know no one else is going to do it. My father doesn't turn around, doesn't acknowledge I've even said anything at all.

"Go on, give him ten minutes," Tracy encourages. "It won't kill you. I'll be fine to finish up in here."

Every cell in my body wants to walk out the front door and get in my truck, but instead I grab a beer from the massive stainless steel fridge and walk outside. Now that the sun's set you can feel fall coming on. We're close to the time when the heat of summer will be long gone. Not that it becomes a winter wonderland around here, but the change of seasons always makes me feel like there's the possibility of a fresh start. Of making something happen.

Out on the patio it's nothing but old news. My father has the fire pit going, even if the extra heat's unnecessary. Tracy's spared no expense with the decorating out here and I've got plenty of choices for comfortable seating while my father lectures me. I'd like to think there's a chance for a discussion, that he might want me out here just to shoot the shit, but that's never the case. I make sure to look at my watch before I crack open my beer. I'm not spending more than ten minutes listening to what he has to say.

My father's got his usual tumbler of scotch and his feet propped up on the edge of the stone fire pit. He's dressed like he planned on spending the afternoon on the golf course, not at a kids' party. He never made it into the pool, could barely pretend to be interested when Andrew opened gifts. Even now he's still business casual without a hair out of place.

"Go ahead and have a seat. I think we need to catch up." He gestures to the chair next to him and waits for me to lower my butt into it. "Good party?"

"Andrew seemed to have a good time." I take a swig of my beer. I don't want to waste time on small talk and I know my father doesn't have the stomach for it.

"How's business?" He cuts right to the chase.

"Good. Plenty of projects and more in the pipeline." I won't give any more information than that.

My father raises his eyebrows but the surprise only stays on his face for a split second. He'd never say it out loud, but I know he expected I'd be admitting I was in over my head by now. He's been waiting for me to come running with my tail between my legs, begging for his help. But Cruz and Sons is doing well, great even, especially now that I've got Kat helping me.

"That's good to hear. Anything I should know about?"

"About my business?" Now it's my turn for an eyebrow raise. "Obviously not."

"Technically it's a family business. And, as part of this family, I need to make sure you aren't doing anything that would reflect poorly on the rest of us." He takes a slow sip of his scotch and then returns the glass to the little table he has next to his chair. It's a practiced movement. One I'm not even sure anyone else would think twice about. But my father's worked hard to leave all the traces of his working class upbringing behind him, even going so far as to ruin his marriage to my mother. She couldn't get on board with his new needs and wants—the fancy house, the dinner parties, the hired help. She couldn't see what was wrong with the way they'd started out. I can't say I've ever figured out what was so wrong with it either.

"I doubt you'd be anything but pleased with the way the business is being run." I don't say *proud*. Another kind of father might say that—Zach, for example. He'd have no issue telling his kids he was proud of them. I'm sure that word just rolls off Graham's tongue when he looks at his son. But Peter Cruz? Not a chance.

"She helping you out?" He doesn't look at me, just keeps looking at the flames as they lick up the fake logs he's got in the center of this ridiculous pit.

"Who?" I know damned well who, but I ask anyway.

"Your girlfriend. Though she's not really a girl, is she? Wondering what's in it for her."

"Don't see how that's any of your business. I brought her tonight because Tracy wanted me to, not because I wanted your opinion." The angry sip I take of my beer does nothing to quell the hard feelings I have perking up inside of me.

"It's my job to give you my opinion whether you like it or not." He turns toward me. "I'm still your father."

"So I hear," I mumble under my breath even though I know that will only make the situation worse.

"Look, I've got the benefit of experience here and when it looks like you're fighting above your weight I'm going to say something. There is no way that woman plans on staying with you. What do you have to offer? Right now you're probably a great diversion. Something to take her mind off work. God knows I understand that. But beauty fades, Michael. Just ask your stepmother. Enjoy fucking her while you can. One day you won't be as pretty."

And at that I see red. Who the hell is he to tell me how to live my life? To tell me what's going to happen without knowing anything about me or Kat?

"Excuse me?" I rise to my full height before he has a chance to even get out of his chair. "The hell is wrong with you?" I consider escalating this to something physical, but I don't want to fight with my father. Not like this.

"What? I shouldn't talk about her like that? I'm just saying what everyone else is thinking." He doesn't move, obviously not afraid of what I might do or how I might react.

"You don't know what you're talking about and whatever you think you know you should keep to yourself."

My father snorts. "Guess you got things all figured out, huh? Got the business we know you can't run, the woman we know you can't keep, and the same bad attitude you've had all your life."

"Well, I guess we know where I got that last thing," I retort. "Thanks for the beer." I turn to go, determined to stomp out of here.

"Things aren't as simple as you want them to be, you know? There are complications I never would have dreamed of when I was twenty-eight. But you're gonna find that out *m'hijo.*"

The Spanish does it. It flips the switch on all the anger I've been holding onto for all this time. "Don't do that."

"Don't do what? Don't acknowledge your heritage? You always wanted to speak Spanish with your *abuelo.* Now you won't with your old man? That's a shame." Again he rolls the liquor around in his glass. "Probably not speaking much Spanish with Kat."

"Kat's got nothing to do with this." I ball my hands into fists. "This is about you dredging up the past when it's convenient for you. When it suits your purposes. And burying it whenever it doesn't."

"I've done you a favor." My father's eyes glitter in the firelight. "I let you grow up unencumbered by all the baggage I had. I spared you from that and then you just ran right back to it. Blue collar, working your ass off for nothing just like your grandfather."

"Something wrong with hard work?" I sure don't feel there is, but my father seems to feel differently.

"Hard work? Do you have any idea how hard I work? Private school for you and your brothers, travel sports teams, whatever you wanted. No college loans for you, Michael. Your start didn't come saddled with hundreds of thousands of dollars' worth of student debt. All of that's because of me. Me and my hard work."

"I didn't ask for any of that. Neither will they. You can't try to make me beholden for something that was your dream." I'm sure my brothers can hear us yelling out here from their bedrooms. I hate that they're all tucked in their beds listening to this screaming, but I don't lower my voice.

Neither does my father. "I guess your way's better. Breaking your back. Although maybe now that you've got somebody smarter helping you, you'll see the wisdom in doing business my way. She knows how to run a business. Running you shouldn't be all that hard."

Even the mention of Kat has my nostrils flaring. I'm seconds away from tipping my smug father right out of his deck chair and onto the stones of the patio. Only Tracy hurrying down the stairs saves me from doing something I'd surely regret.

"What are you two doing?" she hisses. "The entire neighborhood can hear you."

"The houses are too far apart for that," I snarl. "Great party, Trace. Sorry for the disturbance." I touch her shoulder as I pass, aiming for the street and my waiting truck.

"We're not done with this," my father calls after me. I ignore him and keep my eyes trained straight ahead. I'm more than done with this and I let my retreating back tell him so.

37

Kat

When Michael comes home that night, I'm still wide awake. I hear the key scrape in the lock, the jiggle it takes to actually loosen the bolt, and his boots hitting the floor. He's in the bedroom before I know it, skipping his usual routine in our shared bathroom. In the moonlight I can see the way his face changes when he realizes I'm not sleeping. There's so much need there that even if I thought it was possible for me to resist him, tonight I wouldn't. I need him as much as he needs me after the disastrous evening we've had. I'm sure from the outside all seemed fine—the party, the kids, the family time—but he's looking like his night didn't get much better after I left, and that's saying something.

I've been alone with the unshakable fact that this thing has to come to an end, and sooner rather than later. There's too much at stake now and I can't be responsible for my own heart much less Michael's. The idea that he'd get sucked into a family he doesn't want and can't possibly love... Knowing he deserves the chance for a family of his own making has kept me tossing and turning here on the sheets that still smell enough like his skin to keep me from forgetting for even a second. I have to do it because he won't.

But my brain can't override my body as he climbs in next to me. He's gentler with me since I've been on the fertility meds. The bruises always make him cautious and even now that we've stopped the shots and given my body a break, he hasn't returned to the way he was before. He's still the kind of lover I can't get enough of, he's just always holding back now—more emotion than passion. I'd worried it was the possible change from single girlfriend to mommy that was doing it and had vowed never to bring it up. Obviously, all the extra complications were making it hard for him to see me the way he had in the beginning. He's got his preoccupations too.

But after the disastrous birthday party, Michael's not interested in whispering sweet nothings in my ear. He strips down to nothing in two seconds flat, giving me the kind of view that always leaves my mouth dry and my panties wet. I'm nothing but emotion as he presses up against me.

He doesn't waste any time getting me naked so we're skin-to-skin. I give into the feel of his hands on my body, his lips on mine. Only this can keep me from the thoughts in my head and the terrible inevitability that he won't be here much longer. He slides down, nipping at my breasts, my hip bones, the skin of my thighs. I let him take control, happy to hear nothing, only the appreciative sounds he makes as he worships my body.

"Need this," he says just as his mouth finds my clit. I close my eyes and fist the sheets, holding on for dear life. Michael doesn't tease, just works me toward an orgasm that comes barreling through me with surprising speed. Before I can get my bearings, he's got one nipple in his mouth.

"Flip over." His stubble grazes the sensitive skin of my

chest and the warmth of his lips leaves me. When I don't move fast enough, Michael's big hands engulf my hips and turn me onto my belly. "We're gonna be like that, are we?" His body covers mine and then leaves me wanting.

I turn my head to see him reach into the drawer of the bedside table and fish out a condom. Watch as he opens the packet and rolls it down the length of his cock. I wriggle, but can't move, the weight of one of his hands still heavy on my hip and his legs still straddling me.

"Hold still, baby."

I try, but I can't keep my hips from moving, can't stop myself from grinding just a little. I keep my head turned so I can watch him, so I can see the want on his face.

"Somebody's not being a good listener," Michael taunts. His hand moves from my hip and glides up between my shoulder blades. His fingers are feather light and leave a trail of goosebumps in their wake. I gasp when those same fingers suddenly dig into the flesh of my hip and give me a good yank. His other hand comes down hard on my ass and I groan. "You gonna need more than one of those to convince you to be good?"

I give my ass a wiggle. I'm completely on display for him here. Completely under his control and there's nothing I want more in this moment than for him to use that hand again. "Please," I gasp out, the side of my face rubbing against the bedsheets.

"Please, more?" he asks and I can feel the smile in his voice.

"More."

Two quick slaps follow—one on each cheek—and I groan again. When his fingers dip down between my legs, I push back against them, needing more of him, all of him.

Michael swears under his breath and slides one finger

inside me. "You're so wet, baby." Another finger joins the first one, sliding in and out in a rhythm that only makes me hungrier.

I grind against his hand, the friction not nearly enough. I'm mewling in a way that probably should make me embarrassed, but there's no way I can control myself and I'm not sure I'd even want to. There's something about the way Michael works my body that always leaves me begging.

He drapes himself over me, his lips grazing my ear. "I need to be inside you, Kat."

I push back against him, my intentions obvious, and when he rises up and plunges into me, I nearly shout from relief. His hands grab my hips as he pounds into me. He's not holding anything back and I try to meet him thrust for thrust. My face grinds against the sheets and I knock the pillows to the floor. He wraps my hair around his fist and pulls. My scalp sings, a second of pain butting up against the pleasure of everything else that's happening to my body.

When Michael's hand finds its way from my hip back between my legs, I'm already seconds away from coming apart again. I don't know how I ever managed with only a single orgasm with other men and now I'm ruined because of it. No one will be able to live up to the expectation of Michael, but I try not to think about this as his fingers find my clit and start rough circles. My mouth hangs open and all I can think about is chasing this high, letting my body feel as free as I've ever felt.

I try to stave off my orgasm to make the moment last, but Michael doesn't give me that chance.

"You like the way I'm fucking you?" he grinds out and I can barely get my response out before I'm gasping again, my entire body going tight. "Kat, you're going to make me come."

And then he does, grunting as he pushes into me one final time before we both collapse onto the mattress. The sheets are a tangled mess and we pant, sweaty and spent.

Michael kisses between my shoulder blades and smoothes some of the damp hair from my forehead, spooning me. "Was I too rough with you? I got ahead of myself there." He runs his hands over my body like he'd be able to tell if he's broken me in any way. But he can't tell. I am broken and I don't know how I'm ever going to put myself back together.

"No, that was perfect." I turn my head toward him and capture his mouth with mine. "You don't have to worry about me." But I know that's wishful thinking even as he dozes off, one arm still slung over me. His breathing steadies and I try to commit this moment to memory.

In the morning I tell him it's over.

38

Michael

"You look like shit."

"Thanks," I growl out and even that one-word answer makes my head hurt.

"If you're sick or something I can take over today. Wasn't really expecting you to come by at all." Danny gives me a quick glance but looks away just as quickly.

"I'm fine."

"You don't look fine. Not that it's any of my business, but if you're sick you shouldn't be here. Go home and have Kat spoon feed you some chicken soup or something."

Just hearing her name makes my heart start banging around in my chest. Kat's not going to be feeding me any chicken soup. She's not going to be so much as looking at me. "There is no Kat. Not anymore."

Danny raises an eyebrow. "What'd you do?"

"Nothing. She's just done." Or at least that's all I could get out of her when she told me it was over. She gave me the expected excuses, but I couldn't get her to commit to much more than that. And I'd tried like hell. I'd begged. I'd pleaded. Shit, I'd cried. I'd fucking *cried* and she'd still shown me the door. Claimed I'd "thank her one day." Well, it's been a week and I'm still not feeling very thankful. What I'm feeling is hollow. And hungover.

"Are you drunk?" Danny leans in and gives me a sniff. "How bloodshot are your eyes behind those sunglasses?" His nose wrinkles in disgust. "Man, you cannot be here at the job site looking like this. Let's get some coffee in you. I'll put Patrick in charge."

"Patrick can't be in charge," I protest and get only an eye roll from Dan.

"He'll be fine for an hour. Wait here while I tell him about his temporary promotion to management."

The coffee doesn't help. As my head gets a bit clearer that only makes it more difficult to ignore my heart. That sucker wants to quit beating, to quit feeling as banged up as it does right now. And with a clear head I can start going over everything again. And still not know exactly where I went wrong.

"You want to go ahead and get all those feelings out? I can try my best to listen but I can't promise I won't laugh. Or give sage advice." When I don't even crack a smile Dan lets out a sigh. "She really did a number on you, didn't she?"

"Please don't tell me you told me so. I know you're dying to." I take another sip of my coffee and hope that no one in this diner can see how close I am to losing it. Breaking down in a public place is not on my list of things to do today. Should have gone home to lick my wounds in private.

"I just don't understand why Kat would call things off. I've seen the way she looks at you and that's not how a woman looks at a man she's about to cut loose. You sure nothing happened?"

I've been wracking my brain for the answer to that question. She'd met my family and gotten a reminder of our age difference, but she'd seemed to roll with it. I'd gone to bed that night surer than ever I was right where I needed to be. Sure she felt the same way.

"We went to my dad's and it turned out she and Tracy went to high school together. But at home everything seemed fine so I don't think that's it."

"You check with Tracy to make sure she didn't say anything crazy?" Dan swirls the coffee around in his cup. "She's a talker."

"Even if she did, why would Kat decide to cut and run? She's pretty level-headed and that's not how she works. She's a planner." One who had maybe been planning on not keeping me around for a while. The thought rolls around in my gut, threatening to send this coffee right back up.

"Just explain it to me. She said you'd thank her later, right? Why would she think that? She thinks she's doing you a favor. But she's gotten over the age difference?" Dan adds more sugar to his cup.

"You're going to give yourself diabetes. And, yeah, I thought that wasn't an issue anymore." I pick at a hangnail around my thumb. "But she thinks we don't want the same things. That I can't give her what she wants, I guess."

"Well, what does she want? In my experience you're supposed to figure out what the lady wants and then give it to her." Dan shrugs like it's the easiest thing in the world. Like Kat wants flowers or a puppy.

"She wants a baby."

Coffee comes spewing out of Danny's mouth all over the tabletop. Our waitress is over in an instant, scowling as she wipes the surface dry. When she refuses to refill Danny's cup, he barely even protests. "A what? You've been trying to get her pregnant?" He's loud enough that a few heads turn in our direction.

"No, she's getting pregnant by herself." I scowl across the table. I'm giving out too much of Kat's personal information here.

"You realize that's not how it works, right? No wonder she decided she was done with you."

I frown.

"Because you can't *get* her pregnant? How long have you even been trying? Because I'd have thought those swimmers would get the job done. I guess you never know. My cousin had a problem with that and let me tell you—"

I slam my cup down on the table. "I haven't been trying to get her pregnant. She's doing it all on her own. Using a donor. It's separate from what's been going on between me and her." As it comes out of my mouth, I realize how ridiculous that sounds. Even more idiotic than the time Kat told her family the exact same thing.

Danny shakes his head. "Even you should have been able to see how that was never going to work. You were gonna let her have another man's baby? And then what? Just hang around while she raised it? That's not how I would have imagined you doing things."

That's not how I imagined things either. It hits me squarely between the eyes. I've been imagining a life with Kat. A family. But she doesn't know. She has no idea how much I want that baby—any baby of hers—to also be mine. Not just the making of it, I want the raising of it. I want the late nights and the diapers, the birthday parties and graduations. I want all those things and I want them with her.

"Ohhh." Danny's mouth quirks into a half smile. "You just figured it out, like right now?"

"She thinks I don't want what she wants."

"Duh." Danny shakes his head. "The question here is whether she's right or whether she's wrong."

"She's wrong."

"Well, then you'd better figure out a way to let her know." Danny swirls the last two sips of his coffee around in his cup before tilting it up to finish them off. "You're paying for the coffee, by the way. That's a million times cheaper than the therapy you need."

I scowl but throw a few bills on the table. I don't have time to argue with Dan over who's paying for coffee. I have a woman to win back.

39

Kat

I've been staring at the blinking cursor for thirty minutes when Mark pops his head into my office.

"You ready? They're in the conference room."

"What? Already?" I look at the blank page in front of me where my presentation's supposed to be.

"We said ten. It's five after. Do you need a few more minutes? I can stall them with fancy coffee or something." Mark's mouth works its way into a concerned pucker. "Do you want to show me what you've got?" He comes around the desk and furrows his brow. "Nothing?"

"No, no, I researched. I just can't get my ideas out." I turn my face up toward his. Mark's trying not to show his displeasure, especially after the past few weeks here in the office. I've been scattered and unfocused, and Mark's had to pick up the slack. "Just go and entertain them for five or so and I'll get something together."

I can tell Mark isn't excited by this idea. He starts to open his mouth, then shuts it, nodding his head. He leaves my office and goes back to the conference room to save my ass once again.

Once I muddle my way through the meeting, I go back to my office on autopilot. I freeze in the doorway when I notice the new bouquet of flowers my assistant has placed on my desk. I don't have to look at the card to know who they're from. And I already know why they're here.

He remembered.

He doesn't know for sure, of course, but if everything goes according to schedule, tomorrow's the big day. Time to finally try to get myself knocked up. Time to bite the bullet on the thing that's made me give Michael up for good. And he's sent me flowers to commemorate it.

"Do you have time to..." Mark stops behind me. "Why are you standing out here in the hall?"

I turn to look at him and burst into tears.

"I'm so sorry. This is unprofessional. I shouldn't be doing this at work." I sniffle and wipe my nose again with the tissue Mark's provided, one of about one hundred that now litter the top of my desk. The tears are relentless.

"It's fine." But Mark's eyeing me like he's discovered me in here gnawing on my own arm. "You have been a little... off lately. Is there anything you want to talk about? I'm not trying to pry, but as your friend I'd like to be able to help, if I can."

"Can you turn back time and make my uterus twenty-five again?"

Mark sighs. "I think the hormones are doing a number on you right now. It's tomorrow, right? Is that what they decided at your appointment today?" He hands me my water bottle from the edge of my desk. It's plain. No more special flavored water now.

I take a sip. "Yep. I'll be out all day."

"I don't care about that. I'm more concerned you're hell bent on doing this alone. Who's taking you in the morning?" Mark's face shows more concern than I'd like.

"Amy's coming with me." I don't mention the fact she'd strong armed me into letting her be my support person. And I leave out the fact I'm still wishing it was Michael instead of my sister. That fantasy isn't going to come true and wouldn't be fair to him if it did.

"You going to call him?"

I know good and well who "him" is, even without Mark giving me a hint. And he knows good and well I'm not going to be doing any calling. No calling. No texting. No in person face-to-face. Even if it's killing me.

"You could call him; it wouldn't be the end of the world. You could thank him for the flowers. Those are from Michael, right?' Mark gestures toward the bouquet.

"I can't call him." Not even to exercise my good manners and say thank you.

"Why not? This still doesn't make any sense to me, Kat. You're miserable without him and he's obviously still thinking about you. Whatever happened between you must have been pretty dramatic to have you calling things off. I've seen the way he looks at you. Whatever he did must have been pretty terrible to make you give that up."

I blink. "Michael didn't do anything. It isn't like that."

Mark startles. "I'm sorry. I just assumed." He's waiting for more information, hoping I'll tell him why I've put myself through all this, but I'm not sure I can give it.

"I ended it because it wasn't fair to him." I fold my hands

in my lap, let my thumbs rest on the spot where tomorrow there might be a baby.

"Excuse me?" Mark looks at me in disbelief. "What does that even mean?"

"He's young, Mark. And I'm trying to have a baby. He doesn't need that." I keep my voice firm, telling myself almost as much as I'm telling Mark.

"Did he say that? He's not interested in a baby?"

"He *is* a baby. He didn't need to tell me he doesn't want to be forced to help me raise one."

"But he never actually said that?" Mark's brow furrows. "Did you even ask him?"

"Ask him what? If he wanted to stick around while I got hugely pregnant and then help me change diapers? I don't need to ask to know the answer to that question." I tighten my grip on my middle. Hearing Michael tell me he wasn't interested would have been unnecessary in this heartache.

"Kat..." There's more than a twinge of pity. "You didn't even give him a chance, did you?"

I frown.

"And now you're going to try to do all this by yourself rather than accept that he might be interested in being with you?"

"I'm not going to trap him into this," I huff and glare at Mark. What does he know anyway? I'm the one making decisions here. And I've already made this one.

"He wasn't acting trapped, from what I could see. He was trying to help you get ready for this. That doesn't sound like someone who was looking for the exit."

"That doesn't mean he would have stuck around. None of this is easy and it's not going to get any less difficult. He'd be signing on for a relationship with a woman who had someone else's baby."

Mark lets out a sigh. "Plenty of people raise children who aren't biologically theirs, Kat. That isn't something so unusual you'd end something good over it." He pauses, his eyes widening. "That isn't what you did, is it? You didn't break up with him because you're worried about the baby not being his, did you?"

I can't look him in the eye, because, yes, that's what I did and I'd do it again if it meant giving Michael the opportunity to make his own family.

"Did you ask him if he'd consider being the father?"

My eyes snap up to Mark's face. "Of course not! I wouldn't have put Michael in that position. That's too much pressure when we're so new." Even if I've been dreaming of what a great dad Michael would be, imagining him with our baby in his arms. Even if I've started thinking about what that would be like to have him as the father of my child.

"If you say so. But you keep acting like he's a kid, Kat, and I think you know he's anything but. I asked Rachel to marry me when I was twenty-five. We had two kids before I was thirty. He's plenty old enough to decide he wants to start a family. You just need to let him. If he's not into it then fine, but denying him the chance? That's selfish, and it isn't making either of you very happy."

My eyes start to get that familiar prickly feeling and I know I'm about to cry again. I don't want to think about how I might have screwed up the possibility of a life with Michael. I can't think about that right now, not when I should be trying to relax and get myself ready for tomorrow. "It's too late now," I say and the defeat in admitting that gets the tears started again.

"Maybe not." Mark hands me another tissue. "But I can't make you do what I think you should. I'm going to go back to my office and iron out the rest of the proposal. Why don't you go on home and rest up for tomorrow?"

I nod, unable to talk through the tears.

"Let me know if you need anything. Rachel and I would be happy to help."

I nod again. I'm sure Mark's rethinking his business decisions right about now. Who wants a partner who can't make it through the day without sobbing?

"I still think he deserves a phone call, but I'll let you figure that out on your own. Good luck tomorrow. Call if you need me."

But I don't pull out my phone and dial Michael's number. I have to stick to my decision, no matter how much it hurts, because anything else is only going to hurt him in the long run.

40

Michael

Ringing the doorbell takes more effort than it should, but I make myself do it. I don't have a key to unlock the door anymore. I'd left that on the kitchen counter when Kat had told me we were through. Which should mean that coming over here unannounced is probably not the best idea. I've tried to let her know I've been thinking about her, but not pushing. I know how stubborn she can be once she's set her mind to something. Her determination is one of the reasons I actually have this excuse for face-to-face contact. I'm not sure if I should be grateful or sad.

Amy's the one to answer the door. I should have expected that, maybe. I'm thankful Kat's not alone, but I know her sister's not going to be able to take care of her the way I would. Or the way I used to. But I try not to dwell on that as I smile at her, her surprised eyes opening a bit wider when she realizes who's standing out on the porch.

"Well, hello. You are not the pizza delivery man." Amy takes in the bags I'm holding and the bouquet of flowers. "Kat didn't tell me you were coming over."

"Kat doesn't know. I'm just dropping some things off for her. Thought she might like some comfort food." I hold the bags out for Amy to take. "I made her favorites."

Amy takes the bags and peeks inside, her lips thinning. "You cooked?"

"Sure. I know what she likes and she's probably pretty tired. I also know she can't feed herself so I figured I'd go ahead and do it." I manage a little smile. "How's she doing? I mean, if you feel comfortable telling me."

"She's fine. A little crampy... Why don't you just come inside? You don't have to stand out here on the porch." Amy moves a little to the side. "She's taking a nap, if you're worried about upsetting her."

More than anything I want to come in off the porch, but I want to be welcome in Kat's house—not sneaking in when she's unaware. "I shouldn't. I don't want to have her think I'm taking advantage. If you could just make sure she eats? And let me know if she needs anything?"

Amy nods. "I can do that. Thanks for stopping by, Michael. That was really thoughtful of you. I'll go and put these flowers in some water." She stares at me for a beat and gives me a sad smile. "You're a good guy."

"I try to be." I shrug and then make my way back to my truck.

The next day when I ring the bell I brace myself for more of the same. I'm not coming by with expectations, so I try to keep the possibility of seeing Kat out of my mind. I'm here to make sure she's well-fed and I can do that without catching a glimpse of her green eyes or being tempted to run my fingers through her hair. But I wait until I'm sure she's home from work before I drive over so I can't deny I'm hoping to see her for just a second or two rather than having to leave the food on her porch. And operation "how can you live without me?" probably works better with a little in-person time.

Kat's face is surprised when the door finally opens. She's in a pair of those soft sweatpants she likes to lounge around in and her face is bare. I suck in a breath that I hope she can't hear and try to keep myself from reaching out for her. Luckily, I've got my hands full of these bags to prevent me from doing something stupid.

"Hi." Kat pushes a strand of hair off her forehead. "I wasn't expecting you to come by again." She folds her hands in front of her and I notice her twisting her fingers just a bit.

"I brought you dinner." I hand the bags to her and she unclasps her fingers long enough to take them from me.

"You didn't have to. I can order in, you know. I can feed myself."

I give her an incredulous look. "Now's not the time for takeout, Kat. You need to have nutritious food and not have to worry about where you're going to get it. I also put a book in there. It's supposed to be good. I haven't read it, but..." I shuffle a bit on my feet. "And I put a puzzle in there too. I know you have work to keep you busy, but sometimes it's nice to have other distractions." I wince at how this explanation is sounding and know I need to get off this porch and back in my truck before I make myself look like more of an idiot.

"Thank you. That was really nice of you." Kat stares at me for a beat too long, her cheeks pinking up a bit.

"How are you feeling?" Once I know this, I'll be able to leave. At least that's what I'm telling myself as I try to prolong the time I'm allowed to be this close to Kat.

"Fine, actually. Yesterday was a little hard, but today I can barely even tell any difference."

"That's great." I don't even have to fake my enthusiasm. "Two weeks until you know, right?"

"Yeah." Kat answers me in that soft voice I love, the one that used to mean she was getting ready to love up on me. My heart starts to beat a little faster and I know it's time to leave. Yes, I want Kat to want me like she used to and I know what's happening right now is the kind of need that I don't mind her having either. But I want both. I want her to need me and to want me and not just because she's terrible in the kitchen.

"Do you want to come in? Have a beer?" She gestures toward the living room.

I fight the urge to waltz right back into Kat's house and make myself at home on her couch. "No, I need to get going. Make sure you rest a little, okay?" I keep my hands firmly at my sides.

"Okay." Kat's bottom lip comes out a bit and for a split second I think she might be a tad disappointed. But I don't dwell on that. Now's not the time to get my hopes up. I give her a nod and climb back down the steps for the longest ride home ever.

The third night's the same.

And the fourth.

And the fifth.

But by the sixth night my resolve crumbles a bit. Making her dinner every day is overkill. So's adding extra things like the soy milk she likes for her lattes and the decaf version of her coffee. And sometimes making a lunch for the next day is definitely over the top. But I can't help myself. Yes, I've got work and I could be hitting the bars with Danny any night of the week—hell, every night of the week—but there's only one thing I really care about and that's making sure this time's as easy as possible for Kat. So when she invites me in on Friday night, instead of doing what I know I should, I let her open the door wider and I go on in.

"I have some of your dishes and things. Come in and I'll get them for you."

That's a reasonable excuse to walk through the living room and into the kitchen, right? And, when she hands me a beer before I can protest, I certainly don't want to hand it back to her and have it go to waste. *The cap's already off! It'd be rude not to drink it.* But I don't have any excuse for how slowly I sip on that thing, making it last far longer than it should.

"Have you eaten?" Kat's unloading the bags I've brought over.

"I have." And I should not even be entertaining the idea that I could sit down at the table with her.

"Oh." That lip comes out again. "Want to keep me company while I eat?"

More than anything. "I shouldn't. I'll just finish this beer and get out of your hair." Even though it's killing me.

"No rush. You keep spoiling me with dinner every night, the least I could do is let you watch me eat it." She reaches up to pull a plate from the cabinet and I can't help but look at her stomach. If everything's gone according to plan, there's the beginnings of a baby in there.

"Making you dinner's hardly spoiling you." I don't remind her that I used to do it every night before she decided to cut me loose. "Feeding you's just being a concerned citizen. Can't have you starving when you're supposed to be creating a baby."

Kat freezes. She blinks a bit before she looks at me again. "Well, I appreciate it."

I nod, keeping one hand on the beer and the other jammed in my pants pocket. "No problem. I should get going." I finish the beer and put the bottle on the counter. I'm not even going to tempt myself by rinsing it out in the sink. Kat's entirely too close for me to be able to handle that. The urge to hold her's getting damn near overwhelming and I need to get out of this house before I give in and wrap my arms around her.

Kat frowns but lets me go, closing the door softly behind me, leaving me on the porch with nothing but the crickets and the fireflies.

41

Kat

I now know I'm the most selfish woman in the world. Maybe the universe. I shouldn't invite Michael in, shouldn't offer him a beer, and most certainly shouldn't ask him to have dinner with me. I shouldn't be accepting these home cooked meals and presents, shouldn't be smiling when I think about them during the day. But, that's exactly what I'm doing. All of it.

When Michael tells me he's going, I want to pull out all the stops to make him stay. I'm lonely and a little scared and he's just what I need to make myself feel better. But the little twinge I see on his face as he's turning to walk out the door reminds me why I can't reach for him, can't grab his hand and pull him back to me. I've made this choice so he can find someone better suited to him. If there's such a thing as soulmates, I have to keep believing Michael's is still out there. I don't bother thinking about mine.

I go back to the kitchen and finish what I started. I open the containers he's left for me—he's outdone himself tonight with the Asian theme—and pile my plate full of sesame broccoli, chicken in spicy sauce, and the brown rice he keeps making me eat instead of white. Technically it's not even rice although I couldn't tell you what it's called. But apparently I need superior nutrition so that's what I'm getting. And it's all delicious, of course, so I'm not complaining. I get the slightest guilty pang as I picture Michael making this dinner for me and the lunch I'm sure to find at the bottom of the bag. This is all in addition to work and I'm left hoping that doesn't mean he's falling behind on the things he needs to be doing. I contemplate this as I chew, the sounds of my fork hitting the plate ringing through the empty house.

I scroll through social media on my phone, knowing that most of these happy photos and declarations of love are probably just for show but finding myself unable to look away. Once this baby's born who will take all the celebratory photos? Me and the selfie stick, I suppose. I pat my stomach. *We'll be fine.* Although right now this loneliness is swallowing me up. Late night with a crying baby is sure to be much harder than dinner alone on a Tuesday is turning out to be. I think about posting a picture of my plate but decide to call Amy instead. Maybe she can get me off this rollercoaster I'm hoping is just pregnancy hormones.

It rings more times than it should for Amy "always available" Winston, but she eventually picks up with a flustered, "Hello?" There's music in the background that abruptly stops two seconds later.

"Hey, just calling to see what you're up to." Amy doesn't immediately respond and I hear what sounds like scurrying on her end of the phone. "What *are* you up to? It sounds like you're hiding a body."

"Just trying to get a few things ready for school," Amy huffs. "You know how much planning that takes."

"Were you listening to music for inspiration? I thought I heard some guitar or something." I push the remaining food around on my plate.

"Guitar? No. Well, maybe. It was the radio." Amy breathes into the receiver. "But enough about me, how are you feeling? Any pregnancy symptoms yet or are we not supposed to talk about that?"

I let Amy deflect even though I'm suspicious. I did call her, after all, and I am wallowing in some serious self-pity over here. I'm more than happy to talk about myself. "We can talk about that but most of the symptoms now are the same as PMS, so I'm not getting my hopes up. I am hoping that this hormonal funk means there's a bean in there, though."

"A bean? We're going to call the baby 'bean'?"

"Just at the beginning. You don't like 'bean'?"

"It doesn't matter to me; it's your baby." Amy's still moving around. "Are you enjoying another gourmet meal courtesy of your not-baby-daddy?"

I groan. "Can we not right now? I'm already feeling guilty. I actually tried to get him to stay and eat with me tonight. I'm a hot mess. See how hormonal I am?"

"Oh, we're blaming that on hormones, are we?" Amy laughs. "That's got nothing to do with you possibly being pregnant, Kat."

"Of course it does. What else could it be? I'm a little lonely and pumped full of fertility drugs and maybe a baby. It's expected that I'm going to make a few strange decisions." I look down at my almost empty plate and feel a second of longing. It's fine to have those feelings, right? To miss what I had even if I know I made the best choice for me? Made the best choice for Michael.

"You miss him. He misses you. He's still coming around

even after you cut him loose and you're letting him. Sure some of that's loneliness but you made yourself lonely on purpose. You aren't regretting that, are you?" I can picture Amy pushing her glasses up higher on the bridge of her nose. She's getting ready to deliver one of her helpful life lesson lectures.

"Of course I'm regretting it, Amy. I wish I could have it all, but I can't, not if it means Michael misses out on what he deserves to have."

"Seems to me he's missing out on having *you*. That's what he's missing and you're both missing out. What did he say when you asked him to stay tonight? That was a little manipulative, by the way, especially if you want him to be out finding some hot younger girl to knock up."

I gulp because I know Amy's right—and because the idea of Michael with another woman still makes my throat close up. "He said no and then he left. And can we not talk about Michael? I want him to find someone who's a better match for him." *But I don't want to think about it.*

"He said 'no'? Really?" Amy gives a little *harumph*. "That's not what I would have expected. I'm still surprised the two of you have held out this long."

"What's that supposed to mean?"

"You know what it means. I don't have to tell you." Again the music starts in the background, the unmistakable sound of a lone guitar, but then it's muffled again. "Sorry about that. I meant to turn that off."

"That doesn't sound like the radio—"

"Kat, you need to really think about this, okay? I don't have time tonight to walk you through it. I know you think you're loving him enough to let him go or some shit like that, but maybe that's not what's needed in this situation. Maybe he's okay with raising Russell Brand's baby. He doesn't seem to be going anywhere and you've tried—sort of —to convince him to. Maybe reconsider this great plan you've got for him and let him tell you what he's got planned for himself." There's a distinct crash from somewhere in Kat's house. "Oh God, the cat. I have to go."

"Wait, you have a cat?"

But Amy's already hung up.

That night I dream of a little wisp of a girl with dark curly hair and dark eyes. We're at the playground and I'm pushing her on a swing. Her little legs pump furiously every time I send her soaring high into the air. When I stop pushing, she cries out for more and I send her up again and again until the sun starts to set and it's time to go home.

"Aren't we going to wait for daddy?" the little girl asks me. She can't be much older than four and she puts her chubby hand in mine as we walk toward the parking lot.

I frown down at this imaginary daughter. Doesn't she know—shouldn't she know—there is no daddy coming to meet us? That it will be the two of us, and just the two of us, tonight and every night after? I start to open my mouth to explain this, to tell this little girl that she doesn't actually have a daddy—not one who can push her on the swings or meet us at the park—but the sound of a male voice calling out my name stops me.

"Sorry I'm late. What a b-i-t-c-h of a day."

Michael.

He swings the little girl up on his shoulders and takes my hand in his. "Glad to be with my girls now, though."

I smile up at him, at those perfect teeth and the warm

brown eyes. The same eyes looking down at me from the face of our daughter.

When I wake up, I type a text to Michael. I thank him for the dinners but tell him there's no need for him to bring them by anymore.

I let my finger hover over the screen for a second before I delete it.

Michael

It is never a good sign to have my father's truck in the driveway of a new client's house first thing in the morning. Aside from the fact that he's parked in the spot where my truck should be sitting, having him standing around casually shooting the shit with my crew as I drive up is guaranteed to take away any happiness I had been harboring this morning. And I did have just the tiniest smidgen of it as I drove to work, because after having Kat invite me to stay for dinner, I woke up to a thank you text that made me feel just a little better about turning her down. And she's reminded me that tonight's the night of the boxing match I've been waiting all summer for. You see, Kat's got it on Pay Per View and her mentioning it has to be a good sign. I'm playing the long game here and hoping to wear her down a bit. I can't tell yet if it's working, but having her thinking enough of me to remind me about the fight and to maybe hint that I could stick around tonight to watch it has a tiny bubble of hope bouncing around in my chest. But that bubble pops as soon as I see my father leaning against the side of his truck holding court with my guys—guys who should be getting the fuck to work.

Danny jogs to my driver's side door, looking more than a little sheepish. "Sorry, man. I tried to get him to leave, but he cannot take a hint."

"It's alright." I slam the door behind me. "Any idea what he wants?"

"Nope. Just said he needed to talk to you. Probably wanted to have an audience." Danny shrugs. "Anything I can do?"

I shake my head. Dealing with my father's my responsibility and mine alone. "I'll take care of it. You just get the guys back to work." I take a deep breath as Danny walks back to the crowd of people around my father. No sense in dragging my feet, better to get to the bottom of whatever my father thinks deserves a discussion at eight in the morning.

"Michael," he calls out to me once I get close enough. "Sorry to bother you at work. Can I have a minute?"

He's asking but I know that's not really a question, and as much as I'd like to tell him to go to hell, I'm not doing that at work. Not in front of any of the guys who think of me as their boss. I'm not giving him a chance to make them see me as the kid he still thinks I am.

"Sure." I jerk my head to the side. I want distance for whatever conversation he's planning. I move farther out into the yard of the sprawling house with the defective roof to give myself a little space away from Danny and the guys, and to give me an opportunity to call at least one of the shots. Surprisingly, my father follows without an argument.

"Looks like you got a good crew," he says once we're a little away from the house. "Plenty of new guys."

"Yep. They're all pretty solid." I shove my hands in my

back pockets. "You come all the way out here to inspect my crew?"

"Of course not." My father rolls his eyes. "I came out here to talk to you."

"About?"

"About how we left things the other night."

It's been weeks since the birthday party and my phone hasn't exactly been ringing off the hook. Not a text from my father since, either, so showing up today means more than just clearing the air. I've been busy with other things and thankful that Peter Cruz apparently had more on his plate than just setting his oldest son straight. My luck's finally run out on that one.

"You have something more you need to say? 'Cause I feel like we've exhausted that subject."

My father's jaw tenses and he folds his arms across his chest. The blue button down he's wearing pulls tight across the front. He's more casual today than usual—no suit and shiny shoes—but I don't take that as a sign of him being any more relaxed than any other day. "I have a few more things I'd like to talk about."

I shrug. "Have at it then, but I don't have all morning."

"It's been brought to my attention that I was a little harsh with you after the party."

I can't help the sound that escapes my mouth. It's a combination of a snort and a scoff and it makes my father's jaw set even harder and his eyes narrow.

"I'm here to apologize for that, I guess, and to see if there's anything you need from me." His face remains impassive and he rocks on his heels a little. "I know you think you can run this business on your own, but I do have some knowledge that might benefit you, despite what you might think."

"Well, I appreciate the *apology*." I can't help but emphasize the word because if that was an apology then I'm Willie Nelson, but at least I know he has an inkling of what he's supposed to do when he's in the wrong—even if he's not actually doing it now. "But I think I've got the business stuff well in hand."

"Kat helping you out?" He raises his eyebrows a fraction.

"Don't." The way my father spoke about her last time we were together still burns and I'll be damned if I'm going to let him do that again.

"Fine. Not my business." My father lifts his hands in surrender. "But you'd be wise not to get too high and mighty over there. I know you think that woman's it for you for some reason, but be careful you're not staying in something just to prove a point. Don't stick just to prove you aren't me."

I blink.

The idea hovers there for a second, shimmering between us. I'll admit that in life I do make an effort to do the opposite of whatever I think Peter Cruz would do. I'm the antithesis of my father in nearly every way that I think counts. But standing across from me, I can see the parts of him that are reflected back in me: the dark eyes, the strong chin, the tilt of his mouth. I get my build from my mother's side, so I'm taller than my father now, and broader, but some of that's also about the other choices I've made: the manual labor, the time outside, the refusal to sit still. It's easy to see that we're related, though, the same way it's easy to see Will and Andrew are my family, too. But with my father the similarities end there. They're physical, unless you count the stubbornness and the temper, both of which might be genetic. I've been thinking more and more about this whole fatherhood thing—this whole family thing—and how it all fits together. There's no denying I'm a part of my father, but there's more to me than that. I'm not limited by the things I've learned from him.

But my relationship with Kat isn't a reaction to my father. It isn't something I'm using to prove a point or make a statement. It isn't in opposition to anything at all unless you count Kat's reluctance to let me in, to let me love her the way I want to. There my father's stubbornness just might come in handy. But I'm not trying to make a life with Kat out of anything but my own desires, my own feelings, my own ideas about the future. My feelings for the baby she may or may not have growing in her belly aren't all that complicated either. She might not have my genetics, but she's a part of Kat and I've got nothing but love there. I'd love that baby—will love her—automatically. There's none of my father in that and the realization feels surprisingly good, gives me a little boost that has me wanting to pull out my phone and dial Kat's number just to hear her voice, just to let her know I'm thinking about her. There's something so pure in that second—something so easy—I almost want to thank my father.

"She's got nothing to do with you, but I'll keep that advice in mind." I try to signal we're done here but my father doesn't move.

"That's it?" He seems genuinely surprised, letting his lower lip fall just a touch before he straightens himself back up.

"Unless you've got something else. I need to get back to work; I'm sure you've got places to be." I don't need to let the old anger get the better of me, don't need to let it ruin the good that's starting to run through this day. "I appreciate you stopping by."

My father snorts. "We both know that's not true, but I'll get out of your hair, I guess. Crew's looking good." He's surprisingly docile, moving back toward his truck. Like it or not, that man's always going to be my father and I have to find a way to reconcile that with the kind of father I want to be.

The kind of father I'm going to be, if Kat will let me.

43

Kat

Be kind, but firm. Be friendly, but not too friendly. I repeat this over and over to myself as I wait for the inevitable knock on my front door. I have myself prepared for the moment when Michael arrives and I have to protect him from the thoughts in my head that have me wanting to invite him in and convince him to stay forever. Almost equally important—I need to protect myself from this idea I could make Michael a permanent part of my life. I've already made this decision, but I need to keep reminding myself that it's best for everyone if I stand firm. No Michael staying for dinner. No Michael hanging out in the kitchen. No Michael ending up in my bedroom. Especially not that last one.

But maybe I've read too much into things because at 8 p.m. my mantra's starting to wear a little thin. I check my phone again for texts. None. Make sure I've got cell reception. Four bars. Consider the possibility Michael's been in a horrible car accident and is at the hospital right now. Unlikely. What's much more likely is that he's busy. Busy with something other than making my dinner and catering to my every need. Busy with something other than me. Which is all I've been focused on: *me*. Maybe he's wised up and found someone who has the wherewithal to think about his needs for a change.

The loneliness of that realization hits me hard. Michael doesn't owe me anything. His time is his own and he's supposed to be out living his life. That's what I told him to do, what I made him do and gave him no choice. But now here I am, waiting for the man I convinced I wasn't interested to hurry up and get here with my dinner. Pathetic.

And I'm a self-sufficient woman. I can take care of myself and have for years. Sure, someone else doing that has been nice, but it was never part of the plan. I square my shoulders and get up off the couch, walk into the kitchen and start to rummage around for something I can cobble together for dinner. There's not much and I start to wish I'd been a little stingier with the leftovers when my sister stopped by yesterday. There was feast but now it's looking like famine in this refrigerator.

The sound of boots pounding up the front porch stairs makes me jerk my head out of the crisper. The knock on the door that follows gets me nearly running through the living room. I throw the door open without even bothering to take a look through the window.

And then there he is. Still in clothes that have obviously seen a day's work. That dark scruff lining his jaw, highlighting the white teeth he flashes at me when he sees me. Those dark eyes that crinkle at the edges as his smile spreads and gets wider. It's the same smile I'm wearing now, even though I know I shouldn't. His hands are full, multiple grocery bags hanging from his fingertips.

"Sorry it's so late. This job today ran long and I didn't get a chance to get home in time to make anything. But I got a rotisserie chicken, if you haven't eaten yet, and I can make those potatoes you like, if you don't mind waiting. Are you starving?"

Suddenly I am starving—starving to rush out onto the porch and wrap my arms around Michael's neck, starving to run my fingers through his hair and put my nose in the crook of his neck. I keep my hands by my sides but can't wipe my goofy grin off my face. He's here. So much for *friendly, but no too friendly. Kind, but firm* has already left the building.

"I should have called first. I don't have to come in and make anything. Here." Michael holds the bags out for me. "You can take these and I'll leave you to whatever you were doing. God, sorry, I stink." He gives himself a sniff. "You should try to stay upwind of me." He smiles again and my brain whirs to a stop.

"You can take a shower here." It is the most dangerous idea on the planet—Michael naked here in this house with me—but I say it anyway. "And stay for dinner. Is there salad stuff? I can make a salad."

"Are you sure? I don't know if I should..." Michael's hesitation is just enough to have me digging this hole deeper.

"Yes, yes. You went to the grocery store instead of going home." I take the bags and usher him in. "The least I could do is make a salad."

"Um, okay. If you're sure." Michael stands in the middle of the living room, hands shoved deep in the front pockets of his jeans.

"Help yourself to the shower. You know where everything is." I turn my back so he can't see the creep of pink climbing from my neck up to my cheeks. I know what's under that T-shirt, those jeans. I don't need to be thinking about any of that if he's naked two rooms down the hall.

Salad. Think about salad.

"That won't make you uncomfortable?"

"Nope." I try to wave dismissively behind me without turning around. "You won't be comfortable if you have to stay all sweaty." I try not to think about other ways we could get sweaty. *Please let these crazy thoughts be the result of pregnancy hormones and not just my brain operating on its regular old wavelength.*

"Give me five. I'll be quick."

I unload the bags on the kitchen counter, trying to ignore the sound of the water running in the bathroom down the hall. This is a very bad idea. It's playing with fire in every sense of the word. I'm the queen of mixed signals and I can't explain this away—even to myself. But just having him in the house is already making me relax, making all the thoughts of having ruined things with him for nothing move to the back of my brain.

"I'm going to run out to the truck real quick. I think I've got a clean shirt in there."

I turn and get the full force of everything I've been missing. Michael stands a few feet in front of me, shirtless, jeans low on his hips, water still dripping from his hair. My mouth goes dry and all I can do is blink for a second. Already certain parts of my body have forgotten the reasons Michael can't be here every night of the week, why I can't go over and slide a hand over his chest and up to that wet hair, forget about dinner altogether and get busy with other things.

"Kat?"

"Oh." I try to get my brain back on track. "I actually think you might have a T-shirt in the bedroom. Maybe a clean pair of jeans, too."

"Really? Sorry about that. I thought I got everything when..." He doesn't have to finish. *When I threw him out on his ass without any good explanation.*

"I think they may have been in the hamper. It's fine. They're in your drawer."

If Michael finds that at all strange, he doesn't let on. Of course he's still got a drawer in my dresser because he's still got a place in my heart. And I haven't had the energy or willpower to excise him from either spot.

Once he's back and smelling like soap and that fragrance that can only be his skin, he gets to work on the chicken. He looks at my sorry excuse for a salad—randomly cut tomatoes and entire leaves of lettuce—and manages only a slight smirk.

"What?" I ask, already knowing what he's biting back.

"Just glad to see some things never change." Michael shrugs and carries the platter of chicken he's carved over to the table. I can picture the smile he's hiding without even seeing his face. "You want to grab plates?"

Dinner's less awkward than it should be with Michael filling me in on all the new business developments I've missed since I broke his heart. He's got things running without my help now and sounds so smart I can't imagine that he doesn't have a line of women waiting outside his door. I push my chicken around on my plate and try to keep from asking the questions I really want the answers to, like, is that assistant I helped you hire still too cute for her own good, and have you been out trolling the bars with Danny? Both things I have no business asking and should not be thinking about as I try to make a single bite out of one of the lettuce leaves I serve myself from the salad bowl. As I try to cut it to fit on my fork, I can't help but notice how nice it feels to have company again and then chastise myself.

Michael's only here for tonight and only because it's convenient, though these feelings are anything but.

And he's being so polite. Too polite to still be thinking about anything but dinner. More than cordial here sitting at this dining room table, putting forkfuls of chicken in his mouth in the very spot where he'd had me bent over just a few weeks ago. This table has seen its fair share of escapades, only Michael's sitting here like that's the furthest thing from his mind.

"I'm sorry. I'm terrible at this." He puts his fork down with a loud *clank*.

"What?" I look up from my lettuce leaf and see the obvious distress on Michael's face.

"I promised I wouldn't do this."

"Do what?"

"Come in here. Get all attached. Start thinking things I shouldn't." He runs a hand through his hair, the ends still damp.

"I don't understand." There's a little bit of panic rising up toward my throat but there's also a tiny bubble of hope there as well. Selfish hope that he might not be quite as over me as he seems.

"I took a shower. Goddamn." Michael shakes his head. "I want to make sure you're eating, but you've made things clear. I just don't want to accept them."

I open my mouth but nothing comes out.

"I know you don't think I'm long-term material, Kat, and I get that. And I'm hoping that right now you've got that big dream of yours growing like a weed in there, I really do." He gestures toward my middle. "But I need to say something."

I open my mouth again, but he raises his hand.

"Just let me get it out and then we can move on. Baby or no baby I want to be with you. You think I'm not old enough to make that decision, I guess. I'm telling you right now you're wrong. I don't care two licks that you might be having a baby that isn't technically mine. I've thought about it. None of that part matters to me. And I'm always going to be here for you and for her, no matter what. I'll try to be friends if you won't give me more, but I need you to know that I'm capable of making a commitment. I've been trying my best to show you. And now I'm going to get out of here before I make even more of an ass of myself than I already have." He pushes his chair back from the table and stands.

Before I can wrap my mind around anything at all, Michael's kissing me on the top of the head and walking to the front door. He turns to look at me one more time and I want to tell him to come back. That I've made a terrible mistake in pushing him away. But I can't get any words out. And everything he said is still banging around in my head twenty minutes later.

Her.

He made the baby a girl.

44

Kat

I feel the first twinge as I'm getting out of bed in the morning. It isn't much, but it's enough to have me putting a hand on my belly. Today's the first real day I should be able to take a pregnancy test and know for sure if the IUI has worked. But cramping's not a great sign. Not the end of the world, as Dr. Sharpe has told me, but possibly the end of my pregnancy dreams for this round as the Internet so helpfully supplies. My period's not late yet, so there's nothing to keep Aunt Flo from showing up right on time if my donor sperm hasn't done the job. *Or if your elderly body hasn't worked the way it should.* I try to stay positive but that voice in the back of my mind keeps popping back in with commentary.

At work the cramping gets worse. I make it through the first round of meetings no problem, but by lunchtime there's no denying the inevitable. I debate staying to finish out the day, but with nothing on my agenda it seems masochistic to stay at the office. I don't want to be sitting at my desk when I'm faced with the cold hard truth that I'm not going to be welcoming a baby in nine months. I've been warned that this might take time, but the realization is still painful and I'd rather be at home if I need to start eating ice cream out of the carton.

At home I change into something comfortable and settle in on the couch. The pregnancy tests I bought in a more hopeful moment taunt me when I go into the bathroom to wash off the make-up I no longer need on my face. Michael's toothbrush manages to get in a jab or two as well, making sure I remember that I've given something up for this opportunity. In a weak moment I consider calling him, asking him to come over and keep me company. Instead I find a *Real Housewives* marathon on TV and commit to an afternoon of mindless entertainment.

But my brain doesn't seem to be on board with this whole idea of shutting off for a bit. It just keeps whirring and humming, turning over the next steps of my baby plan. *If* I'm not pregnant now, when can I try again? *Could* I be pregnant? Do I need to call Dr. Sharpe to get organized for next steps? Or should I wait it out to be sure? The plan is solid and requires me to keep my focus on the end result without getting bogged down in the details or the waiting. But I'm terrible at waiting and obsessed with the details, so this is all I think about as I try to forget everything and watch a group of New York ladies cut each other to the quick.

And I think about Michael. Every other thought goes back to whether or not he's going to show up tonight on my front porch, and what that means going forward. If there's no baby there's no need for him to keep dropping by to feed me and he can't keep being my personal chef forever. His declaration from the night before is still playing on repeat in my head. Could he really commit to life with me? To life with a baby? He seemed so sure, but the reason I set him free in the first place still matters. He deserves the chance to have a family of his own making. One that works with his timeline, not the rushed one I've had to commit to. Still, his sureness was convincing and has me thinking all sorts of things I probably shouldn't, and hoping for all kinds of things I should never consider.

After the third episode of my reality TV show, I cave. The lure of possibly knowing if I'm pregnant wins out over my stoic attempt to wait for the inevitable. I march myself into the bathroom and get ready to pee on a stick. The directions on the box seem pretty straightforward. I'm days past when the test should be effective, but there's still a chance I could get a false negative. I tear open one of the foil packages and pull the plastic cap off the top of the stick. I only have to pee on the thing for five seconds so I'm pretty sure I can manage that. The box recommends that I wait until morning and use the first pee of the day, but I'm too impatient for that right now.

I'm trying to figure out how to keep from peeing all over my hand when I notice the spotting in my underwear. Again, Dr. Sharpe had warned me that a little spotting might happen so I try to keep myself from getting too anxious. I know that plus the cramping probably means something decidedly not great, but I soldier on.

Waiting the three minutes it takes for the test to be ready feels like an eternity. Is this how other people do it? Sitting by themselves as the seconds tick away? Most people have partners, I'm guessing. Maybe counting down the minutes with them, maybe about to be surprised with results when they walk in the door. Positive or negative, someone else to share it with would make the waiting easier. When my three minutes are up, I flip the stick over.

Negative.

I blink for a bit, squinting to make sure I'm not missing some imaginary second line there, but there's nothing. Not even the faintest suggestion of a second pink line. I wait for the tears to start because I know they're coming and when they do, they do not disappoint. Big fat tears roll down my cheeks and spill onto the bathroom counter. They last through the next test and then the next. All negative. I'm like a faucet turned on full blast and when I hear a knock at the door, I can't even pull myself together enough to get them to stop. I answer it and find myself face-to-face with my sister. Amy's shock only registers for a second before she's muscling her way inside. I wave a white plastic stick at her and she peers down at the results window.

"Oh shit," Amy whispers. "Okay, okay." She puts me on the couch and stands there, hands on her hips. "This calls for wine, I think." When I don't contradict her, she heads off to the kitchen.

Amy returns with two glasses and an open bottle of white. I probably shouldn't be drinking—I might not be pregnant but I'm not going to be giving up on trying. Still, my hand shoots out to take a glass and I let my sister fill it up.

"You can try again," Amy says as she fills her own glass. "You knew it wouldn't be easy and that it might take a few tries."

I nod wordlessly because I do know all these things, but I can't explain to Amy the real reason I'm crying. I can't possibly tell her that mixed in with the disappointment at not being on the path to motherhood, there's a healthy dose of relief banging around inside me. Not because I don't want to have a baby. Not at all.

But because I want Michael to be the father.

45

Michael

"Thank God!"

It's a more exuberant welcome than I was expecting.

"Hurry up and get your ass in here. I need to tag out for a second." Amy gives me a yank and pulls me into Kat's living room.

"What the—" That's when I notice Kat crumpled on the couch, her face red and swollen. I drop the bags I'm carrying, not caring that the cupcakes I stopped to buy at Kat's favorite bakery are probably now all stuck to the top of the pink cardboard box. By the time I scoop a bawling Kat into my lap, Amy's halfway out the door.

"I'll check back in when I get a chance," she calls over her shoulder.

Kat's blubbering into my shoulder and mumbling something about things being broken. "Amy? What the hell's going on in here?"

"I accidentally got her drunk. Sorry. I think her tolerance is pretty low since she quit drinking. But she can explain the important parts. I've got to run; I'm already late. You're a lifesaver, Mike." Amy blows me an air kiss and shuts the door, leaving me with whatever's happening with Kat and these uncontrollable tears.

"Babe?" I look down into Kat's tear-stained face. Her mouth's worked its way into a pout that makes me want to press my lips against hers, despite the copious amount of snot she's got happening. "What's wrong?"

Kat furrows her brow and hands me one of the white plastic sticks she's got clutched in her fist. She frowns. "That's exhibit A," she explains.

I don't know much about pregnancy tests, but I'm pretty sure that's what I'm holding, and I'm pretty sure it isn't good news. The single pink line, coupled with Kat's sad face, tells me a story I know is probably breaking her heart.

"Is this definitive?" I have no idea how this works. Does one "no" mean it's absolute or is it like the magic eight ball at this point and we could ask again a little later and get a different answer?

"I started my period too," Kat wails.

"So, a pretty definite no?"

Kat's face crumples.

"Oh, I'm so sorry, Thumbs." I cradle her up against me, rocking her a little bit. I can't fix the real problem, but I can do everything in my power to let her know she's not alone, to let her know I'm here for her no matter what.

"Don't be sorry. I'm the one who broke it."

That makes no sense to me, but I don't stop rocking, moving just a little bit as I think about what she's said. "You didn't break anything, Kat. This isn't like scrambled eggs. It's gonna be fine. You can try again." None of this is the end of the world, but I'm sure that's how Kat's feeling.

"No." She sits up in my lap. "I'm not talking about that."

She takes the stick from my hand and tosses it across the room. "Who gives a shit about that?"

"Um, I thought that was the thing we were caring about the most right now?" I can't keep the confusion out of my voice. She's been living and dying by this baby and now we know it isn't happening yet. "What's more important?"

"What's more important?" Kat looks at me like I'm the dumbest man on the planet, and maybe I am because I have no idea where she's going with this. "Really, Michael?"

I shrug. "You tell me, Kat. What's more important to you than having a baby?"

Kat lets out a sigh. "This is how I broke it," she says and then clamps her lips shut.

I wait for a few beats, hoping she's going to enlighten me about whatever she's talking about. That never comes, of course, because while the wine's loosening her tongue somewhat, it isn't making things any clearer.

"Did you mean what you said yesterday?" she asks and I feel a little hitch in my chest. My crazy declaration from last night was one hundred percent true, but can't be something Kat wanted to hear. I'm trying to make her see me differently and blurting out a bunch of teenage feelings can't be selling me too hard.

"Which part?" I ask, stalling.

"The part about the baby."

I know exactly what she's talking about, but I want to pretend I have no idea. I know what I said and I stand by it, but right now it might not be what Kat wants to hear. But one thing I'm not is a liar, so I answer her as best I can.

"The thing I said about not caring that the baby wasn't mine?" I'm pretty sure that's what Kat's remembering.

"Yes."

"What about it?" I shift her in my lap so I can see her face better.

"Did you mean that? About it not mattering?"

"Yes." Maybe I'm a fool for letting Kat know that there's not much I wouldn't accept to be with her, but accepting her child, no matter where it came from? That's an easy answer. "I told you I'd love you and her no matter what."

"You made the baby a girl?" Kat's green eyes look up at me, questioning.

I hadn't given much thought to it, but, yes, I'd been thinking about a little girl with dark eyes and two brown pigtails. The best combination of me and Kat even though I knew there'd be none of my DNA in there. "Yeah, I'd been thinking about a daughter."

Kat shifts in my lap. "And you would have loved her?"

"Kat, I would have loved her no matter what. Because I love her mama." It comes out easy. There's no need to hide it. I love Kat. I've been keeping it in too long, protecting her and trying to protect myself. But she had to have known. The only question now is if she's going to return the sentiment or leave me hanging out here.

Again that brow crinkles. "You love her mama?"

"More than anything. But I'm not sure how she feels about me." I cock an eyebrow in a last-ditch effort to protect my heart from what's about to happen, from the moment when Kat confirms she doesn't feel the same way.

"I was thinking about a little girl too," Kat confesses and I try to give her a little space to maneuver away from my body if she needs it. But she doesn't move away, she pulls closer. "But it was all wrong."

I cock my head to the side. "What do you mean?"

"She wasn't yours."

"And you wanted her to be?" I feel my heart starting to

swell. It's more than pride, more than arrogance. It's that feeling I get when Kat looks at me and smiles, when she's got nothing but good things to say.

"More than anything."

The way my heart constricts has me wondering how I'm still breathing. She hasn't said the words, but she's given me something better. Kat wants a family and she wants me to be part of it.

"But you know that might not happen. Right?" Kat's all apologies when she doesn't have any reason to be. And I know how deep that worry goes, that she'll be keeping something from me. But I know there's a million ways for us to make a family and DNA's got nothing to do with it.

"Kat, I love you. Kids are just the icing on the cake, no matter how we have them. I'm not worried about that part."

"No?" She seems unconvinced.

"No. If you love me then I've got nothing to worry about." I leave it out there. All Kat's got to do is pick it up.

"Why wouldn't I love you?" Kat looks at me like I'm crazy, like she hasn't been pushing me away for weeks now.

"Well, because you've never said it. And because you told me you didn't want to see me anymore. Those are pretty strong indicators that you might not."

Kat's face crumples back up again. "See? That's how I broke it."

"Broke it? I'm still here, Kat. It can't be that broken." I nuzzle my nose up against her cheek. I've missed getting to hold her close like this, missed getting to touch her.

"You think it isn't too late? That we can fix it?" Kat's hopeful eyes look up at me. Like I'd ever be able to say no to her looking at me that way.

"I'm confident we can fix it, Thumbs. Not going to take too much work at all." I give her a kiss on the forehead.

Relationships might not be roofs, but I'm sure I can figure out how to repair things between me and Kat. "Let's get some food in you first, though. Then we can get this repair job started." I ease her off my lap and start to move from the couch. Kat grabs my hand.

"Hey," she says before she gives me the most serious look I think she can manage with all the wine. "I love everything about you."

"How about you tell me that in a few hours, once we've had dinner?" Oh yeah I'm going to make her tell me that again. Probably several times. With details. And I'm going to make sure I get those three little words on their own a thousand times or so before I leave this house again.

At least a thousand.

Later that night when I've got Kat safely tucked up against me in her bed, I bring it up again. "I am sorry about the baby being a no-go this time, Thumbs."

Kat wiggles closer and presses her head against my chest. She sighs and I feel her body relax into mine. "It wasn't meant to be this time, I guess."

I pull back and look at her. "That's an unexpected answer from you."

"Oh?"

"I thought you were all about planning. Crushing those goals and all that."

"I think maybe some things just have to happen when it's time." Kat gives a shrug, still mashed up against my side. "I need to relax and just let things happen a little more, maybe. There's a reason to rush, but I can't make this happen just by sheer force of will. And, like you said, there's more than one way to make a family."

"And you want to try to do that with me? To do that together?" I hold my breath while I wait for her answer.

"If you do." Kat tilts her head up, those full lips just begging me to lean in and kiss her.

"Of course I do. You want to start right now?"

"There's no way I can get pregnant right now," Kat whispers against my chest.

"Then it'd just be practice." I'm already way too excited to get to the baby making part of this discussion.

"You're not... I mean. It's shark week, Michael."

I laugh. Kat's obviously forgotten who she's dealing with. "Kat, that absolutely does not matter to me. Come here and get me messy."

And to Kat's credit, she does.

EPILOGUE

Kat

"See right there? That's the spine. Which looks great, by the way. No issues. And I think baby's going to move for us here. Maybe give us a chance to see if we're getting a baby sister or a baby brother. Do we want to know if we're having a boy or a girl?" Dr. Singer looks up at all three of our expectant faces.

"I don't know," I confess. "Maybe we should ask Lucia? What do you think, ladybug? Do you want to know if Bean is a little brother or a little sister?"

My daughter wiggles excitedly in Michael's arms, nodding so vigorously that her chubby cheeks shake.

"I think that's a yes," Michael laughs, shifting the toddler from one hip to the other. We'd debated bringing her to this appointment. She's a ball of energy and hard to contain under the best of circumstances, but in the end, we decided we didn't want to miss the chance for Lucia to get a glimpse of her little brother or sister. She's so excited about the new baby.

We're all excited and still a little shocked. When I'd

found out I was pregnant I'd thought there'd been a mistake. After all the fertility treatments I'd undergone in an effort to have a biological child, it was a huge surprise to see two pink lines without any help at all. And at forty-three? There was no way anyone was expecting that. We were already pretty deep in the adoption process in the hopes of welcoming baby number two when we got thrown this unexpected curve ball. Not that I'm complaining. I'm sure my body's not thrilled with this "geriatric" pregnancy, but I'm thrilled to be able to go through this at least once.

I'm pretty sure this will be the one and only time I carry a baby. And that's fine. I didn't give birth to Lucia but I couldn't love her more if I'd made her from scratch. When we finally got to hold her for the first time, I knew she was meant to be ours. After all that waiting and hoping, I couldn't believe that someone had chosen us for that most precious gift. And she's been a gift every single day even if she is moving into the terrible twos.

Michael tries to keep Lucia marginally still as the doctor slides the probe over my slippery belly. On the screen we can see the grainy image of this baby he and I have managed to make. A little miracle that's wiggling as much as his or her big sister. Michael whispers something in Lucia's ear and she instantly stills. Her brown eyes focus on the screen and her little hands clench into fists. She's concentrating like crazy and I can only imagine what Michael's promised her to get her to behave.

The two of them together look like two peas in a pod. He's not her biological father, but you would never know. She's got the same dark hair and eyes, similar complexion. When she calls out on the playground, everyone would know which man's her daddy, even if you couldn't already guess from the way he was running to get to her. She's most certainly a daddy's girl, wanting him to be the one to read her a bedtime story and put her hair in pigtails. He's surprisingly good at that, actually, even if the part sometimes ends up a little off-center. Now we get to see if he'll get the pleasure of having a new customer at his salon in a few short months.

"Okay, I think this is the best we're going to get, but I'm pretty confident I can tell you if you want. You sure you want to know?" Dr. Singer gives us one last chance to change our minds.

Michael looks at me and shrugs but Lucia's all business. There's no way she's leaving here without finding out if she's getting a brother or a sister. Michael whispers for her to settle down in Spanish—he's been trying to speak Spanish to her as much as possible. She's as likely to respond to Spanish as she is to English.

I think it surprised Michael how much he wanted to make sure Lucia had a connection to her roots and how much it made him miss his own mother and his grandfather. Lucia's had plenty of visits from her grandmother, visits that have done as much for Michael as they have for her. Even Michael's father has turned into a surprisingly involved grandparent. Tracy isn't so thrilled to have been made a grandmother earlier than expected, but what's she going to complain about? Lucia's the world's cutest kid, if I do say so myself.

"Well, Dad, what does that look like to you?" Dr. Singer points to the screen and Michael leans in for a better look, still holding Lucia on one hip.

"If I had to guess, I'd say that was most definitely a penis." Michael looks over to me, eyes wide. "That looks like a boy to me."

"Good guess. That's what I think too. I could still be wrong, but I'm pretty sure you're having a boy."

"A boy?" I can't believe it. A son. One of each when I thought there might never be a chance for me to experience motherhood at all. "What do you think, Lucia? You're getting a baby brother."

Lucia doesn't seem bothered one way or the other since she's discovered the slimy gel all over my stomach. She slides her tiny hand over my belly, leaning off her father's hip to get closer. "Baby," she says and my eyes fill with tears.

"Baby *brother*," Michael tells her and I can hear the excitement in his voice. When he locks eyes with me, I can see the happiness there. I'd thought he wouldn't be ready for this, but he's been my rock. He's the kind of father I could have only dreamed of for my children, and the kind of partner who makes it look easy. There's nobody better than Michael Cruz when it comes to loving me.

"We're going to have to tell all your cousins there's going to be another boy in the mix, *gordita*." Michael pulls Lucia back up and grabs a tissue to wipe her hands as he plants a kiss on the top of her head.

"Aunt Amy's going to be excited to have another nephew to lead astray." I say it jokingly, but Amy's still committed to the title of fun aunt.

"I can print out some images of the baby, if you'd like." Dr. Singer's already pushing print.

"I need one for my desk. To add to the one I have of Lucia so that everyone can see the future of Cruz and Family." Michael's smile is wide. He officially changed the name of his company once we adopted Lucia. He wanted to make sure daughters were included too, even though he'd never pressure her to join the family business. If she wants to he'll be thrilled, but he'll be just as happy having her doing anything else she loves.

Once I'm cleaned up and my next appointment's scheduled, we walk back out to the car. Michael's got Lucia on his shoulders, bouncing her a bit to make her laugh. It's like my dream, but better because this is as real as it gets. I've got the little family I thought I'd never have walking along beside me, its newest addition growing safely in my belly.

Later, it will be the three of us piled in our bed when I feel the baby move for the first time. Lucia's sweaty head on my shoulder and Michael's arm thrown over the both of us.

Perfect.

ACKNOWLEDGMENTS

As always, there are people to thank! The world's on fire, but *Fix It* still managed to make it into the hands of readers. That all by itself is amazing. I hope Kat and Michael's story gave you a bit of a break from the gloom and doom that is 2020.

Thanks to Tamara Mataya for her editing expertise. She's the best at giving those little hints that make a book better, not to mention plenty of dad jokes.

Austin Ryan read an early version of this story and was kind enough to give her feedback. Thanks for helping me have faith that Kat and Michael were hitting the right notes.

Thanks to Laralyn Doran for reminding me to relax and for offering support and feedback on the nitty gritty. I'm so happy to be riding this publishing ride with you.

Finally, many "tips of the cap" to my patient kids. From offering construction puns to helping pick a cover model, they've learned so much about publishing. They didn't want to learn it, but too late now. Hope you and your friends never actually read this book!

ABOUT THE AUTHOR

Jessie Harper writes steamy, contemporary romance with a slightly Southern flavor. Originally from Nashville, Tennessee, she has lived all over the world—from Europe to Asia. She currently resides in Park City, Utah with her husband, three children, and more rescue animals than she ever intended. She appreciates a nice glass of whiskey, homegrown tomatoes, and well-delivered sarcasm. She hopes to never have to "bless your heart."

For updates and more visit www.jessieharper.com.

facebook.com/JessieHarperAuthor
twitter.com/jessiehromance
instagram.com/jessieharperromance
bookbub.com/authors/jessie-harper
amazon.com/author/jessieharper